SLOUGHING OFF THE ROT

SLOUGHING OFF THE ROT

Lance Carbuncle

vicious galoot books, co
tampa, florida

Sloughing Off the Rot
© 2012 by Vicious Galoot Books, Co.

ISBN: 978-0-9822800-4-1 (paperback)
ISBN: 978-0-9822800-5-8 (ebook)

Vicious Galoot Books, Co.
412 East Madison Street, Suite 1111
Tampa, Florida 33602

PRAISE FOR
SLOUGHING OFF THE ROT

"Once again, Uncle Lance has asked us to pull his finger. But this time it doesn't go the way we think. Carbuncle is still the cunning linguist we love and loathe, using blood and body fluid with a painter's precision. This time around, however, his canvas is rich with biblical allusions, dark satire and one unreal road trip. To read *Sloughing Off the Rot* is to watch of one of America's most original humorists growing up, kicking and armpit-farting the whole way."

—Patrick Wensink, author of
Broken Piano for President

"Woof."

—Idjit Galoot,
fictional basset hound

"Carbuncle is a writer who gets you in the gut. He writes with a raw energy that tells it like it is, warts and all. In *Sloughing Off the Rot*, Carbuncle has conjured a fascinating vision, an epic, Biblical quest for identity and meaning. His books are obsessed with our physical, bodily nature, but here he's managed to fuse the physical with the spiritual, seeking out answers to the big questions. His journey is worth taking."

—David David Katzman, author of
Death By Zamboni and
A Greater Monster

"I don't get it. Is this supposed to be funny or something?"

—Uncle Hank,
octogenarian curmudgeon

"Carbuncle's writing has always infused the grotesque underbelly of our world with an inherent beauty only a careful eye can perceive, and while *Sloughing Off the Rot* continues this trend, giving us more of what we've come to know and love in his previous works, Carbuncle turns over a new leaf in his latest, a tale of self-discovery rich with metaphor in the vein of Frank L. Baum & Lewis Carroll . . . then he bursts that vein, infecting the reader with his own unique brand of fantasy. This is not to be missed!"

—Kirk Jones, author of
Uncle Sam's Carnival of Copulating Inanimals

"I'm not a real strong reader, but those are real pretty words you wrote there. It's a good thing that you done that, Son. It's a real good thing that you wrote that book."

—Enid Carbuncle,
mother of the author

"Another masterful and shocking story. Lance Carbuncle is a genius. Lance Carbuncle could write about rubber band ligation of hemorrhoids and it would put all other written works to shame. Lance Carbuncle could train monkeys in the deadly art of Krav Maga. Lance Carbuncle is the King of All Authors. I want to ride him, rim him, and give him a reach around with both hands, all at the same time. I love this brilliant man."

—Lance Carbuncle, author of
Sloughing Off the Rot

"Lance Carbuncle channels the Book of Revelation, Carlos Castaneda, Cormac McCarthy and Fat Elvis in his rudest, weirdest, richest book yet."

Mykle Hansen, author of
Help! A Bear is Eating Me! and
*Rampaging Fuckers of Everything on the
Crazy Shitting Planet of the Vomit Atmosphere*

And that night John went to bed without eating his dinner. Zonked on zolpidem and single malt scotch, wrapped tightly in his super-special 1,000 thread count sheets and nestled comfortably on his newfangled memory foam-reclining- adjustable king-sized bed, John blacked out just after lying down. Peaceful nothingness swirled around him, tossing off flecks of gold and strands of cool blue. The ten thousand things fled and left in their place a cozy void.

And that night a screeching horn section from below jarred John from his warm nothingness. Dissonant, jagged saxophone, rending the night and prematurely tearing the morning from its belly. Screaming brass devil, like the Demon Zorn ass-raping Kenny G with a chainsaw. Raw blistering giggle-jazz.

And that night John heard a voice, as a trumpet in his head. And the voice commanded: "You shall henceforth be known as John the Revelator. And you shall walk 500 miles. And when you wake up, you're gonna be the man that wakes up next to me."

"Who are you? What are you?" asked John.

"I am the alpha and the omega, the first and last."

"I don't understand."

"I am you as you are me as you are he and we are all together."

"What is that even supposed to mean?"

"Enough of your questions and your havering. There is important business before us," the voice demanded.

And that morning, when John received his walking orders, he asked no questions. He did as he was bade by the commanding disembodied presence that he assumed to be the God he never really believed in. Surveying his surroundings, John realized that his room was no longer a room, but instead a craggy cave. His bed was now indiscernible from the dusty ground, his memory foam pillow now a rock. And beside the spot where he awoke was a hole five cubits in diameter. John peered into the pit but saw no bottom. He dropped a rock but the sound of it hitting bottom never came to him. At the edge of the pit were claw marks in the sand and a trail that dragged itself to the spot where John awoke.

The voice, now speaking in a gentler tone, said, "You have not been true to me, nor to yourself. But, you are a good soul. Now is your chance for redemption. Before your journey, it will be necessary to polish thy rod and salve it with balms and ointments. Do this and your seed will find purchase, thus populating this desolate land. Be true with the stroke on your sanctified rod and your issue will increase exponentially and be fruitful."

On the floor at his feet sat earthen jars filled with aromatic balms and ointments. The perfumed scents of frankincense, and myrrh and patchouli wafted from the containers. John's member stood erect against his stomach when he bent and he noticed his nakedness for the first time. Inexplicable shame first gripped him but was quickly dashed by his arousal. Glancing around the cave, John confirmed that he was alone and dipped his hand in one of the clay pots. The golden goo from the pot warmed his hand and pleasured him greatly as he rubbed it on his loins.

With each slow stroke of his hand John brought himself to ecstasy, and his loins issued great spouts of crimson spuz, like a massive bloody font. And a gory puddle formed at and around John's feet, like the blood-soaked floor of a slaughterhouse. From the rippling surface of the blood-puddle, small unrecognizable forms dragged themselves, clawing madly at the ground, grimacing and pulling themselves through the dust, growing in power and size while leaving behind them rust-colored trails and torn membranes as evidence of their birth. And their screams, their wonderful horrible screams, gasped from newly formed throats. New jagged teeth cut through fresh pink gums. Some of the creatures stretched, morphing into muscular serpents, and slithered from the cave. Others took on three legs, four legs, five legs, more. Thick pelts of fur coated some while others were pale and wrinkled and unfinished in appearance. Horns and tusks sprouted from their faces and heads. Incipient bipeds, visibly growing and drunkenly stumbling away on awkward and uncoordinated spindles, instinctively sensed their superiority. A two-legged being fell on a small, bushy-tailed creature and beat at it, discovering the destructive power of the balled fists that had just formed at the ends of its arms. The biped, triumphant over the smaller creature, tested his pointy teeth and tore at the creature's flesh, devouring it, fur and bones and all. Other two-legged creatures, some simian, some hominid, tore at the smaller creatures, rending their forms. And as the lesser creatures were destroyed, torn at, and stomped out, they reverted to bloody puddles, and new, different forms crawled from the pools and grew and moved out of the cave.

Spent from onanism and birthing, John collapsed in a corner of the cave, and watched in both horror and fascination at the genesis of some creatures, and the death and rebirth of others. When the last of the beings slithered, slunk, scrambled, walked and crawled away, and the bloody puddle of mess was nothing more than a stinking brown taint on the ground, John wrapped his arms tightly around his knees and wept until all feelings deserted him. And he relapsed to the swirling nothingness of the void left in the absence of the ten thousand things.

In a space of time that stretched out infinitely, but also contracted into a sliver of a moment, John wept away his fears and trepidations. And he rose and stepped wide around the rusty blot on the floor. And the commandment that he begin his journey rang in his head. And that morning, before dawn broke, John dressed in the white robe and breeches of fine twisted linen that were left for him. He slipped on leather sandals, exited the cave, and started walking.

The red brick road snaked before him, a loopy serpent slinking its lazy way toward the horizon. John knew not the country around him and marveled at the alien landscape. Rust-colored rock formations presented with arches carved out of them by time and wind and water. The barrel cacti, in full bloom, birthed blood red flowers. The black and twisted skeletons of dead juniper trees silhouetted against the red sky. It all looked as arid and dusty as John's throat felt.

And as he walked along the road, the clanging tone and drone of an out of tune guitar tweaked John's ears, the hint of a melody drawing him in while, at the same time, the slightly out of tune chords setting him ill at ease. An intermittently off-key twang of a voice crooned about garbage dumps and their previously unsung benefits. The grating voice finished the song with "and that sums it up in one big lump," as the high E string snapped with the last strum.

"Ah, it will be fair weather, my brother, for the sky is red." The voice, with forty grit coarseness and dry as the red sand around them, issued from a slight figure with a crusty tangle of a beard and the mystical bearing of a holy man. With merely a girdle of skin about his loins and a leather pouch hanging from his neck, and holding a weather-beaten guitar close to his chest, the bearded man sat atop a balanced rock and bored into John with bulging, unblinking eyes.

"Who are you?" asked John. "Where am I? What the hell is going on?"

"I'm the son of man, son." The man went silent and his face contorted, cycling through and miming random emotions. All the while, his intense unblinking eyes stayed locked on John. The face emoted confusion, switched to astonishment, followed by sorrow, glee, horror, amazement, anger, and settled finally on contentment. "I am nobody. I'm a tramp, a bum, a hobo. I'm a boxcar and a jug of wine. And I'm a straight razor if you get too close to me. I go by many names. Santiago. El Diablo. Jerry. Whatever you want to call me, I'm sure I've been called worse. Santiago will be just fine for our purposes."

"What are our purposes?"

Setting his guitar beside him on the rock and cocking half of his bushy unibrow, Santiago smiled broadly and answered, "well for now it seems that our purpose is for you to toss questions at me as if I'm somehow obligated to give you all the answers. And then I'm supposed to spoon-feed you the meaning of life. Right, Johnny?"

"Why do you call me Johnny? Is that my name? How do you know it?"

"See, there you go again. All pushy with the questions. Yeah, your name's Johnny, for our purposes. And how do I know? Shit, boy, I've been waiting for you twenty and five days and nights. I've been living on the desert jive, just stayin' alive. You took long enough to leave the cave, didn't ya?"

"You've been waiting for me?" said John. "But why?"

"I've been fasting. And waiting. And walking. I spent a little time on the mountain. I spent a little time on the hill. I knew you'd be here. I just didn't know it would take you so damn long. I'm starving, Jack." Santiago leapt from his rock, ratty guitar held to his chest, and stuck his landing right next to the pinyon pine several feet to John's side.

"I don't get it," said John. "I don't know who I am. I don't remember anything. I woke up in a cave and I must have been hallucinating because I can't believe the things I saw. And now you're here, telling me that you've been waiting for me."

"Right on," said Santiago, cocking his eyebrow to the point that it looked painful.

"So tell me again, what are our purposes?"

"You're going on a journey. Dig? A helluva trip. One big mind-fuck and I get to tag along." Santiago accented his words with a fluttering hand and circled John. "Ain't that a big kick in the nuggets?"

"A journey?" John rolled his eyes, threw back his head and sighed deeply, trying to get on top of the panic that was rising in him. "You're telling me I'm going on a journey. I'm in no shape for this. Obviously I must have suffered a head injury or something. I need to get to a hospital. And you say I'm going on a journey. Says who?"

Santiago's mouth snapped shut and a bland blankness washed over his face. Although his eyes lacked expression, Santiago's fingers flew over the fretboard of his guitar while his right hand feverishly plucked strained strings, plinking away at a jangling staccato, ostinato arpeggio and ignoring John's questions, circling John, dancing faster and faster as the tempo of his disharmonious notes quickened.

"Stop!" shouted John, reaching out and trying unsuccessfully to grab the nimble little man by his hair. "Stop now and answer me."

Santiago danced and dodged and plucked the repetitive spastic notes, the strings going more and more out of tune and spitting out a warped, grating song. Born of his complete frustration, John mustered the speed and agility to finally grasp

Santiago by his tangled hair and wrest the guitar away from him.

"Ahhhh!" screamed John. "Ahhhhh!" and he bashed the guitar against the balanced rock, reducing the instrument to jagged fragments and splinters. The guitar's wooden body lay in horrid disrepair at John's feet as he stood, hyperventilating and grasping the broken guitar neck in his hand. Pathetic metal strings dangled from the neck, as if trying to drop to the ground and take root.

"Oh. You wanna play rough, Johnny?" An almost joyful glint in his eyes, Santiago leapt back and dropped into a wrestling stance. His feet spread to shoulder width, one in front and the other lagging back, knees bent with elbows near the thighs, and hands held out in tensed claws as if to fend off any further attack. "I was just trying to play some music to help you calm down. And you attack me? I see how it's gonna be. Well let's roll then."

Before John could say "no" or even brace himself for the attack, Santiago sprang and was on him, a maddened savage gripping John's torso and sweeping his legs. Face down in the red dust and choking on a mouthful of earth, John swung his arm back behind himself in an effort to elbow the bushy-headed wild man off of him. Santiago effortlessly dodged the elbow and grabbed at the arm, twisting it high behind John's back and dozing the red dirt with his face. With John's arm still wrenched, Santiago mounted his back, wrapped his legs around and locked them on John's inner thighs, rendering the larger man helpless.

"Say uncle, Johnny," Santiago whispered into John's ear, the stench from his rotten mouth making John's eyes water.

"Get off of me." John wriggled in Santiago's hold but was unable to free himself. "Get the fuck off of me."

"Just say uncle and I'll let you up."

"No!" John struggled and rolled but Santiago clung to his back, like a dog locked in coitus with a bitch.

"If you won't say it, then you're escalating this thing." Santiago leaned in with brown stumps that used to be teeth and tore off the top of John's ear. Blood dribbled down his chin as he chewed on the gristle of the ear and swallowed.

Blood rained from the remainder of John's ear and soaked into the sand. "Owww! Fuck. Okay. Okay. Uncle. Get off of me."

Santiago sprung from John and reverted to his defensive wrestling stance, hands out in front and clawed for another attack. His unblinking eyes locked on John's. "Are we done with this nonsense? Are we cool?" asked Santiago. "Can we get on with things now?"

John rose unsteadily to his feet and wobbled, almost falling back down. Backing away from Santiago, John said, "You ate my ear. You ate my fucking ear. You're crazy. Just leave me alone." He continued to shrink back from Santiago, shaking his head in disbelief. "You ate my fucking ear."

Thin, dry lips parted, revealing Santiago's moldy smile. "Come on, man. It doesn't matter. Your ear will grow back. And besides, I warned you that I was hungry. I'm always hungry, man. You should have said uncle."

"What do you mean my ear will grow back?" John held his hand tightly to the side of his head to stanch the bleeding and felt the *thub, thub, thub, thub* of the injury throbbing on the palm of his hand.

"That's the way things work here."

"Where is here?" asked John, waving his free hand about around himself.

"That's what you need to find out," said Santiago as he climbed back atop the balanced rock and sat, Indian style.

"I need to be anywhere but here," John said. He turned and started to walk. "I certainly don't need to be attacked and chewed on."

"Wait up, man," Santiago shouted from the rock as John continued to walk away. "Don't you want to know what our purposes are before you split?"

And John paused his retreat, stopping but not turning back. "Why should I believe that you have any answers for me?"

"Because I'm spiritually allied with the desert, Jack. I'm spiritually allied with the scorpion and the wolf. You live in your physical realm. But, I'm in the spiritual, baby. I walk and talk and do all the physical things. But that's only because I want to. Dig? If I don't want to do something, I don't have to. I'm not stuck on that trip. See?"

"No, Santiago or whatever your name is, I don't see," said John, flapping his arms about spastically as if slapping Santiago's words from the air before they could reach him. "You don't make any sense. If you have some answers for me, please just give them."

"I have no answers."

"Then why did you ask me to stop?"

"Because I know where your answers can be found."

"Well, tell me then," said John.

"You must climb the mountain and seek the counsel of the burning thorn bush."

"Okay, so you're just talking nonsense again. I get it. Thanks for nothing." John turned and began walking again. Almost immediately, Santiago appeared at his side, grabbing his arm to stop him.

"For real, man," Santiago said. "Just turn around and look."

With the last of his patience, John stopped and turned around. Santiago's buggy whip arm extended his hand and pointed toward the mountain from which John exited. A stone's throw above the cave entrance sat a thorn bush, alight with great blue and orange flames, but the bush itself did not burn.

Flames flicked and swirled about the crucifixion thorn. Flares from the fire licked at John's face and clothes, cauterized his wounded ear, the intense dry heat applying a natural rouge to his skin but not drawing blisters. "I am the god of hellfire. And I bring you fire," boomed the voice from the bush. "You are lost, and I am found. You are death and I am life. I am rubber and you are glue. I'll be your mirror, reflecting your life back at you."

The voice and its words gripped John's throbbing curiosity and rubbed at it in a most stimulating way. With his desire to know now aroused and standing at full attention, John spasmed and spurted his words, "Tell me. Who am I? What is happening? Why am I here?"

"All in good time, my son. All in good time." The bush flared and threw off sparks. Then, resuming a low burn, it continued, "For now, you are just John. A blank slate. Tabula rasa. An uncarved block. To tell you too much about your past would condemn you to relive it. To tell you too little would be doing too little. For now, just be. Your history will be revealed to you in due time. For the time being, suffice it to say that in your previous life you were a miserable son of a bitch. An emotional cripple. A user and an abuser. A destroyer of hope and happiness and all that is good. A loser and a wuss and a whiner. But that is not you now. This is your rebirth. You, rising from the ashes and becoming."

"Becoming what?"

"Yes. That is the question, isn't it?"

And the flames flared up again and forced John's eyes shut. He cringed back and away from the bush. The light burned his retinas through the thin, clenched eyelids.

"What do I do?" John shielded his face from the fire. "How do I get home?"

"You follow the trail."

"What trail?" asked John.

"Look toward the heavens."

A westerly flowing river of bright, white clouds cut through the sky, flowing faster than the other cumulo fracti hanging in the air. Looking from the heavens, and to the ground and back again, John saw that the river of clouds traced the same path as a red brick road on the ground.

"Follow the red brick road, El Camino de la Muerte. Follow

the trail. He who follows the trail is at one with the trail. He who is virtuous experiences virtue. He who loses the way is lost. When you are at one with the trail, the trail welcomes you. Follow the trail."

"Where will the trail take me?"

"To a man who will help you get home."

"Where is home?" asked John.

"That is the question. Isn't it?"

The red road swerved and swayed for miles, tapering off to a point at the top of a slight rise. John sat at the mouth of the cave, leaning back on his hands with his legs splayed out before him, tracing the path of the clouds above and then looking back to the crumbling brickwork path. The shift of his eyes from the ground to the sky and back again enhanced the optical illusion that the road was slithering like a snake to its sharp culmination miles in the distance.

"Well, what are you waiting for?" Santiago squatted in front of John, arms wrapped around his knees, and wiggled the furry caterpillar above his bulbous eyes. "Your journey can't start until you take the first step. So let's do it, pal. Put one foot in front of the other. Where are we going?"

"I don't know that I'm going anywhere. This doesn't make sense to me. I know I must be dreaming, or hallucinating, or something, because none of this makes sense." John waved his hand, indicating the arid landscape in front of him. Scanning the horizon, John noted two crescent moons in the sky. "Oh boy. None of this makes any sense."

"It don't have to make sense, Johnny," said Santiago. "If you hadn't noticed, you ain't in Kansas anymore. This is your reality. It's as real as the infection that is already setting in on your ear."

John pressed his palm to his ear and winced. "Ow. How the hell can an infection set in so quickly?"

"Two reasons," Santiago held two fingers up in a reverse peace sign. "One," he curled his pointer finger toward his fist, leaving the middle waggling in John's face, "you were talking to that bush for a hell of a long time. Much longer than you probably realized. And, two," the middle finger curled in to make a fist that Santiago waved much too close to John's nose, "bites from humans are far worse than those from other animals. I mean, who knows what the hell kind of diseases I might have. Right?"

"Great," snapped John. "What the hell am I supposed to do? I can feel my ear throbbing and getting hot. It really hurts."

Santiago said, "There's only one thing to do about an infection like that." He pulled the leather sack from around his neck. His thin fingers uncinched the sack's rawhide tie and dug around. "Alright, open your eyes wide and look toward the sky."

"What are you going to do?" asked John, looking upward as he was told. "Why should I trust you?" Directly above him, a blood red sun tossed off great orange flares. The direct glimpse of the burning star heated John's retinas and caused temporary partial blindness, leaving him with only a glowing halo of peripheral vision.

John did not see Santiago dangling plump grubs just above his head. He did not see that the larvae were pale, moist, and wrinkled, or that they had disproportionately large, fierce pincers that reached for his eyes as the maggots wriggled and tried to escape Santiago's grasp.

Santiago said, "You should trust me because it doesn't matter. It's all a dream, right? So just go with the flow as it washes you along. Follow the trail where it takes you. And, brace yourself, Sonny, because this is going to pinch a little." Santiago released the grubs from his grasp, dropping them directly into John's eyes. "It might even be excruciating."

And John screamed. He rolled on the ground and clawed at his eyes, but to no avail. He shouted the names of fifty different gods in vain, but the gods paid no attention to his cries. Upon making contact with the sclera, the grubs locked their pincers on the whites of John's eyes and pulled themselves under the lacrimal sacs and into the sockets. John felt the creatures squirming behind his eyes, into his head, tearing at him and feeding as they explored his skull. And then he felt numb and dumb. Absolute blackness that began to shift again toward light. From the blackness, the ten thousand things reappeared. His vision returned with great clarity, as if a curtain had been lifted from his eyes. A warm, satisfied, and safe feeling caressed him.

At some point during his ordeal, it rained. John lay on the rock, feeling the natural sauna of sage scented vapor leaving the rock, warming him, opening his pores, cleansing him. As he tried to sit up, Santiago placed a hand on John's forehead and another over his ear. Santiago said, "Not yet, Johnny. Stay down on the ground and look toward me."

John looked in Santiago's direction. Detachedly, he watched Santiago raise his hand and smack down at his uninfected ear. John remained calm and accepted the slap as if it were expected. With another whack to the side of his head, John felt something stretching and a wiggling in the canal of his infected ear. Santiago cupped his palm to the side of John's head and left it there until the discomfort in John's ear ceased.

"Wow, look at those babies," said Santiago, pulling his hand away and looking at the engorged, thumb-sized larvae in his hands. Their now-black bodies oozed an oily substance. Their horns tore at Santiago's palm. Their bodies squirmed and mutated abruptly, sprouting legs. Brown armor and wings, tinged with the virescent hues of death, formed around the previously fleshy bodies, metamorphosizing the creatures into fierce, enormous beetles. Santiago shook the scarabs from his hand and they skittered away along a zigzag path toward the red brick road, the chitinous clinking of their tiny feet tap-tap-tapping out their retreat. "It's a good thing they cleaned you out because there must have been a lot of mung in there. I've never seen them grow so big."

"What the hell were those things? What did you do to me?" said John.

"What the hell were those things? What did you do to me?" Santiago mocked, and then laughed nervously. Twisting at a tangle of hair hanging in his face, and then rubbing his beard, Santiago grinned and said, "Those were lunkworms. A miracle and a curse, depending on your general makeup. The question and the answer. They can cure what ails you. They can be the worst things to ever happen to you. Just depends on how you deal with them. Those two babies I dropped on you, they gorged on your infection. You are clean and not infected with any defiling mold or fungus."

Santiago dumped his sack into his palm, shaking out a hand-ful of the lunkworms for John to see. The small mound of lar-vae wriggled. Maggots unsuccessfully strove to crawl to the edges of Santiago's cupped hand but ultimately tumbled back into the squirming clump of grubs. John watched in horror as Santiago threw his head back and dropped several worms into his own eyes. As John did before him, Santiago clawed at his eyes when the worms locked onto the sclera and tunneled be-hind the eyeballs, back into his head. The madman tore at his hair and rolled about on the ground, throwing up a cloud of dust and shrieking at the heavens. There was much weeping and gnashing of the teeth. When it looked as if he could take it no longer, as if his heart or his brain or some other major or-gan might explode, Santiago stopped and stiffened, his arms locked straight and to his sides, his legs extended and motion-less.

John stood above the thin, petrified form and looked down, wondering if Santiago died. Not a muscle on the little man moved. His chest did not swell and fall with respiration. His body froze in a pose. His eyes remained closed. And then they opened, flipping from side to side. Santiago laughed nervously, tugged at his beard.

"Holy moly!" said Santiago. "I just flipped my friggin' wig, Johnny." His face rapidly contorted and cycled through his range of expressions.

John sat again, right next to Santiago, looked over the little man, and said, "I get it that the worms ate my infection. I understand why you gave them to me. But you're not ill. Why did you drop the worms in your eyes?"

Santiago sprang to his feet and raised his voice, almost yelling, but not in anger, "It's not all about infection. Those that are whole don't need no doctor. Yeah? It's about reflection and introspection, baby. It's about inflection, detection, rejection, and the house of correction. It's about injection and the violin section. It's about my erection." Santiago grabbed at the swelling in his loincloth. "It's about perfection."

With a startlingly stunning clarity of mind, John understood Santiago's rant. John noticed everything. He marveled at the shape of the individual grains of sand. He was amazed at the points on the thorns and the spikes on the cacti. He scanned the world around him and noted the slightest of color variations in the rocks and the sky and found novelty in everything he saw. He gawked at the trail in the sky and felt its movement. "Trails," he murmured. The sounds of insects on the rocks and small desert animals chittering registered in his head and took on new meaning. John studied the dirt-clogged pores on Santiago's cheeks and forehead, the strands of beard as they intertwined and knotted into an intricate mess.

"I see you digging on the cut of my jib, Johnny. You're starting to understand my jive. I can see it in your eyes. Well that's all just great and groovy. But you still don't really dig it yet. Do you?"

"I think I do," said John, tearing his eyes away from an intriguing clump of discolored skin on the side of Santiago's nose. "You gave me those worms. They made my ear feel better. Thanks for that. I'm just glad that we're done with the worms."

"You ain't done with nothing, brother. And those worms ain't done with you." Santiago's voice rose to urgency again and he flailed his arms about wildly. "They're still a coming at you. It's a coming at you. A big wave is coming and you better lash yourself to something strong cause we're gonna be tossed about and it's gonna be a hell of a night."

Santiago flung himself backward toward the ground. His words spat rapid-fire from his mouth in a frothy logorrhea and fluttered about in front of John's face. He saw the madman's random utterances taking physical form, spelled out in the air in great bold, thick, capital letters. The word LAPIDATE shot from Santiago's beard-crusted orifice and pinged off John's forehead, leaving a welt and a small scrape. Next BLOOD spewed from Santiago's mouth and soaked John's face and chest. BIRD flew from his mouth, coasted on the wind currents above John and dropped a SLOPPY SHIT, which bespattered his shoulder. MIGHTY FIST OF RAGE hammered the side of John's head and knocked him on his back, right next to Santiago.

John closed his eyes and shielded his head. And though Santiago continued to rave, his words no longer physically assaulted John. Without open eyes to give them power, the words dropped and thudded on the ground, became two-dimensional lower case phrases, and expired. A tugging at his belly, like a hook on the end of a rope pulling at him, yanked John into the air. He dangled there, looking down at his supine, motionless body. His tall, thin form, arms outspread, looked as if it were welcoming the abusive words as they rained down upon him. His eyes clenched. His stubbly face twisted up in a smile. Next to his body, John saw Santiago, still flat on his back, his mouth erupting a gush of unconnected, bolded words into the air. Many of the words were emphatic and given great force by gargantuan exclamation marks. Still, with his eyes closed, the words did John no violence. They merely bounced off of him, scattered about his body on the ground.

And then, John saw both his and Santiago's bodies lifted from the ground as if they were marionettes on strings. Their bodies jerked and lurched about awkwardly, as if trying to fight off some outside force that was making them move. As they moved, their bodies gradually took on more fluid, lifelike movements. The men jumped and ran and flailed about. John watched on from above, feeling detached from the action. With a powerful whoosh, he felt himself sucked back into his body, felt the strain of his muscles and the compulsion to move forward, to run and jump and dance. No longer a spectator, John felt the frenzy of random emotions and the need to groove.

Red and gold brick roads, starting at a center point and spinning outward, expanding as they swirled, set out two separate paths, the red opening up to the west and the gold spreading out in the opposite direction. And starting at the center of the two-toned swirl, John and Santiago bounced and jumped and kicked up their heels and allowed themselves to be washed along with the wave that pushed them down the red brick road. They whirled down the road, spinning madly, pulled by the current of the river of clouds above them.

Along the road, they encountered other men and boys. Santiago plucked an everlasting supply of worms from his bottomless bag and dropped them in the people's eyes. And the men and boys joined them and danced along the road, spinning and circling around John, as planets orbiting a sun. The dancers, their arms raised to the sky and grooving to some cosmic jam, spun and jumped and kicked up dust, ushering John and Santiago along.

The road curved and swelled and welcomed the frenetic swarm of dirty, sweaty bodies. Along the way, members of the crowd picked up instruments and began to play. Bouzoukis and baglamas plinked and sang and dueled feverishly, the three-stringed instruments reverberating and complementing each other, driving the pace of the dancers faster. Flutes fluttered frenetically above the din. Those without instruments picked up sticks and clinked them together or beat on drums or jars. Some chanted and moaned in unison. Others clapped their hands until it hurt. Still others just danced.

Santiago, in a trance, ripped a leather belt from the robe of one of the dancers. In time to the beat, Santiago whipped the strap at his own bare back. The scourge drew welts and blood and exclamations of joy. Some of the dancers ventured too close to Santiago and felt the sting of the leather that he flung about. Following Santiago's example, some of the dancers stripped off their shirts and beat and slashed at their own backs with belts and branches and straps made from the hides of goats. The rhythm of the music urged the flagellants on, driving their self-abuse to greater extremes. Occasionally a spent and bloody dancer dropped by the side of the road, his body still twitching despite the lack of energy to continue on, left to watch helplessly as the surging, spinning, dancing crowd of men moved away down the road.

The men danced through the night, following the red brick road. Above them, where the trail of clouds flowed during the day, a river of fire mirrored the snaking road. The star Wormwood winked a hypnotic green strobe down on the crowd. And the road welcomed the throng of sweaty, dirty, beaten and bloodied men. It drank their sweat and blood and gave back its own energy to urge the crowd on. It worked in concert with the river of fire, reflecting energy to the trail and receiving the rebounding aura. El Camino De la Muerte drove the clamoring mass through small villages and over hills picking up more bodies along the way, sweeping the men along treacherous mountain roads, sometimes tossing weakened and useless husks of men off the side of the road and down the steep drops. All the while, John spun and leapt and moved forward, and Santiago followed, dropping worms in the eyes of newcomers and providing John with lunkworms when his energy waned.

After three days and two nights of manic dancing, the crowd dwindled to nothing. A trail of broken and spent bodies, some dead but most not, littered the brick path for miles and miles behind John and Santiago. And the two men found themselves alone on the road again and lacking the energy to go any farther. After three days in the desert fun, John's face began to turn red. After three days in the desert sun he was looking at a riverbed. He threw himself to the ground and lay on his back in an area where the red brick road crossed the dry riverbed, staring up at the flickering light of Wormwood millions of miles away. From his peripheral vision, he saw Santiago walking around their stopping point and pissing a circle around them.

"What the hell are you doing?" John asked.

Santiago shook off the final drops of urine that he could muster and answered, "Setting up a perimeter. And I'm dry. I need you to finish up wetting the circle around our camp here."

"For what? I'm too tired to stand."

"To save our lives. To make it through the night. To keep us safe, man." Santiago walked in a circle around John's unmoving body. "You need to get up and finish the circle that I started to keep us safe. And I ain't gonna let you sleep until you do." He poked at John's ribs with his big toe and jumped back when John swatted at him.

"What is our piss going to keep us safe from? This is ridiculous. I want to sleep."

Santiago nudged at John again with his foot. "Get up and I'll tell you. Otherwise I'm gonna pester you and not let you sleep."

With a great effort, John rose to his feet. "I'll try if it will shut you up. But, I don't think I have enough piss to complete a circle around us." Much to his surprise, John loosed a high-pressure flow of urine that more than finished Santiago's protective ring around the men. He shook off several times, giving it an extra effort so as not to dribble on himself. "So what is our piss going to protect us from?" John returned to his resting position on the ground and resumed his gaze at Wormwood's green flicker.

"Lunkheads, baby. Lunkheads," said Santiago. He settled in on the ground next to John and stared at the green star, too. "If you wanna make it through the night, don't step outside of that piss-circle. Don't put a hand or foot or any other body part outside of the perimeter or you're likely to lose it."

"What are lunkheads?" John asked.

Santiago sat and scratched at his beard momentarily, putting together an acceptable answer to John's question, and said, "Lookie here, man..."

But, before Santiago said any more, John fell fast asleep on the ground beside him, mumbling incoherently to himself.

And John awoke with his eyes gummed up and a rotten mouth. A low drone of grunts and groans and snarls and moans stirred him as the flammeous daylight broke. Just outside of the piss-perimeter stood a shifting, stinking wall of men and boys, their skin greenish and pocked with sores. Their soulless eyes passed over John and Santiago but looked right through them, the giant dilated pupils having taken over most of the whites of their eyes and showing as stagnant pools of numbness. Those black eyes betrayed no emotions. No feeling showed itself on the lumbering creatures' faces as they remained just outside the circle and shifted slowly back and forth on their feet. But there was a hunger, an urgent need for something that was clear from how their numbers were pressed in on each other around the circle but held back only by some invisible barrier.

"Santiago! Wake up!" John rolled toward Santiago and shook him awake. "What is this? What the fuck? What are these people doing?"

Santiago sat up slowly. He rubbed his eyes. He rejected the urgency in John's voice. He scanned the slow-moving throng around him. He stretched. "What the fuck, Johnny? That's a hell of a way to wake me. I told you about lunkheads last night. Remember?"

"I don't remember anything. We stopped. I was beat. I slept. We didn't talk."

"We did, man," said Santiago. He squatted low to the ground and tugged at his beard. "We did. And I'll hep you to it all again. But first, you gotta tell me something. Do you want more worms? Are you jonesing for one more lunk?" He tittered his nervous laugh and watched John's face closely.

"I don't ever want to see those stupid worms again," John snapped. "My body aches all over. I feel empty inside. My skin is torn and scabbed and burned. My head is throbbing and the ground feels like it's moving. I want nothing to do with lunkworms."

Santiago jumped up again and slapped John on the back. "That's the answer I was looking for. You ain't gonna be no lunkhead. If you don't want more, then you ain't a lunkie."

The gape-jawed men stood just outside the circle, watching and waiting. Santiago approached the edge of the perimeter and stood in front of a short, crumpled man. The man's eyes were devoid of any emotion or recognition, but they locked on Santiago. The man's jaw repeatedly shifted and chewed at his ragged tongue, his lips pursed and slackened, pursed and slackened. His arms twitched and thoughtlessly slammed balled fists against his own sides. The right side of his face hung, palsied and dull. Infected claw marks crisscrossed his bare chest.

"These," said Santiago, waving his hand to indicate the men who surrounded them, "these are your sins and your shame and your guilt, guy. These are the things that will dog you until you deal with yourself. These are the manifestation of your fucked up past. This is your shit looping back around and smacking you in the back. These are lunkheads. Some people take the lunk once and never have a need for it again. Some get helplessly addicted. Some suffer almost immediate mental incapacitation and only certain parts of their brains seem to work."

Santiago swaggered around the circle and waved his hand in front of an emaciated lunkhead's face. Angry red patches of flesh marked spots on the man's head where he had torn out his own hair. A red sore throbbed and oozed on one of the bald patches. "Look at this sorry sack of shit. Lets just call him Gary," Santiago said. He balled up his fist and threw it within inches of Gary's blank eyes, stopping his hand just short of the protective perimeter. Gary did not flinch. His only reaction was a cruffulous cough, and then he stared straight ahead, his brain turned off.

"Hey, motherfucker, Trix are for kids!" Santiago shouted, blasting a fine mist of spittle in Gary's face, trying to get a response. But the man did not answer. The man did not wipe the spit from his face. The man took no umbrage at Santiago's abuse. He did not blink. The man stood and stared at Santiago. "Look at him," said Santiago. "He's cuckoo for Cocoa Puffs, baby."

Santiago paced at the edge of the circle, stopping to taunt the creatures. Scooping up a handful of sand, he threw it in the face of a drooling lunkhead. The recipient of the sand stood slack-jawed and unaware of the mistreatment, not even blinking to clear the grains of sand from his eyes. "Look at these. These are lunkies. And what do they want? They want my Lucky Charms, don't they? They want my worms. But I don't have any more."

"Well, why are they here then?" said John. "Just show them that you don't have any more worms." John stood toward the center of the circle, repulsed at the shuffling swarm of bloodied and bruised meat surrounding him.

"They don't just want my worms," tittered Santiago. "They want you. They want to tear you down. They want me. They want to fuck us and kill us and eat us. And not necessarily in that order, baby."

"So, what? They're like, zombies or something?"

"They ain't zombies, dig?" said Santiago, stopping to pick up an apple-sized red rock from the ground. Winding up like a major league pitcher, he flung the rock with all his might at a tall, gangling lunkhead who stood shifting his weight from one foot to the other. The rock smashed the lunkhead's nose and provoked a flow of blood. The victim of Santiago's attack shook his head and then resumed his back and forth shifting. "They're not dead. You won't turn into one if they bite you. Their affliction ain't contagious, or infectious, dig? It's more pathetic and outrageous. They're just missing a part of their brains, brother. For some reason, lunkworms affect some people differently. I don't know if they change the chemical balance in the lunkies' brains or if the worms just eat an essential part of the brain, or what. I just know that when some people ingest a worm, it turns out that the worm is actually ingesting them. It's like the basic needs are all that drive the lunkies. And all thought and reason go out the window. These bad boys just want to eat, shit, fuck and kill. Dig? Let me show you."

As the crowd swayed back and forth outside of the invisible barrier, Santiago ran around near the border of the circle, picking up speed and tittering his nervous laugh all the while. With a sufficient head of steam built up, Santiago launched himself into the air, throwing his feet in front of himself. His feet broke the protective border of the circle and smacked into an elderly lunkhead's bare chest. Upon making contact, Santiago allowed his legs to bend slightly and then pushed off with all of his might, springing himself back into the protective perimeter and, in the process, knocking the brain-dead old man to the ground amongst the groaning crowd of lunkheads.

And a violent and lustful blood orgy erupted. The lunkheads converged on the fallen man and tore at him. And there was much screaming and gnashing of the teeth. The savages ignored the man's screams and devoured his flesh, quickly tearing him down to bones and a puddle of gore. Some, as if in a drunken barroom free-for-all, turned their frenzy on each other, reeling about, randomly striking, scratching and biting at any bodies close to them. John's eyes reflected the horror as he watched one lunkhead smash a rock down on the head of another lunkie who was bent over and chewing on an unconscious victim. The rock caved in the back of the man's head and he dropped face-first into the dust. Other lunkheads fell on him and ripped at his flesh. His side was gashed open and the viscera tumbled out, slopping onto the dusty ground. One of the creatures, his hunger for flesh sated, tugged the pants off of the fallen man and mounted the prone form, dry-fucking the already-dead lunkie's ass. And his lust incited the base needs of the others, who gathered and penetrated the newly formed openings in the dead man's body. The ass-fucking lunkhead put his hand in the dead man's crotch and performed a vicious reach-around, ripping off his victim's genitals and tossing them into the air, bouncing the rent organ off of the forehead of another lunkie. One of the combatants, upon being struck in the face with a log, tripped backward across the piss-barrier and fell into John and Santiago's circle. The lunkhead immediately dropped to the ground, clutched at his face and yowled a high-decibel scream, rolling out of the circle and back toward the fray. Once out of the circle, he rolled up, fetal, and continued to clutch at his face and scream. Others fell upon him and shucked him like an ear of corn, painfully and permanently relieving him of his suffering.

"What the fuck?" gasped John, shocked at the horrid display of violence and lust. "What did you do?"

Santiago tugged at John's arm, pulling him away from the bloody melee. "I just bought us some time, dig? They're all focused on each other and have forgotten about us. Let's split this scene A.S.A.P."

Allowing himself to be led away from the horrors, John realized that he and Santiago were walking away from their protective circle. They were again walking the red brick road.

John stopped, ignoring Santiago's insistent tugging at his arm. "Shouldn't we stay in the circle? Can't they get us now?"

Santiago answered, "They're all focused on each other. They'll probably tear themselves down, every last one. And even if they do break from that shuck and jive to hassle us, they don't move very fast. Dig? So as long as we keep moving down the line, we won't have no troubles from those boys back there. They'll trail us like the stink of your shame. But, they won't catch us as long as we're careful. We just need to keep an eye out for other lunkies up ahead of us. Let's go, the night is far spent and the day is at hand."

And they were on the road again. Behind them, the lunkies fought and they fit, and they scratched and they bit. And because the mindless violent hunks of meat ripped each other down to scraps and snips on that location, the spot is called Elmira Gulch.

The path now welcomed them. It twisted and wound its way over the red rocks and hills in the distance. The river of clouds rushed by overhead, clearing the way of bad mojo. Bloodcurdling shrieks and howls of combat filled the air behind Santiago and John, the screams fading out as the men distanced themselves from the self-destructing band of lunkheads. The fresh air and the disappearance of the rabid meat-puppets helped John to clear his head. The unthinking exercise of briskly walking away and the clear skies above him lessened the lunk-hangover. His steps fell in rhythm with Santiago's and they beat a steady retreat from the danger behind them. John allowed himself to concentrate only on the rhythm of his march and cleared his mind of everything else. The men headed west, not talking, just walking.

And John and Santiago walked the road for forty days and forty nights. In the desert there were plants and birds and rocks and things. There was sand and hills and rings. Every so often they saw a small village or gathering of people in the distance, off of the path. In the villages the houses were built of unsplit logs and the sod roofs grew thick and green. The aroma of good meat cooking drifted to them on the wind, making their mouths water and their stomachs rumble in hungry protest. But John and Santiago kept walking, eschewing the temptations of a good meal and a comfortable slumber. Instead, they stayed true to the path. When hunger controlled, they dined on desert flora and the oversized dirt-rats whose colonies popped up randomly along the red brick road. Santiago fetched their food by sitting stock-still in the middle of a colony with a handful of pinyon nuts and waiting for the plump, lazy rodents to approach and sniff him. He would wait for the critters to crawl into his lap and eat from his hand. When they did, he swiftly scruffed them with his empty hand and slammed them to the ground. Catching the rodents by hand and dispatching them gave Santiago a sense of satisfaction. At the end of the slaughter, Santiago, uncharacteristically calm with a beatific gaze, sat with the dead animals piled off to his side and still drawing others in to check him out. Once the killing was done, the remaining dirt-rats settled on his lap and safely ate from his hand. The nights found the large stripped rats turning slowly on a spit above a fire, dripping grease that flared up on the embers. The meat, gamey and tough, killed the hunger but left the men unsatisfied.

Along the road, the twisted juniper skeletons stretched their dead limbs, welcoming turkey vultures to roost in them. John marveled at the birds' hideous beauty as they sat, necks hunched over and feathers ruffled, and stared at him with hollow, piercing eyes. The red wrinkled heads tipped with curved ivory beaks seemed ill-fitted to the oversized brown bodies. The birds' glare always seemed to mimic the hunger in Santiago's eyes. The omnivorous creatures waited for Santiago to do his work with the dirt-rats. He always killed more than he and John needed for sustenance and threw the extra carcasses out for the buzzards to dine on.

One morning, as the men walked, John noticed movement far off on a ridge. A lone figure stood, hand held above his brown eyes to block the sun, and gazed in John's direction. Although John could not tell from the distance, the man on the ridge was tall and strong. His name was Three Tooth.

The lines ran deep and dark on Three Tooth's face. His long black hair, held out of his face by a leather band with feathers tucked into it, flowed most of the way down his back. His thick arms and legs were intentionally branded with hieroglyphics, the raised burn scars telling the tale of his ancestors and their role as guardians of the red brick road. Three Tooth watched the men in the distance plod along the road. He saw the strange little bearded man jumping around and circling the taller man dressed in white. Santiago tossed bits of refuse along the roadside as he jumped about and his littering saddened Three Tooth, drawing one briny tear from the Indian's eye.

Three Tooth gathered his rag-tag band of desert scurves and led them in a vector that aimed to intersect with the course of John and Santiago. Leading the pack was Three Tooth, bareback on his pale white horse named Morticia. Three Tooth, sitting as if there were a board strapped to his back and staring forward, his face tense, his mouth a slit and white lines where his lips should be. Following Morticia was Heap-o-Buffaloes, a stringy Chinese-looking man decked out in buckskins and fringed moccasin boots. Heap-o-Buffaloes, skipping dangerously close to the horse's hind legs but never provoking her to kick backward at him. Trailing Heap-o- Buffaloes were two pale-skinned, toe-headed, glazed-eyed mamelukes – Crazy Talk and Throws-Like-Girl – walking side by side and passing a fuming clay pipe between them. Bringing up the rear, grinning like a village idiot, was the shovel-toothed, squat and swarthy Melungeon sluggard, Two- Dogs-Fucking. A scraggly, sparse beard failed in its efforts to camouflage the lack of a jaw line on Two-Dogs-Fucking and only served to draw attention to the flabby turkey neck beneath it that jiggled excitedly whenever he shook his head. Two-Dogs-Fucking, with his bare, floppy man-tits and his bottom-half wrapped only in a too-small bath towel that constantly threatened to fall off (but never did). In one hand Two-Dogs-Fucking gripped a cooked leg of turkey vulture that he intermittently gnawed upon; in the other he held a rope that led a battered and sickly donkey, Alf the Sacred Burro. In a nearby juniper skeleton, a roost of turkey vultures trailed Two-Dogs-Fucking with resentful eyes.

"And now is the time when we dance and draw upon the energy of the great spirit," said Three Tooth, hopping on one foot and working up the momentum to switch back and forth from foot to foot. With his hips dropped low and his back arched up, Three Tooth jumped from foot to foot, throwing his head and hands toward the sky. And his slow, graceful movements, so unlike the crazed and flailing lunk-afflicted dancers, caught like a slow burn among the men. And all but Two-Dogs-Fucking mimicked Three Tooth's movements and pranced in a circle around Alf the Sacred Burro and Two-Dogs-Fucking. The dancing men chanted in tongues unknown to Alf and slowly moved their party in the direction of John and Santiago.

"Come now, dance my round little friend," said Three Tooth to Two-Dogs-Fucking, slapping him on the ass to infect the slothful slug with dance fever.

Ignoring Three Tooth's call to the ghost dance, Two- Dogs-Fucking adjusted his towel, heaved his substantial gut in front of himself, and slowed the pace of his thick, bare, ham steak feet. "Sir," said Two-Dogs-Fucking to Three Tooth, "I simply don't feel motivated today. Perhaps instead of dancing I could sit a while and enjoy a mid-morning meal."

Two-Dogs-Fucking's seamless transition from sluggard to laggard saddened Three Tooth. A tear leaked from his eye because he found himself growing tired of Two-Dogs- Fucking's lack of motivation and general malaise. The round man's apathy was infectious. It tainted Three Tooth's psyche, making him prone to bouts of melancholy. Three Tooth found that he had developed a sad, leaky eye that watered at the slightest provocation since taking Two-Dogs-Fucking into his circle. The sadness made Three Tooth want to drink chicha much more than he used to. This was a problem. And the tear that trickled down Three Tooth's cheek strengthened his resolve to remedy the Two-Dogs-Fucking situation.

Alf the Sacred Burro and Two-Dogs-Fucking ambled at the most leisurely of paces and were circled by the slow-motion circular movement of the dancing men. Unlike Three Tooth and the others, Alf did not mind Two-Dogs-Fucking's lack of motivation. Alf himself rarely felt the urge to do much besides sit on his haunches, munch at the desert grasses and flowers, and get his mangy head scritched by whomever might be so willing. Two-Dogs-Fucking was often the scritcher, and the scritching came at the expense of making any other contributions to the wellbeing of the crew. The dancing men moved their circle along, slowly, as if Alf and Two-Dogs-Fucking were an anchor they had to drag across the ground. Despite their burden, the men stomped about and threw their heads back and chanted in unison to the sky. Three Tooth and his gracefully prancing crew moved like a great sand-slug across the desert, eventually intersecting the course of John and Santiago on the red brick road. When the two groups met, Three Tooth's eye dribbled a tear. And the sky commiserated with Three Tooth in a brief but heavy cloudburst.

Three Tooth dismounted Morticia and walked toward John, his hands held up, palms out in a greeting and as a show of the absence of aggression. Behind Three Tooth, his men stayed in one spot, chanting and circling Two-Dogs-Fucking and Alf the Sacred Burro (who both sat on the ground, recuperating from their walk). At the precise moment that Three Tooth set foot on the red brick road, the rain ceased. And a bolt from the blue gashed the sky and struck nearby, the lightning forking and striking both a juniper tree and a thorn bush. A loud snap of instant thunder slapped the men, making them cringe involuntarily and raising the hair on their necks. The smell of ozone filled the air. The super-heated juniper exploded into pieces and the sand on the ground around it turned to glass. The thorn bush caught fire and maintained a steady, fierce flame.

The tall, muscular scurve, with his hieroglyphic brands and leaky eye, held out his hand. "How," he said in a deep, soft tone, and then cleared his throat.

"How," answered John quickly, holding his hand up, palm out in what he guessed would pass for a proper greeting.

"You did not let me finish," said Three Tooth, clearing his throat again. "How...do you do? My name is Three Tooth. I've been watching you. My men and I are here to help."

"I'm John. And I guess I do just fine. We've seen you up on the ridges watching us. Haven't we, Santiago?"

But Santiago did not answer. He was already settled Indian style in the middle of a dirt-rat colony, catching the rodents and snuffing them out. Consumed by his ever-present hunger, Santiago showed no interest in Three Tooth and his crew. John noticed a sneer on Santiago's face that did not coincide with the pleasure he usually derived from killing dirt-rats. Santiago would not look over toward Three Tooth or his men. His concentration on the dirt-rats seemed more intense than usual and appeared to be intentional disregard of the newcomers.

Three Tooth stood with his arms crossed, waiting for John to say more. John studied Three Tooth and his men, not knowing exactly what to make of their strange appearance. His brain felt thick, slow, atrophied. All he had been doing was walking, and eating dirt-rats and pinyon nuts, and sleeping and walking some more for forty days and forty nights. And it was as if the repetitive, rhythmic thud of his feet on the ground had shut his brain down, making him only slightly more thoughtful than the mindless lunkheads that he and Santiago occasionally encountered. He had forgotten his journey and that he was a stranger in a strange land and that he had at some point lived some other life (about which he was still entirely clueless). Three Tooth's appearance jabbed at a sensitive spot in John's brain, shocking him back to complete consciousness. And John found himself once again wondering who he was, where he was, why he was, and what he used to be.

And Three Tooth stood, tall and stiff, waiting for something. In the distance, Two-Dogs-Fucking spread out on the desert floor and napped, his ragged inhalations hitching and signaling to his body that maybe he had done enough and it was time to call it quits. Alf the Sacred Burro sat on his haunches like a dog, flicking his ears at a large black munkle fly that flitted about and pestered him. Bald patches on the donkey's hide – worn there by time and mistreatment and (sometimes) his own teeth – marked his many misfortunes and hardships. A bullet scar on Alf's right hindquarter memorializes an old friendship. Ruminating on his life (a donkey lives a long time), Alf dredged up a foul shit-brown lump from his stomach and horked it onto the desert floor. Throws-Like-Girl, Crazy Talk, and Heap-o-Buffaloes, now tired from the ghost dance, settled on a downed tree. They passed their pipe, never having to light it, and bounced their-heads to a beat that only they could hear. Crazy Talk picked up Alf's hairy, brown, charcoal-briquette-sized throat-lump, clicked a fingernail on it, and put it in his pocket. "Bezoar," he said. "Sunny fish melon jelly balling the jack at the meat wagon now." Throws-Like-Girl and Heap-o-Buffaloes nodded their heads and smiled.

A flurry of questions swirled around inside John's head like a dust devil, picking up random debris and then violently casting it aside, only to pick up more of the wreckage of his psyche and toss it about. Gripped by a new yearning to learn about his situation, John resumed his conversation with Three Tooth. "So what's the deal? Why are you here? Why me? What can you tell me?"

Three Tooth laughed gently and a tear leaked from his eye. He waved his hands in the air, beckoning his compadres. All of the men but Two-Dogs-Fucking slowly rose to their feet. With his big toe, Crazy Talk poked at Two-Dogs-Fucking's ribs, waking him and eliciting a machine-gun-like burst of laughter from the fat man.

"Ba-ha-ha-ha-ha!" went Two-Dogs-Fucking's grating guffaw. In response, Alf the Sacred Burro got to his feet and walked away with his usually-erect ears pinned back flat against his head, his irritated bray sounding not unlike the laughter that prompted him to move.

And Two-Dogs-Fucking's friends echoed his laughter, "Ba-ha-ha-ha-ha," finally breaking into their own genuine laughs, satisfied that they had sufficiently mocked their ridiculous companion. Throws-Like-Girl, Crazy Talk, and Heap-o-Buffaloes meandered over to Three Tooth and John. Alf stumbled along behind them, trying to keep his distance from Two-Dogs-Fucking lest the man should break out in laughter again. And, not yet on his feet, Two-Dogs-Fucking rolled around a bit, like a turtle flipped on his back. Flopping his arms ineffectually at the ground in an effort to sit up, Two-Dogs-Fucking eventually succeeded in getting all of the way to his feet and ambling over to the others.

The mongrel tribe of desert scurves standing before John was as motley a crew as he could expect to see: an Indian, a Chinaman, a Melungeon and two blond surfer-types. All of them but Two-Dogs-Fucking dressed like Native Americans. And the Melungeon, wrapped only in a too-small bath towel, reinforced the bizarre impression with a hearty greeting of

"Halloooooo," his voice starting out deep and rising to a ridiculously high warble.

"What is this? Who are you people?" asked John.

The tears leaking from the tall Indian's eye belied the three-toothed smile on his face. "We are the lies you have told, the promises you have broken. The helpless and weak and weary that you have ignored and abandoned. The children you have failed. We are the shame that you have suppressed. We are your low self esteem. We are your self- loathing. We are your sadness." And the donkey stood next to him, nudging his head at Three Tooth's hand for a scritching. The oily tear tracks running from Alf's eyes gave him a look of sadness to match that of Three Tooth.

"Don't listen to them, Johnny. They'll turn you inside out with the trip they lay on you," shouted Santiago from the midst of a congregation of dirt-rats. A writhing blanket of diseased rodents covered his lap and the ground around him. "They speak with forked tongues and will only bring you down. They will manipulate your emotions and fuck your brain."

"Do not listen to him," said Three Tooth. He watched Santiago snap the spine of a dirt-rat and toss it on a growing pile of carcasses. Speaking to John but raising his voice to be heard by Santiago, Three Tooth said, "He's not competent. You cannot trust the counsel of someone who is incompetent."

"I'm not competent?" shouted Santiago, frightening the dirt-rats and sending them skittering for the safety of their burrows. "You bet I'm not competent. If you're competent, there's a lot to do. People expect things of you. Give you responsibilities. You better believe that I'm not competent. And because of that, I don't have to do nothing. All I do is what I want to do. I shit and piss and eat and drink. I fuck blumpkins 'til I'm dehydrated and stark raving mad. And nobody tells me to do shit. I do what I want. I live where I want, fella. I live on the ground. I live on the earth. I'm aligned with the scorpion and the wolf. And that's the way it is. I'm not competent. I don't want to be competent. But I'll tell you what, Johnny, you're better off hanging with me than that sorry ass crew." He turned his back to Three Tooth and commenced his efforts to attract more dirt-rats.

"Please, palaver with me and my men," said Three Tooth, ignoring Santiago's rant. "We want to help. We are the helping kind of scurves."

The day blew its wad and ran out the door with some sorry excuse about an early meeting in the morning. And evening was on them quickly. The men pissed a large perimeter around themselves and the continuously burning thorn bush. Santiago skinned and gutted his kills and turned the dirt-rats over a small fire, deeply concentrating on his chore in an effort to ignore the presence of the others. But Crazy Talk did not want to be ignored. He stood in front of Santiago, demanding attention.

"Word is you not think good," said Crazy Talk to Santiago. "Word is rats nibble your braincheese. Word is your heart was torn out and eaten by buzzards."

Santiago laughed and stood up from his squat in front of the fire. "Word is you not think good," he repeated, tittering, scratching at his beard and screwing his face up in a disdainful sneer. "Word is, you're an old woman. Word is you have turkey in the sky. Word is, you fellas enjoy each other's company a wee bit too much. How you like them apples, you crazy talking In-jun?" Santiago's face flicked through a random series of twitch-es and settled on a half-smile. And he laughed again at Crazy Talk. "Word is you not think good. Now hit the road, Tonto."

But Crazy Talk did his best impression of a statue. He stood across the small fire from Santiago and occasionally uttered his gibberish when Santiago looked up. "Word is you're a bad ba-nana with a greasy black peel," he said.

Santiago wrung his face into a grimace but remained still, squatting in front of the fire.

"Word is your brain is full of spiders and you have garlic in your soul," said Crazy Talk.

Santiago rose to his feet.

"Word is your heart's a tomato splotched with moldy purple spots," said Crazy Talk. "Word is you're a crooked dirty jockey and you drive a crooked hoss."

"I'm gonna tell you something, brother," said Santiago, his eyes wide open and bulging from the sockets like bloodshot tulip bulbs. You got this stuff in your head about me, your pre-conceived notions and judgments and whatnot. But, I'm the man in the mirror, guy. You like me, I'll like you. You swing at me, I'll swing on you. You try to cut me, and I'll hack you to shreds. So let's cut it with this trip you're on. Walk away and leave me to my business and we'll call it all great and groovy. Alright, chief?"

"Word is, your soul is an appalling dump heap overflowing with the most disgraceful assortment of rubbish imaginable and tangled up in knots."

"Word is this. Word is that. Bladdah-don-dooo-doo-dat-didilly," said Santiago, stomping around in a small circle and slapping himself in the face. "Well, I got a word for you: incoming." Santiago bent over and dredged the bottom of his lungs for an infected brown and yellow glob of mucous. After a good deal of grunting and clearing his throat and slapping his hands on his chest, Santiago horked up sputum from his depths and spat the enormous gob high into the air, launching it in Crazy Talk's direction.

And time crossed its arms and became stubborn and sluggish. The airborne loogie moved in a slow-motion arc, first rising high above them and then quickly picking up speed on its downward trajectory. Crazy Talk watched, unable to move as the projectile flipped about in the air and headed downward toward him. He had time to study it and notice the greens and yellows and browns of the globule. He saw a small mist of spittle trailing off of it like the tail of a comet. Before he could jump aside, the spit splattered on his shoulder and a stench fumed off of it. The stank sickened Crazy Talk, and he vomited just a little of his breakfast up in his mouth. The substance that rose from his stomach was a bilious madness, a fetid resentment that had been brewing in Crazy Talk well before he ever set eyes on Santiago. And it briefly rendered him mad and murderous.

On his side of the fire, Santiago set his feet and held balled up fists out in front of himself in the stance of an old-fashioned pugilist. Opposite Santiago, Crazy Talk spat the acid hatred from his mouth and tightened his muscles. He tensed up and readied to leap over the fire to attack Santiago. The hair on the men's necks stood on end and they both broke out in adrenaline shakes. Santiago released a musty scent from his anus and a bitter taste visited his mouth. Crazy Talk's vision tunneled and his pupils dilated. A split second before the men were to become engaged in a bloodbath, Three Tooth shouted something that stopped the imminent fisticuffs.

"Lunkheads!" shouted Three Tooth.

All other goings-on ceased. Feet shuffled. The men armed themselves with clubs and knives and bows and arrows. To the south of the road a gang of lumbering lunkheads shuffled toward the camp. Their raspy breathing and groans filled the air. Three Tooth drew an arrow back on the taut string of his bow and let it zip. An audible *whizzzz* dragged through the air, followed by a *squish-thud* as the arrow struck and parted layers of skin, penetrating one of the lunkies dead center of his chest. The creature dropped to his knees and screamed at the sky. He plucked the arrow from his chest and a gout of blood spurted rhythmically from the wound. His screaming died down. Within seconds, the man dropped over on his side, gasping heavily for air, and then not gasping. Not moving. Not living.

Oblivious to their fallen comrade, the remaining twenty or so brain-dead and bloodthirsty lunkheads continued their dreadful and slow march on the camp. As they neared, John studied the dead pools of their eyes and their festering wounds. Three Tooth and most of his men (excluding Two-Dogs-Fucking, who conveniently left his bow behind at their last camp and was not motivated to retrieve it) felled the oncoming lunkies with spot-on kill shots to the hearts. And the lunkheads dropped and screamed and gave up the ghosts until there remained only one morbidly obese lunkie who persisted in his efforts to reach the men. The end of one of his legs was a shredded stump where his foot should have been. His uneven gait slowed him up even more as he limped along.

Arrows tensed themselves for launch on the men's bows. In some unspoken agreement, Crazy Talk, Heap-o-Buffaloes, and Throws-Like-Girl all released their arrows at the same time. Three arrows struck the one remaining lunkhead simultaneously, one arrow in each shoulder and one in his thigh. And the monstrous lump of herky-jerky meat continued in their direction, oblivious to the shafts protruding from his flesh. Heap-o-Buffaloes drew back another arrow, bending the bow almost to the point of snapping, and set the missile free. It penetrated the lunkie in the lower right part of his abdomen. The tip of the stone arrowhead peaked out through the man's back and the flight of the arrow just barely showed itself at the front of the fat man. Crazy Talk's bow zinged as it released another shot that lodged itself in the man's left bicep. And the men practiced their aim on the lumbering beast headed in their direction, emptying their quivers and sticking every shot exactly as intended.

The lunkhead still staggered in their direction, looking like a horrific bloody pincushion. And he stopped at the protective piss-barrier, wobbling on his foot and footless stump, groaning. Foamy blood bubbles gurgled from his cracked and sore-covered lips. He stood patiently, as if he were a deliveryman who had rung the doorbell and was waiting for someone to answer. Heap-o-Buffaloes left the other side of the circle and looped around to sneak right behind the persistent lunkie. Heap-o-Buffaloes lowered himself to his hands and knees just behind the brainless butterball. At the same time, Throws-Like-Girl flung himself at the lunkie and pushed on the one spot on the man's chest that was not pierced with arrows, knocking the lunkie back, tripping him over Heap-o-Buffaloes. And the man fell to his back. Some of the arrows were pushed from his body when he hit the ground. Crazy Talk moved with the speed of a cat, and he was on the man, hammering at his head with a rock tied to the end of a thick stick. The weapon did what all of the arrows failed to, and finally released the man from the grip of the lunkworms.

Three Tooth's men laughed heartily and heavily at the kill. Two-Dogs-Fucking found the situation especially funny and belted out his staccato laughter. And the men mocked him and the air was filled with the loud sounds of "Ba-ha-ha- ha-ha!" The laughter hurt Alf the Sacred Burro's ears and he brayed in irritation at the men. Three Tooth did not find the situation humorous. The death of the lunkhead did not give him joy. It saddened him and a tear rolled down his cheek.

Three Tooth's men thumped their chests and slapped each other's backs in celebration. And they stacked their victims well away from the camp. While his men cleaned up the mess, Three Tooth again engaged John in conversation. The two men sat on a log and John spoke of his confusion and his desire to understand his situation. Three Tooth nodded, his eye leaked, and he agreed to try to help John get a grasp on his predicament.

A swarm of munkle flies descended on the mound of lunkie cadavers. The giant black flies droned out an undulating buzz as they burrowed into the eyes, noses, and other available orifices, laying their eggs. And the bombination of the flies fluctuated up and down in frequency, intertwining with the chirps and squeaks and tweets of other desert animals and insects. The organic rhythm of the buzz resonated with the gang of men huddled around the fire, the sound mesmerizing them. John sat on one side of the pit, Santiago on his right, both staring through the flames and smoke at Three Tooth and his men, Santiago only agreeing to sit with the group upon learning of the peace pipe.

Crazy Talk smiled a lopsided grin at the men and said, "Rang tang, ding dong, I am the Japanese sandman. I'm in the mood to move my body like a weasel, goddamn it." He pulled one of Alf the Sacred Burro's throat-lumps from the pocket of his fringed buckskin pants. His pale white skin (like porcelain) and whitish blond hair glowed in the flickering light of the fire, giving the impression of an extremely amused ghost. "Word is, bezoar like a bribe to the wise, blinding eyes and clearing skies."

"Word is," said Santiago, cocking half of his unibrow and flashing his own warped rictus back at Crazy Talk, "you got some shit to smoke. So let's fire up the peace pipe, you crazy albina Injun, and commune with the great spirit."

Throws-Like-Girl, sitting beside Crazy Talk, laughed and shook his long blond hair out of his eyes. He chewed on some words but decided to swallow them before they could escape his silently moving mouth. Instead, he laughed and bopped his head to a beat that only he could hear. From a full wineskin hanging around his neck, Throws-Like-Girl took a large drink and then almost coughed all of the liquid out, barely managing to stifle the geyser building in his throat. And he choked and gagged and fought the foul brew's attempt to exit his mouth. Just like with his words, Throws-Like-Girl managed to swallow the liquid before it could escape. Shaking off the contractions of his body's rebellion against the drink, Throws-Like-Girl passed the wineskin to his right. The libation made its way around the men, causing them to choke and convulse, their bodies shaking and shuddering as they fought to keep the fluid down.

And the goatskin sack reached John. He sniffed at the opening gagged. The fetid halitosis funk curdled the dirt-rat chymus gurgling in his stomach.

"It's chicha. Drink from the bag and I will explain," said Three Tooth. "It smells like death, and tastes twice as bad, but you learn to love it."

John closed his nasal passage to his throat, steeled himself, and tossed back a solid snort of the tonic. With all of the power he could muster, John pushed the shot down his gullet and told it to stay. His eyes bulged and his chest heaved in an effort to spew the drink. His cheeks sucked in and his mouth puckered like an asshole. But the drink, although bold, obeyed and stayed as it was told. The putrid morning breath stench wafted away, leaving a burning in John's throat and a warmth in his belly. His lips and teeth numbed and some slight emotion stirred in his chest. The river of fire flowed slowly in the sky above the red brick road.

"It's awful at first, isn't it?" said Three Tooth. John nodded and passed the chicha to Santiago. Three Tooth continued,

"That is chicha, our traditional drink. We drink it as an offering to the Great Spirit. Chicha is strong and sudden. It makes a man brave and confident, long and strong. Drink a little bit more. You might think it's not working. But just wait until you stand. It will smack you in the forehead like the hammer of the gods."

"I can already feel the effects a little," said John. "And, it's kind of nice. But what's with the smell? I mean, we could probably dump that stuff around our camp to keep the lunkheads away." Santiago continued to swig at the leather bag, not passing it, and drawing irritated looks from the rest of the men.

"The smell is our saliva," answered Three Tooth. "We chew the purple maize and spit it in a pot. We seal the pot, bury it in the ground and allow it to ferment. When it is ripe and ready, we dig up the pot and celebrate."

A spray of chicha spewed from Santiago's mouth. Unlike the others around the circle, he made no effort to hold in the fermented spit. And he passed the wineskin to Two-Dogs- Fucking. And when the leather bag was empty, Three Tooth produced another one full of chicha. When the beverage made its way around the circle and back to Santiago, he changed his attitude and tossed back a good slug, gagging and holding it down.

A sweet and mellow glaze settled on the men. They stared into the flickering flames. Like a contortionist dislocating his shoulder, John easily disconnected from his brain, making no efforts at thought. He stared forward and allowed his mind to creep about here and there as it saw fit. Crazy Talk placed the donkey bezoar on a rock and smashed it with a smaller stone. He placed the broken fragments in the bowl of an ornately carved ebony pipe and took a pull. Without needing to be lit, the bezoar bits glowed red-hot. Like a hound pup chasing a cat, the pipe dogged the chicha in a circle around the fire, never catching up. And John looked down and found the pipe in his hand. Without a thought, his hand brought the stem of the pipe to his lips and he pulled deeply, inhaling the fruitlike and not unpleasant smoke. His mouth opened and allowed the fog to creep out. The smoke continued to roll from his lips with each exhalation, until finally it all cleared his lungs and took with it all ability to formulate thought, leaving his head empty but for the buzzing of the munkle flies resonating in his skull.

Three Tooth's hand fell on John's shoulder and nudged him back to a slight awareness. "It is time for you to get up now," said Three Tooth.

And John listened. "Okay," he said. When he stood, his legs slowly marched in place. Three Tooth turned him toward the still-flaming thorn bush and gently pushed on his back. John's sluggish marching legs carried him to the thorn bush where he sat down, cross-legged, and stared into the flames.

The crucifixion thorn lashed out at John with a fiery tongue and its words boomed over the land. The voice was loud and distorted, incomprehensible, like a blown public address speaker. The sound waves blew back John's longish hair and slammed his ears. The deep bass of the voice registered as a physical assault on John's belly and balls.

"I cannot understand," yelled John, his hands clamped to his throbbing ears and his knees ground solidly into the red sand. "It's too loud! It hurts."

And the voice softened. The roar of the flames subsided to a low burn. "It has been many moons now," said the burning bush. "I have gone with you and ahead of you, as a trail of clouds by day and a river or fire by night. You have stayed true to the path. And that is the way. Follow the trail and stay with the trail. To do not is to fail, and all will be lost."

"But what is the point?" asked John. He stared into the blaze and was blinded by its brilliance. His face burned and sweat poured from his pores. "I've been walking. I've followed the path. All that I've seen is misery and suffering. I'm ignorant and tired. I don't know who I am or why I'm bothering with this. I don't even know what I should feel or if I even feel anything. I'm traveling with a madman and trailed by brain-dead monsters. And I'm following a road that, for all I know, leads to nowhere. I need answers or I'm just going to stay right here on my knees and wait for them until I die."

A stabbing pain jabbed at John's side, and blood soaked his white robe from the injury. John did not scream or run. He genuflected before the bush and pressed his hands to his side. Then, as if stained with disappearing ink, the blood evaporated and his robe turned white again. And the sharp pain ceased. He tore back the robe and saw no wound, just a white raised scar in the shape of an X.

"You are on the right path," boomed the voice. "And though you may not realize it, I do. I know you and you know me. One thing I can tell you is you've got to be free. And, the red brick road, or El Camino de la Muerte if you will, is the way and the truth and the life. And there is no conclusion to your journey without the path."

"But what is the conclusion? What is the goal?"

"That is the question, isn't it?" said the thorn bush.

"That is," said John. "So what is the answer?"

"I will lead you to that answer in due time. I will show you things. Now, close your eyes to be better in tune with the infinite."

The bush erupted into a pillar of fire. John closed his eyes as he had been told. The smell of his singed hair filled the air and the fire scorched his face. The fury and flicker of the eruption played out on the inside of John's eyelids as a stroboscopic picture show of shifting images. "This," boomed the voice, "is the effect you had on those who you came in contact with in your other life." A parade of horrid faces flashed on the inside of his eyelids, not horrid because of deformities or mutations, and not infected with a defiling mold, but horrid in the emotions they conveyed. An elderly blue haired woman sneered in disgust. A motherly type shook her head and dabbed at her eyes with a lace handkerchief, her shame and sadness stabbing John worse than the prick of the scar on his side. A man, eyes burning with hatred, stared down at John. Images of children crying and running away. A dead cat on the side of a road.

"These are the women who loved you," said the burning bush. There appeared a row of naked women's bodies, some trim, others pudgy, with all shapes and sizes of breasts and buttocks, and some with large pubic shrubbery and others shaved bald and glistening. And their faces – instead of faces, taut drumheads of skin stretched tight over the places where eyes and noses and mouths should have been. Even in the absence of facial features, John sensed a disgust and shame and rage and hurt, and the emotions were all sharpened darts, heaved at and sticking into him. Clouds of grey, purple, dark green, and brown hovered around and about their heads. Jagged scars of crude stitching gashed their chests and ran the length from the jugular notch of their necks to the bottoms of the sternums. The scars, red and feverish with infections, stood out in contrast to the purple bruising around them. John understood that he was responsible for the women's anger. He understood he caused their injuries. The urge to jump up and flee flooded him, but his body refused to cooperate and remained immobile, glued to the spot in front of the burning bush.

And he shook his head to clear the images. The naked, faceless, scarred females backed away from him slowly, shaking their heads back and forth, and a new scene in the eyelid-picture-show replaced them. More faces, tinted in greens and blues and oranges from the flames beating against his eyelids. Faces tainted with desperation and resentment and bitterness. Grudges and repulsion dripped from the slobbering mouths of those rabid with hostility at John. And then the face of Three Tooth, a tear rolling down his cheek, appeared before John. "This is your influence. These are the people you drained and used. These are your family, friends, and acquaintances. Some of them were poisoned by simple contact with you and nothing more. You made them into this. These are your sins."

The blaze of the thorn bush flared and erased the images from the backs of John's eyes. "Those were your people. And these are the feelings you felt in your other life." A lava flow of despair rushed toward and buried John. His gut cramped. The scar on his side screamed. The thumping of his heart in his head felt like it would blow off the top of his skull and spew out the blood and the evil and a torrent of anguish. He welcomed the possibility of a cranial blowout to purge himself of the creeping rot that he felt inside. He welcomed the cleansing. He embraced the possibility of death because he could bear the agony no longer.

John screamed, "Stop it! Stop this madness or I will end it myself." He struggled to get to his feet but his strength failed him.

His eyelids cleared of the images and all he saw was the flicker of the flames. His pains waned and the psychic wounds quickly healed themselves, returning John to the bland feeling of confusion and emptiness. His eyes opened. He stared into the flames, feeling his skin tighten on his cheeks and around his eyes. "What does this all mean?" he asked the bush. "It's awful and utterly depressing. And if that is what I felt before, then I'd rather be here. What could I have done to those people to cause such hate? I don't feel like I'm that despicable."

"The specifics of your life are irrelevant at this time. It is the feeling, the sense of your self that is important. What you are is what's important. What you can do about it, that's what is important."

"I still don't get it," said John. "I do want to know why I felt the way I just did. You need to tell me..."

"Silence!" boomed the voice. "You do not order me to do anything." A neon red halo flashed above them in the sky, and preceded a cluster of reddish-orange lightning, its tendrils shooting down and surrounding John and the burning bush. The flashes of the lightning and the flare of the fire forced John to close his eyes again.

"Keep your eyes closed," ordered the bush. "I have much more to show you."

The stroboscopic eyelid-movie resumed. John saw himself lying in a hospital bed, unconscious and emaciated. A nurse changed bandages on his side. She pulled away the dressing and uncovered a gangrenous wound. The nurse looked away from the injury and buried her face in the crook of her arm, seeking shelter from the stench of the infected flesh. A man in a uniform stuck his head in the door and asked the nurse something. She waved him away and returned to tending the wound. The pain in John's side lit up briefly and excruciatingly.

"That is now," said the bush. "That is you. You are there. You are here. And you are split. Your experiences and habits, your likes and dislikes, your knowledge, your history, and every thing that made you repugnant, that's all you and it's all there in that bed with you, fouling up that hospital room. The man sitting before me now, is John. You are John. And you are the same man, but you, here and now, are not twisted and poisoned by the experiences of your other half. You are an uncarved stone that is slowly developing its own markings. Tabula rasa. This is a different place. And, you have the chance to become something better and new. The path is the way. Follow the road to the end. Stay true and don't let your path stray."

"But, what am I looking for at the end that is going to be so important?"

"At the end of the road you will encounter this man," said the voice. And on John's eyelids appeared the severe face of a black-haired man in mirrored sunglasses. His features tensed as he laughed and shook his head about. The thick black hair lay slicked back and clinging to his skull as if it were spray painted on. A half-grin sat uncomfortably on his face and gave way to a scowl. The image of the man grew and developed, and he stood before a congregation of cowering parishioners. He towered several feet above the tallest of his followers. His black leather pants, black shirt, and boots matched the slicked back hair. And the white of his priestly collar matched the gleam of his sharp, sneering teeth.

John's balls partially retracted into his abdominal cavity at the vision of the Man in Black. He clenched his teeth and tensed his eyes, trying to wipe away the vision. But the Man in Black remained. His image grew until he appeared to be twice as tall as the members of his cowering congregation. He pounded with balled fists at the podium before him and it crumbled as if it were made of sand. Even with the podium smashed to dust, he continued to pound his hands in the air before him to emphasize each word that he spat from his mouth. The congregation stared, rapt. They swayed from side to side, slowly waving their raised hands in the air, their collective arms like an anemone's tentacles drifting in the ocean current.

"His name is Android Lovethorn. The Right Reverend Android Lovethorn," said the burning bush. "He holds the key to your return. He can help you return to yourself and become whole again. You must find him. But, before you do, you will travel the road. And you will decide who you are and what you are. And the man you become on your trek is the man that you will take back to yourself. The journey will make you stronger than your other half. And you can make amends for everything bad that the other you did. You can rectify the past and make a new future. Until then, though, you are split. And the man you used to be is of no consequence. So follow the road and find the Reverend Lovethorn."

"But he scares me," said John. "He reeks of madness."

"He is mad. And evil, and hateful. And he will do everything he can to prevent you from reaching him. He sends lunkheads to slow you. He floods you with temptations from the villages you pass. He troubles your dreams. He will afflict the land with plagues and send demons to stop you. But, stay on the red brick road and follow the trail. Your travels will end at Lovethorn's door. And you must be strong enough to make him return you to yourself."

"But, when do I find Lovethorn? What do I do when I find him? How do I make him return me to myself?"

John's words fell from his mouth and died a quiet death on the ground as the flames on the bush burnt themselves out, leaving the thorn bush green and unmarked. Rubbing his eyes and erasing the images of the Man in Black from his eyelids, John stood. He wobbled on his feet and put his hand down on something to steady himself. That something was Alf the Sacred Burro's head. Alf liked the feel of John's hand, so he stayed in that place and let John use him for balance. John steadied himself and walked away from the bush and the donkey in a daze. Alf convulsed and twitched and coughed up a hairy lung-ball that he spat on the ground. He slowly approached and walked beside John, hoping that the man would need him for assistance with his balance again.

First the tickling on the face, like a feather duster on his skin. And the buzzing. Then the burn and sting of many bites on his face and arms. Santiago ejecting profanities from his mouth like spent cartridges from a Gatling gun. The irate, strained braying of a sacred burro. Drawn out hisses of turkey vultures. Surprised cries of desert scurves. Crazy Talk screaming, "Boze dee boze dee bop, diddy bop." And John woke up. A black cloud of munkle flies, so thick that it seemed to extinguish the morning sun, had enveloped their camp. John jumped up from his sleeping spot and clawed at his nose, where he could feel flies wriggling into his nasal cavities. He blocked his left nostril and blasted out a snot-rocket of flies and their eggs and then did the same with his other nostril.

Three Tooth ran through the swarm of munkle flies, waving his arms to try to clear the way in front of himself, and grabbed John by the front of his robe. "You have brought this plague on the land. You have polluted our desert. You must move along, go away from here. I am leaving two of my men with you to help with your journey. But I must leave you to your business. So take Crazy Talk and Two-Dogs-Fucking. You can take the donkey, too. We will have scouts tailing you to make sure that you need no assistance. But, we can stay with you no longer."

Through the black cloud of airborne insects, John made out Three Tooth's fly-infested face and saw a tear clearing a streak on his cheek. Three Tooth turned and ran, calling out to his men. The scurves fought their way through the flies, fleeing the stinging swarm. John, too, decided it was time to flee and he called out to Santiago, Crazy Talk, and Two- Dogs-Fucking.

And they were on the road again, sprinting down the red brick trail and swatting at the flies that bit at them. A writhing carpet of munkle flies turned to a black mush as the men ran and slipped on the desert floor, now greasy and slick with the paste of flies smashed underfoot. Two-Dogs- Fucking, despite his rotundity and usual lack of motivation, ran the fastest and slipped the least. Just behind him, the moist clopping of Alf the Sacred Burro's hooves on the ground beat out a hasty rhythm of retreat. The high-pitched screams that exited Two-Dogs- Fucking's mouth pained the men's ears as badly as the stinging of the flies on their skin. The enormous cloud of insects trailed John and his men, buzzing and swirling around them, and departed the pile of lunkie corpses from whence they hatched.

The departure of the munkle flies from the site of the lunk-head-massacre left behind an army of turkey vultures. The buzzards hissed and spat and undressed the corpses, tearing at the dead flesh and devouring it until all that was left was a pile of bones and a fattened flock of vultures. And when there was no more flesh for them to consume, the buzzards briefly turned on each other, hissing and clawing and pecking, until drowsiness from the feast mellowed them.

John, Santiago, Two-Dogs-Fucking, Crazy Talk, and Alf the Sacred Burro raced down the red brick road, dogged by the munkle flies the entire morning. Everything along the path – rocks, cacti, trees, the ground – buzzed with a covering of the nasty biting bugs. At midday, the sun sat directly above the men and sapped their strength with its glare. And though they felt ready to drop, they persisted in their flight. And the swarm of flies abated. The insects' half-day life span fizzled out lamely under the harsh desert sun. With no cadavers to lay their eggs in, the entire swarm expired quietly and left no descendants to pester John and the others. The dead flies piled up, ankle-deep, and John and his crew continued until they were clear of the blanket of insect corpses.

The sweltering sun, dehydration, and fatigue combined to make a persuasive argument that the men should lay themselves out on the road and recover from their flight. When it was clear that the plague of munkle flies had concluded, John threw himself down on the red bricks. His chest heaved with a thirst for oxygen. Every inch of exposed skin swelled and burned from the countless and repeated munkle fly bites. The brilliance from the noonday sun scorched his afflicted flesh and blinded his eyes. But John did not care. His body cried out against any further efforts, being drained of strength by chicha and bezoars from the night prior. And the mad dash away from the thousands of biting attackers exacerbated his weakness. Even if he had the will to move, he had not the strength. So John lay out in the sun, exposed and weak and without a care about what happened to him. The sun sizzled him like a piece of bacon on the frying pan surface of El Camino de la Muerte. He lay there, welcoming oblivion, should he be so blessed. Alf the Sacred Burro lay on the ground beside him, heaving raspy breaths and coughing up puddles of mucus filled with dead flies that he had inhaled. Two-Dogs-Fucking and Santiago took positions far apart and collapsed from weakness. And Crazy Talk sat, not far from John, alert and still energetic, scanning the horizon.

Late in the afternoon, John awoke to the hissing of turkey vultures fighting over the corpses of several dead lunkheads. Crazy Talk sat down beside him and handed John a skin filled with water. John hydrated himself, half emptying the skin without a thought. Crazy Talk nodded toward the lunkie corpses and said, "Word is, man-meat sleeps in open coffins, and it's happening more often." Crazy Talk thumped a fist on his leg and flashed a brown-toothed smile. He held up a thick stick with a rock strung to the end of it and swung it around. "I make boom boom," he said as he slammed the rock-end of his weapon into the ground.

"You killed those men?" asked John.

"I make boom boom," said Crazy Talk, slamming the weapon into the ground again.

"Thank you. I wouldn't have woken up even if they were eating me alive. I just didn't have it in me. You protected me."

"Now, don't go getting all misty-eyed and wet in you panties." Santiago approached and cat-hissed at Crazy Talk. "Cochise there wasn't protecting you. That crazy talking albina Injun is just plain screwy. We're lucky he had lunkies to take it out on or he likely woulda bashed our heads in for game."

Crazy Talk continued to look at John and said, "Word is, Unibrow speak with tongue twisted into pretzel. He think he big man. He think he more bacon than the pan can handle. Word is, Unibrow is nothing."

Santiago recoiled as if he were smacked in the face with a bag of dicks. His expressions ticked through his full range of emotions and settled on outrage. "Nothing. You saying I ain't nothing, Geronimo? Well listen up, I'm everything. I do what I need to do to survive. I live in the desert. I live in the mountains. My mind is big. Dig?"

Tightening his grip on the rock-stick, Crazy Talk stood. He took several steps backward and watched Santiago flap his arms about and pull at his own hair. Crazy Talk said nothing and waited to see if he needed to defend himself.

Santiago calmed and laughed his nervous titter. He did not approach Crazy Talk. He did not carry on with his rant. He merely squatted beside John and said, "This guy's gotta go before he kills me. He ain't helping us here, Johnny."

"Well," said John, "he saved our skins while the rest of us were dead to the world. He stood guard. He stopped those lunkies from getting at us, didn't he? You'd be a goner, too. So tell me, how is it that you are more important to me than Crazy Talk?"

"I feed you, don't I? Without me, you wouldn't have all those tasty dirt-rats to eat," said Santiago. "And I cured that nasty infection you had on your ear, didn't I?"

"You bit off my ear and swallowed it in the first place, you lunatic. You caused the infection. How's that helping?"

Still squatting, Santiago tugged at his beard and said, "Lookie here, let me explain something to you. I'm necessary, man. I'm what you need to survive. You ain't got nothin'. You got no de-

sires. Your emotional range is nonexistent. Have you really got-
ten upset about anything since you've been here? Have you
been mad? Happy? Sad? Have you felt like fucking or fighting
or screaming? No, you haven't. You ain't got it in you right now.
And that's what I'm here for. I'm your wild side, your desires,
your base urges. I make you eat. I drive you to do the things
that your body needs, even though your brain doesn't even realize it. I'm your fucking id, Johnny. I don't give a squeaky shit
about consequences. I seek instant gratification. And you need
that aspect to get you through. Because without the drive,
you're just going to sit here and bake in the heat, not caring,
because it all seems so meaningless. Ain't that right, Johnny?"

"I don't know what you're talking about," John said. He tried
feebly to manipulate his face into a look of indignation and realized that Santiago was right. He was numb. He moved along
because he was pushed in a direction. He ate because food was
given to him, but didn't have the urge to seek out anything for
himself. He had no urges or desires.

"I wanna ask you something personal," said Santiago. "We've
been all alone, and I bet you haven't tugged your pud since you
left that cave, have you?"

"That's none of your business," replied John, again with the
faux-indignation.

"Well, you haven't and you know it. How in the hell do you
just ignore the urge to gratify yourself? Or, let's be honest here,
you don't really feel any urges do you?"

"I don't want to talk about this any more," snapped John. And
he was up, walking away from Santiago, avoiding the conversation. He wanted to tell himself that maybe he was afraid of

blasting out another bloody spooge puddle. And maybe that was part of it. But not really. He simply felt no sexual urges at all. And the thought of it shocked him. He ambled away from the group, trying to force himself to feel something, anything.

John tossed and turned during the night, his skin prickly and uncomfortable from the swollen munkle bites that were forming into pus-filled carbuncles and furuncles all over his body. The conversation with Santiago echoed in his head. He felt nothing about his situation. The burning bush told him to walk, so he walked. Santiago led him into temptation – food, lunkworms, physical altercations – that he cared nothing about otherwise. Crazy Talk saved his life while he was sleeping, but John would have been just fine with being murdered in his sleep by the worm-addled lunkies.

As he drifted in and out of his fitful sleep, John saw the face of Android Lovethorn. The Reverend Lovethorn's head, laughing and ringed in a halo of red flames, floated as a hypnogogic apparition before John. "Thrive and drool on," said the apparition. "I will thrive and drool on." And strings of foamy slobber oozed from the corners of his mouth. The flaming black-haired head doubled in size and thrust itself in John's direction. Lovethorn ripped off his mirrored sunglasses and empty black eye sockets stared at John. And the void in the sockets reflected John's emptiness and blackness right back at him. And John flinched, found himself falling backwards, flailing his arms and legs at the hazy space between sleep and alertness, then jerking back awake and realizing it was just a dream.

Then the cycle started again with the discomfort and agitation and stinging of the munkle fly bites. He felt the boils on his flesh bursting and seeping out the pus. But, he did not care. And the seepage drained him not only of fluids, but also of his energy. And with the flowing river of fire above and Wormwood casting down its green aura, he drifted back toward sleep, only to be accosted again by Lovethorn's horrid, laughing countenance. Then the falling. And the jerking back awake. And the discomfort. And so it went through the night for John.

On the ground around John, the others lapsed in and out of sleep and were also visited by Lovethorn's empty eye sockets and his mocking laughter. They all squirmed restlessly and fought and fit with sleep. Like John, the men all found sleep elusive until just before sunrise, when exhaustion finally won out and the men achieved the empty, dreamless slumber.

Santiago shook John awake. The smell of cooked dirt-rat filled the air. Crazy Talk and Two-Dogs-Fucking still lay on the ground, each on one side of Alf the Sacred Burro and cuddling up to the sickly donkey. John's stirring awakened Alf. The burro choked on a gob of mucous and coughed it out onto Two-Dogs-Fucking, waking the bulbous slackard. Crazy Talk did not move.

"Crazy Shit over there didn't make you any breakfast, did he, now?" Santiago said, and he handed John a pointed stick with a fire-grilled dirt-rat impaled on it. His mossy smile sought John's approval.

The fat rodent's eyes bulged and remnants of singed hair stuck to its head and ears. Grease dripped from the rat's face. The smell of the rat-kabob tickled John's salivary glands and a borborygmus rumbled in his gut. He ingurgitated all edible parts of the animal before rising and relieving his morning wood with a drawn-out arc of urine.

Even after pissing a quart of fluid, John's erection remained firm. He felt the tickle of arousal in his loins and found privacy behind a thick saguaro cactus. With a fervor that he had forgotten, John scratched his prurient itch, assailing his loins repeatedly. And the bloody slush at his feet once again spawned new and sundry creatures that crawled across the desert floor and evolved before John's eyes. Several of the smaller jizz-critters scaled the towering cactus and perched on its arms, high above and staring down at John. Some of the creatures expired in the morning glare and others sprouted springy legs and fled across the landscape. John heard the excitement of Santiago and the others in the distance as they clubbed the beasts that invaded their camp. The men split and gutted the jizz-critters and fed on their meat for breakfast. John said nothing when he returned to find them cooking the creatures over the fire and eating them. Even if he thought to warn them, he had no idea what he would say.

With their bellies full and heads dopey from fitful sleep, they set out on the red brick road again, with a direction and intent toward Android Lovethorn. The roiling river of clouds flowed rapidly overhead in the same direction as the men. Bloodwood trees occasionally shot from the ground along the side of the trail, spreading their limbs in a welcome gesture to the sky above, their rough bark oozing sweet, rubious sap. And they came upon a bloodwood tree with a man dangling by the neck from a rope, his face pecked clean by scavengers but the rest of his body intact and mummified by the desert sun. The man wore clothes of fine white linen, just like John's. His feet sported sandals identical to John's. His hair, crusted with sap from the tree, approximated the same shade and length as John's longish brown hair.

Crazy Talk stepped off of the path and peeled bark from the tree. He picked tiny pink grubs from the stripped bark and popped them in his mouth like a handful of pinyon nuts. Grabbing one of the dangling body's feet, Crazy Talk set the corpse to swinging back and forth like a rotten-meat pendulum. "Word is, this the tenth specimen of similar linen-wrapped fruit that these trees have borne in so many moons," said Crazy Talk, picking more grubs from the bark and eating them as the body swung behind him.

"Well, halloooo," crooned Two-Dogs-Fucking as he ambled upon the group at the tree, waving his walking stick in greeting. For most of the morning he and Alf the Sacred Burro had trailed the others. They took their time plodding along, sometimes leaving the trail, cutting across the desert, and catching John as he came back around a bend of the red road. Two-

Dogs-Fucking peeled a piece of bark from the bloodwood tree and started in on his own lunch of pink grubs. "I am not feeling like doing this today. I'd rather nap in the shade for a while. As for my donkey friend, this heat is really taking it out of him."

Alf the Sacred Burro plopped his hindquarters on the ground beside John and horked up several stinking bezoars the size and shape of large grapes. Before the stench from the donkey lumps had time to find a good current to drift on, Santiago fell upon them, grabbing the hairy bezoars and shoving them into the bag around his neck. He shook the bag at Crazy Talk and taunted him with a smile. John reached down and patted Alf's ribs, trying to knock out whatever else might be blocking up the donkey. Alf nudged his muzzle against John, who found himself scritching the donkey's head without even thinking about it.

Santiago jumped high in the air and tried to grab at the dead man. "He's holding something," said Santiago, and he leapt again, grabbing at the mummified hand. With his third effort, Santiago sprang high and slapped at the hand, hitting it but failing to dislodge its contents.

"Here," said Two-Dogs-Fucking, handing Santiago the crooked, knotted walking stick he had been using. "Take a whack at it with this."

Santiago stared at the stick, not sure if he wanted to accept it. Two-Dogs-Fucking did not set Santiago on edge like Crazy Talk. But still, Santiago wasn't sure that he wanted to accept help from any of Three Tooth's men. "Go ahead," said Two-Dogs-Fucking. "Take it. It's yours to keep if you like."

Santiago tentatively accepted the stick and found that he liked the way it felt in his hand. He gripped it and, like a kid attacking a piñata, swung it with all of his might at the mummified claw. And the stick smacked the hand, almost knocking it off of the arm at the wrist. With his next whack, Santiago knocked the hand clear off of the arm. It flew through the air and smacked down on the ground at Crazy Talk's feet. Before Santiago could grab the cadaver-piñata prize, Crazy Talk was holding it and prying back the dehydrated fingers, each cracking and falling off as they were pried away. And from the crumbling claw, Crazy Talk plucked an oversized playing card, the ace of spades. And the artwork on the face of the card showed, in Day-Glo colors, a linen-clad, faceless body, hanging from a tree by a noose and gripping an ace of spades.

John took the card and carried it along with him. He, Santiago and Crazy Talk left the bloodwood tree behind them and set out on the red brick road again. Behind them, Two-Dogs-Fucking sat on the ground under the tree and continued to eat the grubs he dug out of the bark.

"I'm not really motivated to walk right now. I think I'll take a little siesta, nosh a little, and catch up with you guys later," said Two-Dogs-Fucking, waving the men away, unconcerned about being alone with just a sickly donkey in such active lunkhead territory.

El Camino de la Muerte twisted and curved and rose and dropped. The challenge of the road and the searing desert heat slowed the men to a crawl. Along the way they encountered more bloodwood trees with lynched bodies dangling from them. Santiago developed a knack for knocking the hands off of the bodies with his new walking stick. And Crazy Talk snapped the dry fingers away from the cards and handed them to John. The cards depicted various images rendered in shocking hues that cast a neon glow. The second card they collected was a joker, and the fool on the image resembled Santiago with his wild hair and beard and unibrow. And the crazed look in the joker's eyes was not new to John, as he had seen that look on Santiago's face many times. Another card showed a man with two heads and a scale behind him. One card depicted a corpulent man with a long goatee and the curved horns of a mountain goat. And the goat-man reclined on a throne with writhing bodies at his feet. The jack of diamonds had two faces on his head, both of the faces somewhat resembling Crazy Talk's. And the faces looked out from opposite sides and spoke, their words forming a black cloud above the shared head. On the two of clubs was a giant with a boulder of a head and stout body. And the giant fought off a gang of men who attacked him and clung to his limbs. His thick head tilted back as he screamed out at his attackers. By the time they settled down under the light of Wormwood and the two quarter moons, John had nearly collected an entire deck of the glowing cards. And he fell asleep studying the images on the cards, trying to derive their meaning.

Sometime during the night, Two-Dogs-Fucking and Alf the Sacred Burro moseyed into John's camp. Wormwood cast a luminous emerald glow over the desert. Two-Dogs-Fucking wandered away from the camp, and out of the protective circle of piss, to find the perfect spot to lay on his back and marvel at the beauty of the sky with its two moons and river of fire. Alf did not follow and instead elected to curl up beside John. Two-Dogs-Fucking lay back, his hands locked behind his head, and fell asleep to the shimmering streaks of a meteor shower.

Crazy Talk shook John awake early in the morning. The sounds of a tussle and muffled grunts and groans came to him. He tried to shake the sleep off and make sense of the noises.

"We have problem," said Crazy Talk. "Temperature's dropping at the rotten oasis, stealing kisses from the leprous faces." He pointed to a spot behind John, from where the groans were coming.

John rose and turned in the direction that Crazy Talk pointed. Outside of the protective circle, where he had fallen asleep, was Two-Dogs-Fucking, stripped of his bath towel and on his hands and knees. A gaggle of frisky lunkheads surrounded him. The lunkies groped and rubbed themselves about his body. One particularly leprous looking lunkie mounted Two-Dogs-Fucking from behind, jackhammer-thrusting his way past hirsute ass cheeks and into the fat Melungeon's shithole. Another lunkie rounded the front of Two-Dogs-Fucking and penetrated the Melungeon's mouth with a swollen, chancrous erection, brutally fucking his throat. The other lunkies stood around in a circle, stroking their meat and grabbing at Two-Dogs-Fucking's dimpled flesh.

Crazy Talk snatched up his bow and a quiver. He took his time aiming an arrow and let it fly. The arrow pierced the back of one of the lunkies and the arrowhead exited the chest, dead center. The lunkie dropped to the ground with his hand still stroking himself. The others continued their bukake session, paying no attention to their colleague spasming in the simultaneous throes of death and orgasm at their feet.

Two-Dogs-Fucking pulled his head back from the lunkie schwanz that was stretching his esophagus. "No," he screamed, his voice sounding rough and gurgly. "They aren't going to hurt me if you just let them finish. But if you throw them off, they might tear me to bits. Just let them finish."

The front-end lunkie stopped Two-Dogs-Fucking from saying anything else by stuffing his bloated nutsack in the fat Melungeon's mouth. And while Two-Dogs-Fucking tried to explain further, his words squished out around the puffy scrotum as a muffled "mnnmmmpppphhsssss mmmmmmnomnomnomnom manommana."

An arrow sat tensed on the string of Crazy Talk's bow. He contemplated the request of Two-Dogs-Fucking. Should he shoot or let the lunkies finish themselves off? Would they just leave after they glazed Two-Dogs-Fucking with their seed? Crazy Talk could not decide how to proceed. He gazed down the shaft of the arrow at another lunkie's back, drew the arrow tighter, and steadied his aim. But, John grabbed the arrow in his hand and stopped the shot.

And though he did not understand it, John simply knew that he could disperse the lunkheads. He stepped over the piss circle they had sprayed the night before and approached the lunkie orgy. "Be gone," he said with an air of authority that surprised him. "Be gone and bother us no more."

The lunkheads at each end of Two-Dogs-Fucking withdrew from the object of their affections and turned toward John. Behind John, Crazy Talk nocked an arrow and trained it on the face-fucker for a kill shot. Despite his dislike for Crazy Talk, Santiago stood right at his side, walking stick in his hands like a club, ready to run in and dispatch the lunkie threat.

And the lunkheads growled at John, but they did not approach him. They stood their ground, hands still unconsciously stroking themselves, and hissed. They hissed out of anger and frustration. They hissed in fear of John.

"Be gone," he said again and waved his hand in front of the lunkheads, shooing them away like bothersome munkle flies. And he spoke in a manner that felt foreign to him. "Be gone or I will lay you even with the ground. I will grind you to dust. I will drink wine from your skulls and suck the marrow from your bones. Be gone and bother us no more." As he said so, John knew that they would listen. And the lunkheads backed away from Two-Dogs-Fucking, leaving him facedown in the sand. They backed away from John, hissing and spitting at him like frightened cats. But they did back away. Once at a safe distance from John, they turned and did their best to run. Their flight was more of a low-speed, limping, zigzagging jog. And, while their pace was in no way speedy, it was the fastest John or any of the others had seen lunkheads move.

Once the lunkies were clear of the area, John assisted Two-Dogs-Fucking to his feet and handed him his bath towel. "Cover your uncomely parts," John said. And Two-Dogs- Fucking wrapped himself in the dirty towel. John expected the man to be in shock or angry or humiliated. But Two-Dogs-Fucking just waddled back toward the camp with a smile on his face, as if he had just awakened from a sweet dream.

That morning they dined on bloodwood fruit and grubs. After breakfast, Two-Dogs-Fucking leaned back against a log, thumped his palm on his taut belly, and said, "It's been a tough day for me already. I don't have the gumption to start walking just yet. You all go ahead and I'll catch up with you."

So they left Two-Dogs-Fucking and Alf the Sacred Burro behind and set out on the road again. The rhythm of his sandals smacking the red bricks drove John forward. And that morning, John felt something stirring in him. Some sort of emotion. He couldn't identify it, but it simmered in his stomach and radiated warmth all the way up through his chest. John thought it might be happiness but couldn't be sure. He didn't feel bad and he knew he felt something. So it was an improvement. He forced himself to try to feel and it seemed to be working. He thought he might feel like laughing but wasn't sure he was capable. Instead, the slightest hint of a smile formed on John's lips.

"What's got you all flighty?" asked Santiago. "You're looking goofy, almost smiling. It don't seem right."

"I don't know," said John. "But I think it's a good thing." And that's all he said. John kept walking, slapping his feet on the bricks, and he tried to hold on to the feeling that was growing in him. Santiago walked beside him, thumping his new walking stick on the ground, questioning John with a sideways stare.

Just before they crested a hill and lost visual contact with Two-Dogs-Fucking, John peered back into the distance and saw the rotund form leisurely ambling away from their campsite in the direction that the lunkies had fled. Alf the Sacred Burro stood on shaky old legs and walked away from Two-Dogs-Fucking, following the red brick road and heading in the same direction as John. It was hard to tell, but it looked to John like Alf was shaking his head in disgust.

John allowed himself to be swept along in the current of the clouds above. His path stayed true to the way of El Camino de la Muerte. The others followed, content with being dragged along in John's wake. Alf the Sacred Burro caught up with them and heeled at John's side like a well-trained dog. As they walked, the men scratched and picked at the festering munkle fly bites. The picking and scratching only irritated the bulbous boils, popping some of them and inflaming others. The sun pummeled them and boiled the fluid in their blisters. And the men became tired, irritable, and ready to turn on each other by midday.

The red brick road collided into a large mesa that jutted ten cubits off the ground. The edge of the mesa was ringed with grickle grass and derelict school buses sitting end to end like a rust-infected elephant chain. Fabric dyed in bright swirls of many colors hung over the buses' windows and blocked the view of any outsiders looking in.

"What's up with the buses?" asked John.

"You're either on the bus or off?" said Santiago.

"Those not buses," said Crazy Talk. "Those the warm cozies where the people eat and sleep and keep their meat."

"Huh?" said John.

"Those are their digs. Dig?" said Santiago. "Those aren't buses in the sense that their wheels go round and round. There ain't no wipers on the bus that go swish, swish, swish. Those mufuggers just sit there and give you a place to crash instead of sleeping on the ground."

John looked and saw that it was true that none of the buses had tires on them. And they had no wipers to swish. The vehicles sat on stacked-up piles of flat red rocks. Tendrils of smoke crept out of a pipe that stuck out of the roof of one bus. Curtains pulled back in another vehicle and a pair of eyes went blink, blink, blink, scanning the newcomers.

The red brick road rose to the mesa and collided into oaken doors that spanned the distance between the buses on each side. John and the others stood, staring at the doors and pondering what to do. The smell of meat cooking and the sounds of men yelling floated over the buses and dropped like a brick in front of the men.

"Let's go in," said Santiago. "It sounds like a party in there."

"Let's dip our heads in hot wax and glarble praises to the blue fadoodle," said Crazy Talk.

Alf the Sacred Burro whinnied and backed away from the door. He opined that they should circumnavigate the village and keep on keeping on. Alf's nerves caused him to heave and seize up until he regurgitated a mess of vegetable fibers and hair all wound into a hard, blackish lump. Crazy Talk pounced on the bezoar with the quickness of a mountain lion, seizing the donkey-ball and securing it for himself before Santiago could lay claim to it.

"Gawdamn albina Injun," Santiago said to Crazy Talk. "Gawdamn."

John scratched at the itch of his thickening beard and pondered the doors before him. He wondered what was inside. The mesa blocked the path, so they had to pass through. But they had avoided the other towns and villages that they saw off of the trail. And they seemed to be better for it. John did not want to be detained or delayed. And he knew not what awaited them inside the gates. But the words of the burning bush rang in his head: *He who follows the trail is at one with the trail. He who is virtuous experiences virtue. He who loses the way, is lost. When you are at one with the trail, the trail welcomes you. Follow the trail.*

"We don't have a choice," said John. "This is where the trail takes us and we have to follow. We have to be at one with the trail. And this village or fort or whatever it is sits on the way. We have to go through." John grabbed the wrought iron ring of the lion-head knocker and banged it against the door three times.

The three sharp claps on the door rang out. The sounds of feet stumbling and somebody mumbling came through the door in muffled tones.

Someone on the other side of the door moved the cover on the Judas hole and placed his eye to it, glaring out at John and the men. The eye scanned back and forth evaluating them. An oafish voice attached to the eye said, "Go away and be gone. You've no business here." The words, gloppy and gooey, poured from the doorman's mouth like thickened honey.

"We're travelers and mean no harm," said John. "Please let us pass through and we won't bother anybody."

"We're not buying what you're selling, good sir," said the low voice behind the door.

"Please just allow us to pass through," asked John again.

"Move it along, sir. There's nothing to see here."

Crazy Talk put his hand on John's shoulder and eased him backwards. He gave John a knowing nod and approached the door. And though John had no clue as to what Crazy Talk was doing, it seemed right. So John stood back and let Crazy Talk take over.

Crazy Talk said, "Baby talk, baby talk, it's a wonder you can walk. Thatwise, little pig, little pig, let us in."

"Who is that?" asked the man behind the door. "What are you saying?"

"I rubber man bouncing down the mushroom gravy highway. In the time of chimpanzees I was monkey. Thatwise, I now slap the dolphin forcefully in your direction." Crazy Talk gripped the skin on his face between his thumb and forefinger and quickly moved his cheek back and forth, slapping the insides of his cheek against his teeth and making a squishy, mock-masturbation sound.

"Come again, sir," said the man behind the door. "Who be you?"

"Thatwise, I dirty brown, flopping around. Puffed up and bloated when the sun goes down," said Crazy Talk, following it up again with the squishy-cheeked sounds of masturbation.

The doorman said, "Wait there. I'll be back shortly."

Crazy Talk stood still in front of the door, waiting. All stood with him, though they had no idea why they stayed. And the sounds of movement on the other side of the portal returned.

First, the sound of something hard scraping on the wood. Then, the Judas hole opened and a milky eye, afflicted with severe cataracts, squinted out at them.

"Who be you lewdies?" breathed a shaky, faint voice. "And why be you here? What be this chepooka?"

"Listen, ded. I viddy your glazzies and hear your burbling slovos," said Crazy Talk. "You need not even be a malenky bit poogly. We the sadness and madness and hope for the land. We the yellow matter custard dripping from a dead dog's eye. We be the newborn dead and the wet sloppy souls. I am a clown and I bring you Crawling King Snake. Thatwise, we inquire that you allow us to pass fluids in your presence." Crazy Talk jumped back, placed his hand under his armpit and quickly brought his other arm down, making moist fart noises.

"Did you say Crawling King Snake?" asked the feeble voice.

"Yes. Crawling King Snake."

"He is the lizard king. Thatwise, he can do anything," said the shaky voice. From behind the door came clicks, grunts, and the sounds of flatulence. And then, "Open the doors for these men and let them in."

The doors pulled inward and revealed an ancient, small man wearing a toga. Perhaps he was a tall midget, or maybe just an extremely short normal-sized person. His size presented as an optical illusion, making it hard to tell if he was a gargantuan dwarf or a diminutive oaf. A thin strip of sparse white hair ringed the man's head, starting just above one ear, swooping down around the back of his dome, and climbing again to sit atop his other ear. And from the front of each ear sprouted a chin curtain of long white hair along his jaw line, covering his chin and flowing to just above his nipples. Frosty white eyebrows sprang from his forehead in a dense scraggly mess, as if reaching out to catch any insects that might buzz by. He held a tin ear horn that started with a tiny tapered piece that fit in his ear and then spiraled around his hand in convoluted bulbous sections that increased in size until they reached the flared bell that captured sounds at the other end. Shouting so as to be able hear himself, the man said, "My name is Chelloveck. I am the town elder. We will welcome you to our village for the night and allow you to pass through because you speak in the old tongue. That is a sound we have not heard in ages and, thatwise, it is dobby to hear even a malenky chumble of aldspeak. Now enter and what say you?" Chelloveck placed the ear trumpet to the side of his head and awaited a response.

Crazy Talk stepped inside the doors and moved his mouth near to the bell of the ear trumpet. "Grapta, Sa," he shouted into the horn. "We gromb on the navels and slaughter baby seals in your honor."

A look of disgust came over Chelloveck's face. He pulled the horn away and snapped at Crazy Talk, "I'm not deaf, you know. You don't need to shout." And he threw the ear horn to the ground and stomped away, mumbling and grumbling to himself.

They all stood and watched Chelloveck as he shuffled into the bus-walled village. Realizing that the interlopers were not following him, Chelloveck stopped and returned to grab his ear horn. "Come on, then," he said to the men, "don't be put off by my behavior. I'm old and cantankerous. And, actually, I am nearly deaf. I don't know why I did that." He gestured to John and his men to follow him. "Come," said Chelloveck, "Come in. You've arrived just in time to celebrate our festivities. We were blessed just this yesterday with a stampede of interesting meat and mighty fighters. Everybody come in. The ceremony is about to begin."

John, Santiago and Alf the Sacred Burro followed Chelloveck. But, Crazy Talk stayed outside of the front gate.

"I viddy you in good now with Chelloveck," said Crazy Talk. He held up his hand in a lazy farewell wave. "My work done for now. My gulliver is gloopy and ready for sleepy-weep. I go for now. Guarding fumes and making haste ain't my cup of meat." And with that, Crazy Talk disappeared from the doorway and left John and Santiago to follow the strange little-big-man into a labyrinth of buses.

They left Alf the Sacred Burro tethered to a bloodwood tree just inside of the front gate. Alf left donkey vomit balls at his feet as an even-up trade for the windfallen bloodwood fruit that he ate from the ground. Chelloveck assured John that his men would tend to the donkey. And then the strange little-big-man escorted John and Santiago through a circular maze of buses that led on an almost imperceptible downward slant. Curtains pulled back from the bus windows and suspicious eyes probed at the newcomers as they passed.

A circular pit, six cubits deep and fifty cubits in diameter, marked the center of the bus-labyrinth. The edge of the pit wore a crown of mud bricks one cubit high. Rows of seats – bus seats, benches, stumps, boulders – ringed the pit in terraced levels leading up to the circle of buses surrounding the amphitheatre. And in each seat sat a large midget of a toga-clad man who looked just like the men to his left and right. The men ranged in age from mid-teens to ancient, but all were younger versions of Chelloveck. Even the adolescents were already bald and graying and sporting the flowing chin curtains.

Chelloveck led John and the others to an open space at the edge of the pit, in between the rows of men. Chelloveck turned and waved his hands toward the surrounding crowd. "These are my sons. I am Chelloveck. These are Chellovecks." And he placed his ear trumpet to his ear to hear the roar of the crowd as the men cried out in response to their father's acknowledgement.

Santiago stood with them, puffing on a bezoar in the peace pipe he filched from Crazy Talk.

"How many sons do you have?" asked John into the bell of the ear trumpet.

"Three-hundred-and-one as of today. I lost five and twenty of them yesterday in an ambush outside of our village. Damn Po'kinhorns."

"I'm sorry to hear that," said John, not knowing what else to say.

"What?" asked Chelloveck, sticking the ear horn in John's face.

"I'm sorry to hear about your loss."

"It's okay," said Chelloveck in a tone that indicated that it really was all right. "I can always make more. And besides, we fought off the attackers and even took some prisoners. Tonight, we celebrate our victory." And the little-big-man placed his mouth to the earpiece of the ear horn and blew a frantic hardcore-avant-jazz screech that slammed the crowd in the face with a dissonant musical fist and screeched at the men to sit down and shut up.

And the screech of Chelloveck's ear horn reminded John of the blistering giggle-jazz that greeted him upon his entry into the new and strange world where he now found himself. John's body tingled with some sort of emotion, though he found that he was quite inept at interpreting the new feelings starting to bubble up in him. Instead, the emotion manifested itself as a prickle on his skin, and as beads of sweat forming in his armpits and dripping down the sides of his ribcage. He felt tense, excited, angry, sad, confused, and the feelings grated at his raw emotional nerves. His mind reeled at the thought of having three-hundred-twenty-six sons. He wondered how Chelloveck could proliferate when there did not appear to be even one female in the village.

John said into the ear horn, "Please don't think I'm rude for asking, but how can you have so many sons when there are no women to mother them?"

"What?" asked Chelloveck, holding the bell of his ear trumpet toward John.

"You have so many sons. Where are their mothers?"

"Blumpkins," said Chelloveck. "That's why we were ambushed. For our blumpkins."

At the mention of blumpkins, Santiago snapped to attention. He craned his neck back, sniffed at the air, and began to scan the compound with a fierce curiosity. And before John had the opportunity to inquire further, Chelloveck once again blew a wet, warbling trumpet blast.

"Now it is time that we feast," shouted Chelloveck, the force of his voice a surprising contrast to the faint murmur with which he originally addressed Crazy Talk. "Thatwise, Chellovecks, let's enjoy yesterday's bread, today's meat, and last year's cider." A roar issued from the crowd in response. Chellovecks carted in roasted earth pig, baby scruff goat cooked in its mother's milk, and other curious meats.

"Yesterday," said Chelloveck to John, "we were overrun with strange new creatures and scruff goats and earth pigs. If you look toward the tops of our buses you will still see some of the creatures running about. And we have found that these strange creatures are most delectable, their meat being sweet and tender and salty. Thatwise, tonight we feast on the bounty of meats that blessed our camp."

John scanned the tops of the surrounding buses and he did see strange creatures that looked most familiar to him. Some of the creatures had three legs and two heads. Some had the heads of a bird and the body of a cat. And others – unrecognizable amorphous blobs of fur and feathers – rolled about and chattered at one another. John recognized all of them as the myriad forms of his jizz-critters.

Chelloveck clapped his hands and several younger Chellovecks placed a table and chairs in the clearing at the edge of the pit. "Sit," said Chelloveck, motioning to the chairs. "Sit and feast and enjoy the festivities with me." He again clapped his hands and several more Chellovecks placed food and clay pitchers of hard cider before the three men at the table.

John helped himself to the baby scruff goat and ribs from the earth pig and found them to be a delicious change from the dry, tough dirt-rats. He avoided dining on his own jizz-critters, as it just didn't seem right to him. Santiago chugged his cider and motioned to a server-Chelloveck to fill his goblet again and again. On Santiago's plate sat a mound of many meats – scruff goat, earth pig, jizz-critters. His appetite overwhelmed him and Santiago tore into the mound of many meats with zealous abandon. Chelloveck gnawed at a large leg bone of jizz-critter. When he had stripped the leg bare of meat, Chelloveck snapped the thick leg bone and sucked the marrow from it.

"Bring more cider for our guests," ordered Chelloveck to a server-Chelloveck. The ancient man gnawed at another piece of meat, getting just slightly more of the food in his mouth than on his beard.

Server-Chellovecks handed out meat and unleavened flat bread and cider to all of the spectator-Chellovecks. And a great gluttonous feast ensued. Chellovecks attacked their food as if they had not eaten in weeks. They tore at the fresh meat and tossed the cleaned bones toward the center of the amphitheatre pit. Server-Chellovecks tossed grilled jizz-critters to the spectator-Chellovecks and filled all empty goblets with strong cider.

As they dined, a thick, sturdy door along the pit's wall opened and three Chellovecks marched to the center of the arena. The three men held horns that somewhat resembled their father's ear trumpet. The horns twisted and turned in tight convolutions and ended in flared bells. Before the assembly stood the trumpet-Chellovecks, old and wrinkled, their dry skin looking as if it were coated in a thin covering of dust and cobwebs. They wore red turbans and over their togas they sported ephods of white, blue, scarlet and purple, and interwoven with gold thread.

The middle-trumpet-Chelloveck raised the mouthpiece of his horn to his lips. He looked to the Chelloveck on his right and nodded and then did the same to the Chelloveck on his left. His foot tapped out a sick, slick rhythm, stirring up a small cloud of dust on the ground. And then his horn blew hot, spewing a torrent of unhinged notes that slammed into each other with reckless disregard, the result being a slurred and climbing trumpet scream that rent the air but still somehow held a compelling melody at its core. The Chellovecks on both sides stood and snapped their fingers to the beat of the bandleader's foot. Right-side-trumpet-Chelloveck picked up on the gist of the screaming horn and started spitting scorching notes himself. And the two horns rose and fell and twisted their tunes around each other, with a *blum-blum-doo-dat-doo* honking out of one while a tremulous sustained *screeeeeeeeee* soared above it. And left-side-trumpet-Chelloveck dug on the chaotic strain and he sprayed steaming arpeggios all over the groove with his *bloo-doo-doo-doo-dat, bloo-doo-doo-doo-dat, bloo-doo-doodoo-dee-dah-di-dah-di-blah-dah.* And the Demon Zorn looked on, snapped his thin fingers, and smiled a pointy-toothed grin.

As if drawn by the pied-piping Chellovecks, a stampede of all shapes and sizes of jizz-critters scrambled through the pit door and spilled into the arena in a massive wave of snarling, scratching, snipping and snapping beasts. The Chelloveck horn section continued to kick out the jams, stirring up a roiling tornado of intertwined musical lines. Physical manifestations of the notes, appearing as proper but mangled sheet music with the notes twisted in the tangled ledger lines, swirled in the cacophonous cyclone that spewed from the Chellovecks' horns.

And the music whipped the jizz-critters into a frenzy. The chimeric animals in the arena pounced on one another and tore at flesh, sucked at the blood from defeated beasts. Bovine creatures with unwieldy horns ran and tossed their thick heads about, goring all that stood in their way. Small simian creatures pounced on the backs of the heavy-footed bull beasts and scratched at the massive animals' eyes. Other animals became tripping blocks for the members of the horned stampede and were crushed under hooves. As the bull beasts slammed into the ground, other jizz-critters pounced on them and tore open the bovine underbellies, unraveling the mess of intestines, feasting on the entrails. And the melee swirled in a bloody current all around the clearing at the center of the arena where the Chellovecks spat their mad shit from blow-horns.

When the song ended, the trumpet-Chellovecks held their horns to their sides and gazed at the fracas around them. Without the horns blowing, the jizz-critters felt no need to steer clear of the center of the pit. The swirling current of animals scattered. The Chellovecks found themselves in no better of a position than the bull beasts as they fended off attacks from all manner of animals. One trumpet-Chelloveck swung his horn wildly at the crush of furry attackers, knocking five-legged dogs and fish-birds to the ground. But, the effort proved futile when the massive longhorn of a bull beast poked through his back and out of his chest. With a Chelloveck-kabob on his spike, the bull beast flicked his head to the side and tossed the little-big man aside, leaving him to bleed out and be trampled and fed on by the panicked jizz-critters. Before the remaining trumpeters could scramble for safety, the frenzied animals knocked them to the ground and tore them to scraps.

"Ah, what is this vonny cal?" said Chelloveck to John. Chelloveck smacked an open hand to his forehead and grimaced. "Such a kick to the yarbles – three more of my sons tossed at the dung heap like nothing more than soiled holy undergarments. Three more sons that I have to replace."

In the pit of the arena the jizz-critters tore each other down until there was almost nothing but carnage. Several victorious creatures still lived but suffered mortal wounds. A new crew of Chellovecks entered the arena and whacked with sledges at the heads of still-alive but dying critters, dispatching them wholly and completely. And the crew tossed the carcasses onto a wagon and dragged them from the arena, leaving a muddy, bloody sludge on the ground. During the cleanup-intermission, Chelloveck called for more food and drink for his guests. And the crowd of Chellovecks roared in approval. John gladly accepted and gorged himself on scruff goat and hard cider. When he started to tell Santiago how nice it was to have a full feast, John saw that his crazy-eyed, shaggy friend was gone. The ebony pipe, still smoking, sat on the table as a marker, holding Santiago's place. John picked up the pipe and drew heavily on the fuming bezoar.

And the feasting continued. Chellovecks chugged cider and gnawed on meat until their bellies grew taut and their thoughts muddied. Although the hunger for food was sated, a desire to witness more carnage possessed the Chelloveck spectators. In their drunken revelry, the Chellovecks screamed for more entertainment. Down in the arena, Chelloveck guards forced prisoners to engage in mortal battle with one another merely for the amusement of the Chellovecks. Men, tied back to back, fended off jizz-critter attacks with their bare hands. Weapons were set in the middle of the arena and the men scrambled to claim their implements of destruction, smashing each other's bones with maces and clubs and bricks, slashing at each other with knives and swords, poking with pitchforks, striking out with sticks. The bloodier the ground became, the more the Chellovecks whipped themselves into a frothy mania.

Just when it seemed that the slaughter had reached a climax, three more Chellovecks in colorful ephods strode to the center of the pit, stepping over bodies and body parts on the way, and started blowing more steaming licks from convoluted blow horns. In answer to the creaching, chaotic horn racket, a platoon of unarmed Chellovecks marched into the arena in two columns. And the soldier-Chellovecks, twelve in all, wore tunics and heavy monstrous boots soaked in bullock's blood. The toes of the boots, having been baked near a fire, were hard and black like flints. And the soldier-Chellovecks stood straight and still, waiting for the buglers to wind down.

But the horn section kept on rocking, going round and round. While the scorching giggle-jazz filled the air, a hunched-over man, dressed in a leather kilt plated with bronze, stepped through the door to the pit. The man did not slump because he was weak, old, or infirm. He doubled over because his enormity did not allow him to merely walk through the large door like a normal-sized man. When his leather sandals stomped into the pit and he cleared the door, the man stood straight. And a collective gasp escaped the Chelloveck spectators. At his full height of six cubits and a span, the man towered above the little-big Chellovecks. His chest was thick like a rain barrel. His neck like that of a bull. His biceps firm and as big around as a grown man's thigh. A mess of kinky black hair helmeted his head and thick sideboards padded his jawline down to the edge of his determined chin. A thickened and widened nose sat in the shade of the man's bulging, bony brow. His piercing eyes peered out from under the rocky outcropping of forehead, the gaze going straight through the soldiers in front of him and weakening the Chellovecks' resolve, making them question the wisdom of coming to battle the afro-capped giant.

Chelloveck accepted the peace pipe from John and pulled on it as if he were drawing his last breath. He exhaled several breaths of thick smoke before his lungs cleared. "That," said

Chelloveck, "is Joad of the Po'kinhorns of Gath. He is a great warrior and he led the attempt to waylay my sons yesterday. Most of my boys that were lost in the ambush were felled in the effort to capture that bolshy bastard."

The lumbering giant lowered his hips and stomped deliberately around the edges of the arena, each step sounding like a board smacking the ground. He scanned for an area of the wall to scale. Joad was more than tall enough to grab the top of the tall wall and pull himself over. But, the Chelloveck guards, armed with spontoons and stationed around the top of the arena wall, stood ready to poke at Joad with their razor sharp tridents should he try to escape. As Joad ambled around the pit, the trumpet-Chellovecks halted their playing and dashed for the open arena door, closing and barring it behind themselves.

Chelloveck handed John the pipe and rose from the table at the edge of the pit. He momentarily felt dizzy from the cider and bezoar smoke. He wobbled briefly and then steadied himself. His raised hand signaled to the Chellovecks for silence, and the crowd hushed. Chelloveck spoke, loudly enough for all to hear, saying: "The man before you in the arena is Joad of the vonny Po'kinhorns of Gath. That brute killed my sons, your brothers, yesterday. Thatwise, I will grant a fortnight in the blumpkin chambers to the man who can lay Joad level with the ground and return him to the filthy muck from whence he came." Chelloveck raised his glass to the soldier-Chellovecks and then downed its contents. The soldier-Chellovecks snapped their heels and banged their right fists on their chests in salute to their father.

The faces of the soldier-Chellovecks beamed with excitement, for the granting of even a night in the blumpkin chambers meant that Chelloveck would be stepping down as head of the village and handing over leadership to a younger Chelloveck. Much whispering hissed around the stands and some spectator-Chellovecks who had high ambitions became angered by the possibility of one of the common soldier-Chellovecks ascending to power. But, mostly, the crowd crackled with excitement at the prospect of seeing the powerful mountain of a man do battle with their brothers.

Chelloveck sat and motioned to a server-Chelloveck for more drink. The server topped off Chelloveck's and John's cups with the strongest of ciders. John passed the pipe back to Chelloveck. The old man sucked nervously at the pipe, firing the bezoar to a blazing lump of donkey muck in the bowl.

"What," asked John, "is a blumpkin?"

But Chelloveck did not have his horn to his ear and could not hear John. Instead, Chelloveck put his finger to his own lips and pointed toward his men and Joad. Chelloveck did not speak any further as the activities in the arena were of great concern to him.

Joad continued to circle the edges of the pit, backing off when guard-Chellovecks leaned over the edge of the wall and poked their spontoons in his direction. And then the leader of the soldier-Chellovecks whistled three sharp, short tweets, and his men scattered and regrouped in a circle around the giant, making Joad as the nucleus in a ring of soldier-Chellovecks. The smaller men darted in and out of the circle, punching at Joad and kicking at his shins with their hardened boots. The giant swatted at the Chellovecks as if waving away flittering

gnats, his massive fists occasionally connecting with the attackers and knocking them to the ground.

Then the leader of the soldier-Chellovecks rushed at Joad,
trying to grab around the elephantine legs and trip the giant to
the ground. Joad peeled the man from his legs, grabbed him by
the arms, and whanged him around in a circle. Chellovecks
rushed Joad in an attempt to free their brother from the swirling goliath but were knocked back as the spinning-
Chelloveck's boots thumped them in the heads and arms. Mid-
swing, Joad let go of the Chelloveck's hands and released him,
flinging the man in the air and smashing him into several of
his brothers.

Unsteady and off balance from the spinning-dizzies, Joad
stumbled before his attackers and tried to regain his balance.
Sensing an opening, one soldier-Chelloveck leapt at Joad and
tried to trip him to the ground so that the other Chellovecks
could set upon him. But Joad had already recovered. With one
hand he grasped the clinging Chelloveck by the head, his
enormous hand covering the face and his fingers wrapping
around the man's skull like a normal hand grasping a grape-
fruit. Joad balled up his other hand into a fist and slammed it
into the Chelloveck's stomach. And the blow battered the man
with such force that his liver popped out of his asshole, took a
quick breath of fresh air, and then retracted into the relative
safety the abdominal cavity. Joad's victim-Chelloveck crumpled
from the blow and he did not move after being flung to the
ground like a piece of refuse.

"Get him!" shouted one of the soldier-Chellovecks, and the
entire group charged Joad. They grabbed and punched and

kicked and bit at the giant. And the crush of flailing Chellovecks overwhelmed Joad, chopping his legs out from under him and knocking him to the ground. There was much hugging and clutching, much weeping and gnashing of teeth. Joad rolled about and punched and kicked at the flailing mass of arms and legs that battered him. He squeezed balls to a mushy pulp with his strong hands and crushed tracheas with powerful throat chops. But the number of men attacking him still overwhelmed Joad. He rolled about, still punching and squeezing and biting and found himself face to face with his own ass. In the twisting chaos, Joad saw a swollen pair of testicles dangling before his face, offering themselves up for a good squeezing. He grabbed the nutsack and squashed as hard as he could, not realizing that he was twisted in such an awkward position that the balls in his face were his own.

And the pain in Joad's groin spread like fire through his gut. A roar of fury blasted from his mouth. He felt like taking a shit. He felt like crying. He felt like dropping. But more than anything, he was livid, and he felt like killing. With the strength born of pure rage, Joad stood. Chellovecks clung to his body like leeches to a host. Joad grabbed one Chelloveck and snapped his back over one knee as if he were breaking a stick. The crack of the man's spine echoed throughout the arena and it sickened the spectators, quieting them for the first time. And then Joad fought without making a single sound. He did not grunt. He did not yell. He did not cry out. He picked Chellovecks off of him like ticks. He snapped necks and stomped the life out of his attackers. Two Chellovecks clutched at Joad's afro and scratched and poked at his eyes. Joad reached up, grabbed the men's throats in each hand, and brought the heads together with such force as to try to make them both occupy the same space at the same time. Joad brought the men's faces together for a blood-smattered, bone-crunching kiss. He held the limp bodies out in front of himself and dropped them to the ground. He plucked another Chelloveck from his back and tossed the little man into the arena wall, and the crunch of the man's bones once again sickened the spectators. The sight of the silently fighting giant struck the Chelloveck crowd dumb with fear. This was a man who would not be defeated by twelve of them. Joad: a massive and unconquerable killing machine. And not one of the soldier- Chellovecks was left standing when he was done.

At the end of the battle, Joad stood silently in the center of smashed, squashed, and splattered Chellovecks. He surveyed the crushed and lifeless bodies strewn about around him and then looked toward Chelloveck and John. Joad crossed his arms in defiance and waited.

Chelloveck locked eyes with Joad and said nothing for minutes. The two men stared, unblinking, unspeaking. And then Chelloveck broke the stare and shouted to his men, "Take out the giant and lock him up. He will do battle with your brothers once again on the morrow. And I am confident that the results will be different. Now get this abomination from my sight."

The arena door opened and spat two rows of soldier-Chellovecks into the pit. The soldiers surrounded Joad. They ducked behind shields and poked spontoons in the giant's direction. Recognizing the futility of unarmed battle with a phalanx of angry, armed Chellovecks, Joad dropped to his knees and put his hands behind his back. The Chellovecks pushed Joad to the ground, face-first, and bound his arms behind his back with thick leather straps. They shackled his ankles with heavy chains and forced him to stand. And then the soldier Chellovecks jabbed at Joad with their spears to direct him out of the arena.

The absence of Joad from Chelloveck's presence. The sight of spent Chellovecks piled on top of each other in a death wagon. The cider and bezoar intoxication. They all mingled in Chelloveck's thoughts. He threw his hands to his face and wept, looking more like a frail ancient than John had yet seen. "Damn that beast. He single-handedly decimated my ranks." And he wept inconsolably, his thin body convulsing with the pain of loss, only pausing now and again to chug more cider or toke on the peace pipe.

Chelloveck wept and screamed at the sky. Sympathy moved John and he patted at Chelloveck's back, saying "there, there." He lifted the goblet of cider to Chelloveck's mouth and helped him to drink his emotions into submission. And while John found himself feeling sorry for Chelloveck and his loss of sons, he likewise felt concern for the lumbering oaf known as Joad. Something about the giant moved John. He did not seem like a mindless killing machine, as Chelloveck suggested. Even in the midst of the battle, John saw a sensitive, thoughtful creature who just so happened to be fighting for his life. Something about Joad felt like family. And the sympathetic notions churned in John's gut, paining him and giving him a feeling of strength at the same time.

And that night, while John, Joad, Santiago and all the Chellovecks slept, The Reverend Android Lovethorn, with a bag of soot from the crematorium of his mountain fortress, stood atop the tallest tower of his fort and summoned the winds of a crossfire hurricane. Lashing himself to the posts of the tower with leather thongs, Lovethorn leaned out over a great drop and felt the storm's fingers pulling at him, trying to yank him over the side, the blasts of wind ripping his sunglasses from his head and tossing them into the void. The slight jowls on the Man in Black pulled back taut with the wind; the loose skin flapped from the backsides of his head like shredded sails in a storm, but his slicked, black hair remained perfectly combed and unaffected by the storm. Lovethorn scooped the ashes of the dead and tossed handful after handful into the churning funnels of wind that twisted and chased each other around the tower. The leather straps pulled hard against the post as the storm tried to drag Lovethorn away. The thongs stretched to the point of almost snapping. Sensing the imminent peril of being plucked from the tower by a cyclone and tossed into oblivion, Lovethorn heaved the burlap sack into the air and watched it hurtle into the blackness, trailing a cloud of cadaver dust behind it. Android Lovethorn locked his hands on one of the tower posts and spat into the wind. He laughed a scratchy, mad cackle that the winds ripped from his mouth and carried far into the night, waking confused desert creatures in the badlands below. And his yellow eyes reflected into the dark night, gazing over the span of countless days' journeys. "Double, double, boils and bubbles," he shouted into the wind.

And an enormous cloud of dust spread over the land, blocking out the light of the star Wormwood and the two full moons in the sky. The blanket of black death dispersed in the swirling gales and gusts. The four winds rose from their caves and carried the clouds of dusty death forth. And the clouds pissed torrents of acid rain on the land and people, burning flesh and causing running sores, infecting and afflicting all whom the dust came in contact with. And where it did not rain, the soot settled on people's skin and in their lungs, causing stinging tumors and mucky death rattle coughing.

The storm passed and calm settled over Android Lovethorn's domain as quickly as it had erupted. Lovethorn unlashed himself and slid to the ground, seated with his back against the wall. His eyelids closed, snuffing out the yellow fire in his irises, and his lips moved silently. Despite the lack of audible words, Lovethorn spoke. And he was heard.

Running sores. Infected running sores. Bubbling abscesses, carbuncles and furuncles. Infected pus-bubbles. Monkeypox. Gangrenous open blebs, blains and boils. Pustules, pimples, ulcers and tumors. These are the things that the Chellovecks found all about their faces and bodies as they rose to the humectrus of the gloomy morn.

The slate sky blocked out the sun. The scant light that did filter through the ash clouds above cast everything in a sinister glow. A purple haze drifted close to the ground, blurring objects in the distance. And the Chellovecks ran from their dwellings and into the open. They stood before each other in gloomy light, inspecting each other's bruises, blisters, and burbling blood bubbles. And it was as if the Chellovecks were staring into mirrors, seeing exact replicas of themselves with similar skin blights. And all but one in the village suffered from the oozing leprous skin rash.

The racket outside of his shelter-bus woke John. He felt refreshed from the feast the night before. A night's sleep on a mattress stuffed with hay was an immense improvement over his nights resting on the hard-packed desert ground. John stepped from the bus door and into the morning. His unblemished skin radiated a rested and healthful warmth. He rubbed his eyes to clear his fuzzy vision, but realized that his eyes were not clouded with sleep. Instead, the haze hanging about the mesa distorted and blurred everything. He momentarily could not tell if it was day or night. John looked to the sky and saw that it was muddled with a cloud of ash. And the ash eclipsed all else in the sky except for the quick flowing river of clouds that ran above the red brick road. The flowing clouds took on a pinkish tinge from the sunlight above and the path below. The soot in the air stung John's eyes and he rubbed at them again. He pushed his palms against the burn and it comforted him. He left his hands applying gentle pressure over the eye sockets for minutes and focused only on the pleasant sensation. And then he pulled his hands away and allowed his eyes to adjust. And until his vision cleared, John did not notice that a gang of soldier-Chellovecks were accosting him and jabbing the trident points of spontoons in his direction.

John gasped at the sight of the Chellovecks. With their running sores and festering boils, the men's appearance shocked John, even more so than the bedraggled lunkheads he had encountered. He looked around at the Chellovecks and saw that all were plagued with horrific pus-dribbling cankers and diseased tissues. He inspected his own arms, put his hands to his face, and found no such blight on himself.

"Our father has ordered us to bring you to him," said the leader of the soldier-Chellovecks, poking his spontoon in John's direction.

Two other soldier-Chellovecks approached and grabbed ahold of John's arms, as if to prevent him from resisting. Instinctively, John gripped his hands on the wrists of the men and squeezed. A soothing calm spread over the soldiers' arms. They released their hold on John and stood slack as he held their wrists. The healing sensation spread up their arms and throughout their systems, washing over them like warm, clean water. The other soldiers looked on in awe as the soldiers' bulging, throbbing cysts and boils melted away and left fresh, pink skin in their absence. And when they were cured, the men dropped to their knees and thanked John. He belched and farted and waved them away. Behind the newly healed soldiers, the other Chellovecks lined up in a queue that grew and eventually extended all about the mesa, until every single Chelloveck awaited the healing touch of John the Revelator.

And for three days and three nights, John laid hands on the Chellovecks and relieved each and every one of their suffering. Instead of tiring from the chore, John drew strength each time that he sucked the poison from a man. There were no ill effects from drawing out the sickness, other than the intense build-up of gas, making John fart and burp continuously as he laid hands on the men. Occasionally, John became so bloated that he had to lay on his back on a stone bench and have Chellovecks sit on his stomach to push out the foul stench that collected in his system as he drew out the men's sickness and took it on himself.

At the end of the third day, they led John to Father Chelloveck's bus. The old man lay on a mattress, shaking and leaking bodily fluids from infected, gaping sores, stuck to the sheets with the coagulated and crystallized blood and pus. A crackling sound emitted from the sheets as Chelloveck writhed and peeled his skin away from the bedding. At the sight of John, Chelloveck sat up, propping himself with his arms, and tried to speak, but the cankers on his face and skin had progressed down into his mouth, stripping his throat raw. He croaked at John but words would not come, only a multi-toned, jangling, incomprehensible rattle that hitched in his throat and pained all that heard it.

"Lay back, old man," said John. And he put his hand on Chelloveck's forehead. John sucked out the affliction. And the energy flowing from Chelloveck nearly knocked John off his feet. John drew out the sickness and sorrow and took it on, farting and burping all the while, as if the release of the gas served to purge his system of whatever malady he was taking in. When it was all over, Chelloveck lay unconscious on his bed, covered in sweat, but cured of the blisters and boils. Finally spent from his three straight days of sleep deprivation, John fell to the ground and passed out. His ass bleated sulphuric puffs and his belly vented rotten, bile-stinking belches. Several Chellovecks picked John up, carried his dead weight to his bus, and put him on his mattress. As the men left the bus, the blurps and blarps of flatulence and eructation boomed out like an untrained horn section. John and Chelloveck both slept as if dead to the world.

And after a full day's rest and recuperation, John and Chelloveck parleyed in the Tent of Meeting. The Chelloveck guards dunked John in the basin outside of the bright red tabernacle to ensure that he was ceremonially clean and gave him fresh clothes of fine twisted linen. Chelloveck guards – dressed in coats of many colors and wearing pale grey metal helmets topped with blue fadoodle plumage – stood sentry on each side of the entryway. The guards crossed their spontoons in a forbidding X that barred any uninvited visitors. From the outside the shelter presented as an optical illusion, looking like little more than a small, single-roomed dwelling. But when the front doors pulled back, John walked into a spacious big top bedecked with plush couches and animal skins. Halls led from the center gathering room to other chambers. Soothing, tuneful hums escaped the chambers and combined in the gathering room in sublime harmonies. Chelloveck sat cross-legged on a puffed cushion, looking rejuvenated. He waved John in to sit with him. John accepted the invitation and sat on a fluffed cushion.

"The Chellovecks thank you for what you did for us over the past couple of days," said Chelloveck. "It was a selfless act that I will not forget." He put his ear trumpet to his ear and waited for John's response.

"It was nothing," said John. He was glad to have helped. With each Chelloveck that he drained of the plague, John felt a stirring within. An awareness. Knowledge. Power. The sickness fed the void in John, threw light on the darkness. It did not so much answer questions about John's situation as it made him care less about his past and more about his future. He instinctively began to understand things that he had no words to explain. "I would have done it for three more days and nights if needed."

"I know that," said Chelloveck, stroking at his frosty chin curtain and furrowing his wiry eyebrows. "I also know that we were stricken with the skin ulcerations because you are here. The Man in Black came to me as I slept and threw ashes of the dead in my face. The dark spirit plagued this land because he wants you to stay away from him. I am supposed to hold you captive here until his men arrive to take custody of you. He is sending a squad at this very moment to get you."

John studied the old man and discerned nothing from the troubled expression on his face. "Well," said John, "what are you going to do? Are you going to take me captive and hold me here?"

"Non," said Chelloveck. "Non, nein, and nyet. You've done us no injury. It is not your doing that Lovethorn fouled the land with the abominable bubbling boils. You've done nothing but help. You may leave this morn to flee Lovethorn's men if you wish. We will give you provisions for your flight."

"Then I will leave," agreed John. "I will take my friend, Santiago, and my donkey. We will leave immediately so that we do not put the Chellovecks in danger."

"Only you and your donkey may leave. Your friend has committed a most heinous affront to the Chellovecks. He has done irreparable harm. Thatwise, he is now being held in a cell with that revolting beast, Joad. And they will fight to the death for our entertainment as the sun situates itself directly overhead."

And panic tickled at the back of John's neck. He fiddled his fingers and nervously twitched his foot. Without being able to articulate why, John knew that he needed Santiago. And, unexpectedly, he found that he considered the bushy-headed lunatic to be a friend, the closest friend that he ever had, as far as John could tell. A feeling of concern and something that John guessed might be brotherly love swelled in his chest. "What did he do that was so awful?" asked John. "Did he steal? I'll see to it that you are somehow repaid."

"He did the unspeakable. I shan't repeat it here, other than to say that his actions are unforgivable and have caused great detriment to my line. Nothing you say will convince me otherwise, so do not try. You must leave here as soon as possible. Lovethorn's men will be here before the sun sets."

"Then let me speak to Santiago," said John. "Let me see him before I leave. At least allow me that."

A subterranean dungeon spread out as catacombs beneath the mesa. And the Chelloveck gaoler gushed with joy in receiving John's company. The gaoler, a stooped, pale, pie-eyed Chelloveck who appeared as if he had not seen the light of day in years, tapped his finger tips together nervously, and said, "Yes. A visitor. We have a visitor. So nice to have a visitor." The long fingernails clicked as he tapped them together. "Come, come, come." Grabbing John's bicep with one hand and gripping a lit torch in the other, he led John along the twisting main hall of the dungeon. Along the track of the main artery, doorways opened to smaller arteries that led to the capillaries of the cells. "'Tis nice to have a visitor, 'tis. Chelloveck likes visitors. Yes, yes."

Shadows flickered in the light of the torch. The dankness of the dungeon triggered shivers in John. At the end of the long, dark hall, a bitch of an oak door blocked their path.

"Yes, yes," said the gaoler-Chelloveck, leaning in with his face close to John's. "Yes, sir. Your friends are inside. Yes. Yes." And he lifted the thick wood beam that hung across and secured the door so that John could enter the cell.

With gaoler-Chelloveck holding the torch in the doorway, John entered the cell. In the low light John made out two forms. The hulking frame of Joad writhed in a corner, a massive mound of muscles and flesh, snoring and gasping in labored breaths. Running sores bespeckled his entire being, the surface of his skin looking like a moldy, cheese-crusted lunar landscape, the stench of skin-rot fuming off of him.

And on the ground beside Joad sat Santiago, upright with his legs crisscrossed and hands resting on his knees.

Though he looked as if he had been dragged behind horses on a gravel road, and his sores were weeping no less than Joad's, Santiago sat, bright-eyed and alert, emanating an inner strength that was not extinguished by the plague of boils and bumpy blisters. In a steady and strong voice, he said, "It's about time, Johnny. I thought you forgot about me or left me behind."

"Are you alright?" asked John, surprised at Santiago's composure. He'd not seen such serenity from the usually frantic little man. "I tried to tell Chelloveck that you don't belong here, that I'm leaving and I need to take you with me."

"I tried to tell Chelloveck that you don't belong here," mimicked Santiago, laughing. He tugged at his beard and rubbed his mouth. "Shit, son, I belong where I go. It ain't no big deal."

"But they've had you in the dungeon. And look at you, rotten with the sickness and pocked and boiled. You shouldn't be in jail."

Santiago's face flicked through a range of emotions and settled on contemplative. "I've been in jail my whole life, Johnny. So, I'm actually at home here. Prison don't begin and end at a gate. Prison is in the mind, dig? It's locked in one world that's dead and dying, or it's open to a world that's free and alive. Dig? It don't matter what they do to my body. It's what I've got up here," he said, poking one finger at his forehead, "and here," slapping a hand against his chest, popping a boil in the process. "But I'm free in the mind and I'm spiritually aligned. So it don't matter if they hobble me or put walls around me or chains on me. I'm free inside, brother. But you can get me out of here if you want. I think it would be a good idea because you need me.

But that's all your scene, if you see what I mean. Do what you think is right."

"The first thing I'm going to do is heal you," said John, and he laid hands on Santiago's head.

"Oh, fuck yeah," Santiago moaned as the warmth from John's hands spread across and under his skin. And even as he lay back and relished the healing sensation, Santiago pushed John's hands away. "Take care of bigg'un first," he said and nodded toward Joad. "He's worse off than me."

John turned toward Joad. Studying the giant for the best place to give the healing touch, John decided it had to be the face. And that enormous face, buried in the crook of his burly arm, was inaccessible. So John and Santiago struggled to flip the sweaty, oozing mound of flesh on its back. With much huffing and straining and grasping and pulling, they rolled him over and bared his festering, mucid face. John plunged his left hand into the puffy black afro and grasped a handful of hair. The hair pulled free from the scalp with a *splooshing* sound. John shook the clump of kinked hair from his hand and twisted his fingers into the coarse whiskers of one of Joad's sideburns. He laid his other hand on Joad's febrile forehead. The jolt of the initial touch rocked both men. And they convulsed and thrashed for several seconds. Joad screamed. John yelped like a hurt dog, eructating and expelling rancid flatus to relieve the pressure on his system. Then the powerful shock subsided and a steady current of sick transferred from Joad to John, healing Joad and charging John with energy beyond anything he could have imagined.

"He's delirious with fever," said John. But as he took on Joad's affliction, the giant's eyes cleared. And Joad's forehead cooled to John's healing touch. John held on, devouring the sickness and contemporaneously venting a steady *pahhhhhhhhh* of foul wind.

"Much better," said Joad, his words slurring in a deep bass tone as they tumbled from his mouth. His speech cleared somewhat as he spoke, although his voice still sounded as if he had stuffed cotton balls in his cheeks. "Thank you for untangling the knot and softening the glare, before I merged with the dust. I was almost gone, but now am here. And the ten thousand things still rise and fall without cease, regardless of my plight. I am indebted to you."

Joad looked at his hands and arms and saw that they were healed. He rubbed his hands on his face and neck and felt that the skin was smooth. He stood, hunched over so as not to knock his head on the ceiling, and offered a hand to John. And John took Joad's hand and shook it. John laughed at how small his hand looked in comparison.

"Thank you again," said Joad, his deep voice booming off of the walls of the cell, bouncing past Chelloveck and down the hall. "I am forever indebted. I am grateful for your help. I am grateful to experience such gratitude. I'm grateful for my gratitude." And he still held John's hand and continued to pump it with his zealous appreciation, ignoring the sour stench of John's intestines that tainted the already-stale dungeon air.

"Hey there, fella," said Santiago to John. "I'm not sure what bigg'un there is saying, but he seems to be better. So how's about doing some of that voodoo shit on me with your hands?"

And John laid hands on Santiago. After the shock of Joad's sickness, the illness flowing from Santiago was nothing, a mere trickle of the sweet sickness. In no time Santiago became hale and hearty with nary a speckle or hairy mole to blemish his skin. And John sat back, hands on his belly, and ripped off one loud burp. And then he was done with the healing. The invigorated men sat and they talked about their predicament. Occasionally gaoler-Chelloveck chimed in from the door with a "Yes, yes, sir. 'Tis good sir. Yes, yes." And Joad nodded and said, "I shall do as you say, for it is the way and the way is the truth and the truth is the way." When it came time for him to leave, John promised he would not travel the road without Santiago and Joad. And though he did not have a concrete plan, he knew that Chelloveck would grant Joad and Santiago their freedom. He knew it as he had known that he could scatter the lunkheads and lay healing hands on Chellovecks. He just knew.

The slamming of the cell door fell easily on Joad's and Santiago's ears. The tone was not so sinister as one would expect from a dungeon door. The sounds of the retreating footfalls slapped out a soothing rhythm. Gaoler-Chelloveck's fading "Yes, sir. Yes, yes," seemed to answer the important question of their freedom from the Chelloveck mesa. The dark returned to the room as a black cloud descending on them, and their eyes adjusted as best they could. Joad bent over and paced the cell, working off the frantic energy of a healthy giant. And he walked to the tempo of Santiago crooning a repetitive off-key song about a big dungeon door going *Clang, Bang, Clang.*

Chelloveck's humorless laughter filled the Tent of Meeting. John requested the release of Santiago and Joad. And Chelloveck responded with an unyielding brick wall of denial. At the mere mention of the subject, Chelloveck crossed his arms, set his face with a stern resolve, and reverted to aldspeak. "The ogre has tolchocked many Chellovecks and I mean to viddy him suffer a horrorshow demise," answered Chelloveck. "And your little droog has committed and affront so abominable, I shall not speak it. May the gods deal with me, be it ever so severely, if I fail to seek the appropriate retribution this day. Thatwise, those two shall battle to the death and the winner will then have to fight an armed company of Chellovecks. Neither of your detestable droogs will see the sun set on this day."

"If you will not grant their release, as I have requested," said John, "then I will stay and be there for their deaths. I will remain to give them comfort in their final moments."

"But you must leave at once," argued Chelloveck. "Lovethorn's men are coming to get you at this very moment and I know not how far away they be."

"Then get on with the festivities. Get on with the duels. Get on with it now and I will do my best to flee after it is all said and done."

"It shall be done," said Chelloveck. He clapped his hands to call in one of his sons. He whispered into the younger Chelloveck's ear and clapped his hands again. The assistant-Chelloveck scrambled out of the tent. "Let us go to the arena, then, my friend."

Chellovecks scrambled into the spectator area of the arena. And there was no fanfare, no preliminary battles, no feasting and drinking. The rushed proceedings were strictly business. Chelloveck guards dragged Joad and Santiago from their cell and pushed them through the dank dungeon halls, poking at the men with their spontoons. The guards escorted Joad and Santiago to the door of the arena and prodded them out into the middle of the pit, into the midday sun. The glare of the daylight blinded both men, scorching their dilated pupils that had become accustomed to the dark dungeon. The Chelloveck guards ran out of the pit and barred the door shut behind themselves.

John and Chelloveck sat at the table at the edge of the pit, watching. From atop the arena wall, a guard-Chelloveck tossed two swords onto the ground in the pit. The swords reflected brilliant beams of sunlight. In the middle of the pit, Joad and Santiago stood, side by side, and stared up at the table, waiting for John's promised solution to their dilemma. Yet John just sat at the table, staring at the sky and mumbling to himself. He made no eye contact with Joad or Santiago and did not even look in their direction. Instead, he locked his gaze on the trail of clouds washing over them above.

The crowd murmured and shifted about restlessly. Chelloveck placed his lips to his ear horn and expectorated a gnarly giggle-jazz scream, signaling the other Chellovecks to sit and calm down. "Quiet!" shouted Chelloveck, his voice powerful and strong, and silence settled over the stadium. The Chellovecks sat waiting for word from their father. "The two men in the middle of the ring shall fight to the death. The winner earns the honor of living to fight another day. So come now, you filthy skags, pick up those swords and tear into each other as if your life depended on it, because it does."

But Joad and Santiago did not grab the swords. They did not even move toward them. They stood, unmoving and unspeaking, silently defying Chelloveck's wishes, their queer appearance – the blockheaded giant and the scraggly madman standing in unified defiance of Chelloveck – digging at Chelloveck's wounds, mocking him.

"Do your friends not understand me?" asked Chelloveck. "If they do not fight each other, I will have them both executed. Please make them understand this." He placed his ear trumpet to his ear, but got no answer.

John continued to gaze at the river of clouds above, muttering incomprehensibly to himself. He showed no concern for Santiago or Joad or the words that Chelloveck spoke to him.

Chelloveck stood and clung onto the edge of the table, his fingertips turning white from the pressure of his grip. He leaned over the table, in toward the arena. And he looked like a frustrated, weak old man, not like the patriarch of a proud and powerful clan. His prideful strength visibly wilted in front of the entire arena. In his frustration, he shouted to his sons, "Send the Chelloveck guards in to slaughter the meddling skags. If they will not quench our dry ground with their blood, then we shall do it for them. Their lifeless bodies will be dragged from the mesa and left on the desert floor, like dung on the ground, only to be eaten by mad dogs and buzzards."

And the pit doors flew back and ejaculated into the arena a load of Chelloveck soldiers wearing helmets and armed with spontoons and swords and shields. And the men smeared their faces with red streaks of war paint and tied their chinstrap beards near the chin with hemp cords. The company of strong, determined-looking little men split and surrounded Joad and Santiago, poking their swords and spontoons at the two un-armed men in the middle of their circle. Yet still, Joad and Santiago stood motionless, stagnant, looking toward Chelloveck and John at the table. And, yet still, John did not look in their direction, but instead continued mumbling to the clouds above and ignoring the proceedings before him.

As John mumbled, a billow of smoke broke off from the river of clouds and descended toward the mesa. And the cloud streaked ribbons of flame as it rapidly plunged toward the ground. John's mumble gradually changed into intelligible words that increased in volume as the cloud dropped and shifted into a scorching ball of fire. And the flaming ball slammed the ground just behind the Chelloveck guards, ex-ploding into a massive pillar of fire. And the explosion threw up dirt and rocks and knocked the Chelloveck guards to the ground, leaving only Joad and Santiago standing.

From the stands, John's voice boomed out over the crowd as a physical force, knocking Chellovecks back into their seats. "Do no harm to the giant and the mystic," trumpeted the voice that John had previously heard from the burning bushes. But the words were John's and they passed through him, emanating from his balls and humming through his body with great energy. And the voice that escaped his mouth was John's, but he gave no thought to what he said, merely allowing the words to flow through him. And he said, "Do them no evil, or the evil will visit upon you threefold for three generations. Do not pass judgment on the men. Cast out thy beams from your own eyes before you deem these men worthy of death. For they are of the tree. And every tree shall be known by its fruit. And the tree is good and righteous. And if the root be virtuous, then so be the branches and the fruit."

"It's all specious claptrap," shouted Chelloveck to his sons. "Sorcery, subterfuge, skullduggery and chicanery. Do not be frightened by this fraud. Do as I say and summarily execute those men."

The ringent O's of the guard-Chelloveck mouths cast their doubt on their father's decision. But when he yelled, "do it now or forever be excised from my ass like a festering boil," the men shook off the shock of the fiery pillar. They rose to their feet and moved in on Joad and Santiago, who stood still as statues. As the guard-Chellovecks wielded their swords and spontoons and closed their circle, both Joad and Santiago shut their eyes and put their faith in John.

Before the Chellovecks realized it, blistering tongues of flame licked out from the pillar of fire and laid the Chellovecks out, dead and smoking in a circle around Santiago and Joad. The odor of burnt meat made Santiago's stomach rumble and he licked his lips as he stared up at Chelloveck. Cluster lightning burst and crackled just above the arena, electrifying the air. Chellovecks fled the stands and scrambled for the safety of their buses.

John's lips moved and his words echoed from the pillar of fire, "I repeat, do the men no harm. Release them and no harm shall come to you. Harm them and your names will be but a blood stain on the pages of the book of the annals of this world's history. Release them and you shall thrive. Harm them, and I will recompense to you, evil for evil." And the pillar of fire exploded, erupting in a fountain of flames and sparks, throwing molten earth and debris upon the emptied spectator area of the stadium. The flaming matter rained down and smoldered over all of the arena, covering all but a circular clearing that surrounded John, Chelloveck, Santiago and Joad.

Chelloveck weighed his options: side with Android Lovethorn or John and his men. And the exploding pillar of fire placed its finger on the scale and shifted Chelloveck's loyalties to John, making it an easy but regrettable decision to free Joad and Santiago. "I viddy that I have no choice," said Chelloveck. And he shouted down at Joad and Santiago, "Come now, you two. Climb out of the arena and be gone. Be done with us and be gone with your master."

As if lifting a bag of feathers, Joad hoisted Santiago high over his head so that Santiago could grab the top of the wall and climb into the stands. And then with a small jump, Joad grabbed the top of the wall and effortlessly pulled himself over. And Chelloveck, knowing he had no choice, led the men from the stands and out, to the Tent of Meeting, where he fed them and loaded them with provisions. And though Chelloveck protested vehemently, John decided to leave the mesa through its back entrance and head out on the red brick road, directly in the direction of Android Lovethorn's approaching men.

Chelloveck led John, Joad, and Santiago to an enormous oak door on the side of the mesa opposite to where they entered the Chelloveck village. Alf the Sacred Burro waited for them at the exit door, loaded down with saddlebags of provisions. The donkey lifted his face from snacking on the grickle grass, brayed with joy and rubbed his head against John's side. And John discovered a certain affection for the broken-down ass. He rubbed at a not unhealthy-looking patch of hide on Alf's head and felt the joy of greeting an old friend. Alf leaned in and wrapped himself around John as much as was possible for a stiff old burro, giving his friend a donkey hug.

"You, I have nothing but respect for," said Chelloveck to John. "You are a virtuous man and I easily choose my allegiance to you over Android Lovethorn. But you must go now. Be gone and be done with us, before Lovethorn's men arrive. May your load be light and your journey short. May your enemies be scattered and may your foes flee before you."

"Thank you," said John. "Thank you truly. I have a feeling that we will meet again and it will be as old friends when we do."

"And as for you," said Chelloveck, shaking his ear trumpet at Joad and Santiago, "you are saved by the good grace of your friend here. I allow you your freedom at his behest. But should you pass through this way again, give my mesa a wide berth, or I will hang you from the highest branches of the bloodfruit tree as birdfeed for the vultures."

"Lookie here, Chelloveck," spat Santiago, and his face began to cycle through its emotional range. "I'm not afraid of you and

I'm not afraid of dying. I'm scared of living, dying is easy. But it don't matter nothing to me. You got your mind made up about me. You've got your inflections in your voice and your implications. You don't know me, brother. I ain't no devil or no god, I'm Santiago, and if we should meet again..."

But before Santiago could truly launch into a rant, John took hold of his arm and dragged the twitching spasmodic away from Chelloveck. And Santiago did not resist. He allowed John to lead him away from the stern-looking Chelloveck and away from the mesa.

The red brick road sloped into a steep, sinuous slant away from the mesa. And they stepped through the grickle grass growing from the cracks in the red brick road. Spiky spurs from the grass stuck to their legs and pierced skin. Santiago's lewd comment about the best blumpkins he ever went balls-deep into trailed behind him and broke up into meaningless grains of sand on the path before it could find its way to Chelloveck's deadened ears. And Joad trailed his new friends, holding onto a frayed rope that gently pulled Alf the Sacred Burro along with him. Alf found that he liked the big, thick-headed man. Joad discovered a fondness for Santiago and John. And John grew in strength and resolve, relishing the ability to feel the sadness at his departure from the Chelloveck village. He worried about the Chellovecks and how they would survive Lovethorn's men. He suffered guilt for slaying the guard Chellovecks with the pillar of fire. He silently wished the men in the village luck. He looked back at the mesa one last time. And they were on the road again, headed straight toward the distant, oncoming patrol of Lovethorn's warriors.

John felt a hot wind on his shoulder, blowing in from a world that is older. He constantly scanned the red brick road ahead of him but did not spy Android Lovethorn's men. The clop-clop of Alf the Sacred Burro's hooves beat out a steady rhythm on the bricks and John's feet fell into time with Alf's. The steady pace and the distraction of watching for Lovethorn's soldiers drew John's attention away from the emotions fermenting in his chest and gut. He still had trouble recognizing and putting names to the conflicting feelings, though he knew he felt them. And without trying, his mind started the process of sorting the emotions out. Had he taken stock of the sentiments, he would have realized that there was dread, sadness, guilt, joy, anger, anticipation, and excitability. But John allowed himself to be mesmerized by the steady metronome of Alf's hooves on the bricks. As well as his blindness to his emotions, John likewise was oblivious to all of his surroundings – the magnificent natural bridges, gargantuan saguaro cacti, bloodwood trees in full bloom, the turkey buzzards in the trees watching them as they passed – focusing only on the path ahead in anticipation of Lovethorn's soldiers. And the emotional blinders blocked out John's peripheral vision, making him oblivious to the distant silhouettes of a leaky-eyed Indian and a droopy basset hound on a cliff, both staring in John's direction.

Ahead of them on the trail, an enormous red, yellow and black snake, its body thick as a log and longer than the width of the trail, slithered its way across the road. Something about the giant snake snapped John out of his walking trance. He looked in the direction that the snake crawled. His vision honed in on a gathering of men all tightly packed in a circle just off the side of the trail. The overcast sky above, and the span between John and the group of men, left much to John's imagination. He pictured an attack by Lovethorn's men. He imagined an ambush by vengeance-driven Chellovecks. Or maybe it was more lunkheads. John felt no worry about lunkheads, for he knew there was nothing to fear from them. But Lovethorn's men would be something to beware of.

The group of men in the distance did not move toward John. It remained a stationary, shifting blob of pink flesh, its actions indiscernible but still somehow lewd from afar. As they gradually neared the gathering, John recognized the herky-jerky motions of lunkheads. The lunkies paid no attention to John and Joad and Santiago as they drew near. Then, as if sensing the approach of some malevolent force, the lunkhead congregation split into many lunkie-pieces and the half-dead men dispersed like crevice roaches in every direction but toward John. They hobbled and crawled and hopped away from their gathering, leaving one figure on all fours on the ground.

At first they could not tell anything about the remaining person except that he was rotund and naked and on his hands and knees. But as they approached, they saw the man stand and wrap a soiled towel around his waist. And even from the great distance, they knew who it was. From afar they watched the tubby Melungeon chase down lunkies, trying to give them hugs as they scrambled for safety. And the lunkies fitfully swung their fists and legs at Two-Dogs- Fucking, trying to knock him away.

"Aw, sufferin' succotash," spat Santiago. "I thought we ditched that guy. But there he is again. Maybe we can sneak off of the path and go around him so he doesn't see us."

John considered the idea but knew he could not leave the trail. He thought about stopping where they were and hoping that Two-Dogs-Fucking would move off in another direction. But, in the distance, after he had embraced all of the fleeing lunkheads, Two-Dogs-Fucking turned their way. He shaded his eyes and stared directly at them. And then Two-Dogs- Fucking jumped up and down and waved. He ran at John and Santiago and Joad, moving quite nimbly for an obese man in sandals and a bath towel.

So they continued to walk the path. And Two-Dogs- Fucking's voice carried over the distance. "Hallloooooo," he shouted and then broke out with his grating laugh, "bwa-ha-ha-ha-ha."

At the sound of the laugh echoing across the desert, vultures lifted from the trees and scattered drunkenly in the air. Santiago twitched and muttered to himself. Joad's face pursed up in confusion and distaste. Alf the Sacred Burro stopped and plopped his hind quarters to the ground, refusing to budge. His ears flicked in annoyance and he turned his head to the side so as to not even acknowledge the approach of Two-Dogs-Fucking.

John knew that he had the power to make lunkheads flee him and to drop pillars of fire from the sky. But, despite his efforts, John could not budge Alf the Sacred Burro. Finding his powers ineffectual over the donkey, John tried to send telepathic signals to turn Two-Dogs-Fucking away from them. And he felt the suggestion seeping from him and carrying across the scorching desert air in waves. He could almost see the message floating just off the ground and flowing toward Two-Dogs-Fucking, but the waves parted and passed the Melungeon without nearing him. It seemed to John that perhaps he never had the powers to disperse lunkheads with his mind or rain fire from the sky. In fact, Two-Dogs-Fucking moved in toward them with greater zeal as if John were waving and yelling at him to hurry up. John decided they needed to keep moving forward. And Joad pulled at Alf's rope, dragging the reluctant donkey along the bricks. But Alf resisted to the best of his ability and the rope snapped after dragging him several cubits.

So they stopped and rested at that spot on the road. They passed around a skin filled with water and awaited the approach of Two-Dogs-Fucking. And the filthy Melungeon approached, stinking of sweat and the musk of lunkhead nuts, coated in a dusty crust of jism and earth. "Hallooooo," he crooned again, his mouth twisted in a large, ecstatic grin. A salty crust and a halo of stretched, chapped, red skin circled his smiling mouth. And his skin bubbled with boils and lesions from the plague that Android Lovethorn cast over the land. Throbbing cold sores dotted the irritated skin around his lips. "Those damn lunkies got me again. I don't know what it is, but they are drawn to me. It's quite a traumatic thing to be manhandled by those fellows. But you have to let them finish or they'll tear you apart. So," he grinned, "how has the road been treating you fellows."

Two-Dogs-Fucking took the water skin from Joad and put it to his mouth, guzzling a bellyful of the water. When he tried to pass the skin, none of the men wished to drink from it any longer and they turned their heads away as if to pretend that it had not been offered to them. "Well, now, who's this big fellow?" asked Two-Dogs-Fucking, nodding toward Joad. "What's your name, amigo?"

Santiago's features ticked through his range of emotions and settled on a look of concern. He grabbed the unwanted waterskin and threw it off to the side of the road. Santiago moved in close to Two-Dogs-Fucking's face and said, "His name is Goobly-Didger-Doodle-Meigh-Geigh-Gong. You call him that, friend. You call him that."

"I see that you have not changed, amigo," said Two- Dogs-Fucking, his tone dripping with condescension. "Well, I think I'd like to hear from the big fellow himself. I don't think his name is May Day Kong Noodle or whatever you said. And quite frankly, I'm a bit concerned about a new person becoming a part of our group."

"What do you mean, our group?" asked Santiago. "You're not a part of our group. Where were you when I was locked up in the Chelloveck dungeon being threatened with execution? Where were you then? Where were you when we needed to gain entry to the Chelloveck village? You're not part of the group. You're a leech, a tick, a blood-sucking parasite. The big man," said Santiago, "now, he's part of the group. He stood and faced death with me. So you show respect or I will X you out of this world. I have a system for dealing with people like you." And Santiago stomped about on the red bricks, kicking up dust and grumbling curses toward Two-Dogs-Fucking.

"Hold on, now," said John. He put a hand on Santiago's shoulder and eased the ranting madman back from Two-Dogs-Fucking. "Take it easy, Santiago. Three Tooth sent Two-Dogs-

Fucking along with us for a reason. He sent Crazy Talk for a reason, and he helped us when we needed it. He kept us on the trail and got us into the Chelloveck village, didn't he? I have to believe that there is also a reason that Two-Dogs-Fucking is with us. Now," he said to Two-Dogs- Fucking, "you clearly have been touched by the plague. Sit down and I will clear up your sores."

"Thank you," said Two-Dogs-Fucking and he plopped himself down for a seat in the middle of the red brick road. "Although I don't think there's much you can do about the blemishes. I get these regularly and they just clear themselves up."

And John laid hands on Two-Dogs-Fucking and consumed his illness. As the affliction soaked into John's hands, his face turned a crimson hue and he vented the foulness in the form of bleating flatulence and booming belches. When he finished, all of the blemishes, save the angry cold sores, were cleared from the Melungeon's skin, and the area reeked of John's sour intestinal turmoil. And John once again felt a boost of energy and power from taking on another's sickness.

"Thank you," said Two-Dogs-Fucking, getting to his fat, flat, four-toed feet, and readjusting his towel. "I still have not been properly introduced to the big guy. My name is Two-Dogs-Fucking," he said to Joad. "And who be you?"

"My name is Joad of the Po'kinhorns of Gath. John saved me from sure death and I owe my life to him. I am his servant and his soldier. I am John's conscience and Santiago's counterbalance. I am the angel to Santiago's devil. I am what I am." Joad smiled and tipped an imaginary hat toward Two-Dogs-Fucking.

"It's a pleasure, amigo," said Two-Dogs-Fucking. "I, too, am what I am. And I am tired and lacking in motivation. I think I will go rest under yonder bloodwood tree until I'm feeling the need to do more." He looked to John. "I will be rejoining your travels, as Three Tooth requested. But you do not need to wait for me. I'm just not motivated right now and I can think of many good things to do other than hoofing it on this hot road. The donkey can come with me if he wishes."

But Alf the Sacred Burro did not wish to remain with Two-Dogs-Fucking. The lazy Melungeon moseyed toward a blood-wood tree that did not have a man dangling from its branches. Alf rose to his feet and led the band of men away from Two-Dogs-Fucking, and on a course toward Android Lovethorn.

Two-Dogs-Fucking and the tree he lay beneath quickly shrank to a dot in the background as John and the men moved on with a new vigor. Alf the Sacred Burro set the pace at the front of the group, moving along briskly. And the men did not speak for some time. Still not understanding the situation back at Chelloveck village, John looked to Santiago and asked, "What the hell did you do to piss those Chellovecks off? They were so angry they couldn't even talk about it."

"I didn't do nothing so bad," said Santiago, and he cast his eyes down at the trail, avoiding the curious gaze of John. "It ain't like I killed nobody. I ain't never killed nothing but some dirt-rats when I'm hungry. But, they act like I boiled their ba-bies in hot oil. It ain't like that, dig? And what's wrong with a little diversity in their lineage anyway?"

"What are you talking about, diversity in their lineage?" asked John.

"I stuck it to their blumpkins," said Santiago with renewed zeal. And his voice rose in volume and pitch as he explained it to John. "Oh, yeah! I shagged the shit out of those babies. And there weren't a damn niksik in the whole bunch. I rolled around in their comfy pools and made those little fuckers sing the songs. And I tapped well over half of their stock before those Chellovecks came in and discovered me laid out on the floor, spent and sloppy and satisfied. And don't tell me you would've done any different, Johnny, because you know you would've laid into those blumpkins, too." Santiago looked to Joad for support.

"I do like blumpkins," said Joad, his voice low and muffled as if it were coming from deep within him. And he flashed a smile of enormous square teeth.

"What, please explain, are blumpkins?" John's voice rose to the intensity of Santiago's. He stopped walking and his eyes burned with a ferocity that demanded answers. Although Santiago and Chelloveck had both mentioned blumpkins, John never received any kind of explanation as to what blumpkins were. His questions were always interrupted and he did not let it worry him because whatever blumpkins were, they did not seem relevant to his journey. But enough was enough. John decided he needed some sort of answers and they were not going any farther until he had them.

Santiago laughed nervously and tugged at his beard. He pursed his lips and furrowed his brow with thought. Santiago tried to explain: "Well, blumpkins are...well...they're put to-gether nice."

Joad grunted in agreement and nodded his boulder of a head.

"They're," Santiago scratched at his head as if trying to stim-ulate thought, trying to find the right words. He smiled and said, "they're all soft and spongy and warm. When you're hold-ing one, you never want to let it go."

"Umm-hmmm," agreed Joad.

"They've got soft fleshy nubs and warm, wet crevices. And you squeeze 'em and poke at them with your fingers and your rod. And, great gods almighty, I'm getting myself worked up just talking about it." Santiago adjusted the swell-ing in his loincloth to allow his erection a more comfortable placement.

"Ah, now I get it," said John. "Women. Blumpkins are broads."

"Okay," said Santiago. "I've never heard them called women or broads. But if that's how you know them, then you get what I'm talking about."

"Yeah," said John, "I was starting to wonder why we've seen no women. But I guess they keep them locked up safe so you can't get at them."

"That," answered Joad, "and you can find them wherever there are hot springs."

John said, "Well, you're lucky that I was able to lay hands on the Chellovecks and suck up their sickness. For the most part, they like me. But, otherwise, you guys would have been in for a hell of a time. Do me a favor," said John to Santiago. "The next time you feel like getting some pussy, try to control yourself. We need to stick to the trail and not get distracted by such things. Just exert a little self-control, alright?"

Santiago shifted his eyes around everywhere but in contact with John's. He scratched at his beard and muttered, "Alright, but them blumpkins was mighty sweet."

"I do like blumpkins, too," agreed Joad.

"And don't you go egging him on," said John to Joad. "I need you to help me keep that crazy little man under control."

Joad continued to keep pace with the steady rolling donkey at the front of the pack. Without faltering in his stride, Joad laughed a gentle, deep laugh, that came out muffled, just like his voice. "Do you need to keep him under control?" asked Joad. "Or do you need to allow him his urges? Aren't his urges what make him a man? And isn't he one of the most honest men you've ever met?"

"I'm surprised to admit it," said John, "but he is my friend. And I don't want to see him die at the hands of angry Chellovecks or other jealous men. So he needs to keep it in his loincloth."

"Would you prefer to see him live an unfulfilled life?" asked Joad. "Would he be a better man if he were deprived of every-thing that makes him happy?"

"That's not what I'm saying," said John. "I just think he has no impulse control and it's going to be the end of him."

And a piece of bloodwood fruit, earlier plucked from a tree that they passed, splattered on the back of John's head. He slapped his hand to the back of his head and whirled around to see Santiago in his wrestling stance, ready for John to jump at him.

"So sorry, Johnny," said Santiago, his unibrow twitching mani-acally above bulbous, lunatic eyes. "I ain't got no impulse control.

I'm just one giant id. Fucking and eating and fighting is all I know. But whose fault is that? You made me. I come from you. I come from the water, dig? I'm just a free spirit in your valley. No impulse control, brother. Why don't you just drop a pillar of fire on my ass. I ain't afraid of dying. Dying's easy. I'm afraid of living half a life. So don't try to control me. Because you can't get at my mind. I'm gonna think and act the way I do until I die. And I feel like tearing into your ass right now." And he leapt, hands out and aimed for the throat, ready to bite off and eat the ear that had regenerated like a lizard's tale on the side of John's head.

And though quick and nimble, Santiago's speed was no match for Joad's reflexes. The lumbering giant demonstrated a spryness belied by his enormity and with one hand snatched Santiago by the arm, midair, and directed his landing away from John.

"Hold on there, friend," Joad said to Santiago, effortlessly restraining the little man. "Don't you think we should talk this out? Can you agree that John has a good point about your impulses if John can agree not to restrict your needs? Don't you think that we're all better off as a team instead of singly? Can't you feel that?"

Santiago struggled against Joad's hold, wiggling and clawing at the massive hand wrapped around his bicep. But his struggles did him no good. Joad stood, stoically, and held Santiago until he calmed. John stood ready, hands raised defensively, ready to fend off Santiago.

"Are you calm now, friend?" asked Joad. "Can I set you loose without you jumping on your friend?"

"Yeah, I reckon you can," said Santiago. And his features

slackened as he calmed himself. "I reckon he may have a point about my impulse control. I'm good now. Sorry about that, Johnny. I get a little crazy sometimes."

Joad released his hold on Santiago's arm. Immediately the little man leapt at John. John slapped his hands over his ears to protect them from Santiago's teeth. And before Joad could stop him, Santiago was on John, hugging him, laughing and crying out, "I didn't mean to hurt you, brother. I's just so crazy sometimes. Help me with my impulse control." And he laughed again and planted a sloppy kiss on John's cheek.

John pulled his hands from his ears and pushed Santiago by the face, knocking him to the ground. "Get off me, you crazy bastard!" But he was not mad. Santiago and Joad felt like family, and John found that he was glad to have them accompanying him on his journey. He looked down to Santiago on the ground. The little man cycled his face through the range of emotions and the expression settled on shock, his eyes bulging and unibrow wiggling in astonishment. Then John laughed. And the laughter caught on with Joad and Santiago. Alf the Sacred Burro brayed mirthful donkey laughter. And all was right between them. They laughed until all of their tensions dissipated. And as the contagious laughter was winding down, a sound boomed out from behind them that terminated the laughter once and for all.

"Bwaaa-ha-ha-ha-ha," blurted Two-Dogs-Fucking, his joviality hitting them like a splash of cold water and promptly ending the laughter.

And from the edge of a distant cliff, Three Tooth looked on with a tear dribbling down his dusty cheek.

El Camino de la Muerte twisted and turned and the dirty old road revealed more bloodwood trees decorated with human piñatas. Mostly the cadavers did not hold cards in their hands, mostly. But when they did, Santiago no longer needed to knock them free with his walking stick. Instead, Joad easily reached the cards and extracted them from the corpses' hands. And John collected the cards until he had a complete deck.

As they wound their way along the meandering trail, Two-Dogs-Fucking intermittently stopped and rested in the shade of the bloodwood trees. He napped and drooled and unconsciously groped at his dick. When done with his catnaps, he would step off of the trail and cut across the desert to intercept the others again on the path. And after several hours without Two-Dogs-Fucking, the men happened upon him snoozing on the ground in the shadow of a bloodwood tree, his bath towel hanging as a circus tent on a fat and short center pole. A lynched man swayed gently in the breeze above him.

John sat with his back to the tree, looking up at the swinging corpse. Up ahead on the trail, the sharp yips of a dirt-rat colony called out to Santiago. Although the Chellovecks gave them ample provisions, Santiago felt the need to slaughter rodents. He needed it not for food but for his nerves. He left John and Joad and Two-Dogs-Fucking at the bloodwood tree and commenced a barbarous dirt-rat massacre.

"Who are these men?" asked John to no one in particular. He looked up at the hanging man. "What have they done to deserve this?"

Joad approached and stood face to face with the dead man, waving away a small swarm of munkle flies and studying the man's features. "Who do you think they are?" he asked.

"I don't have a clue," said John. "I'm only just beginning to learn who I am, or what I am. How am I supposed to know anything about these men?"

"I think they are like you," said Joad, and he moved away from the corpse. He looked down on John from high and said, "I think that they, too, were following the trail. I think that they were seekers who failed to find what they were looking for."

"So they were trying to reach Android Lovethorn?" asked John. "They were trying to get back home?"

"I don't think so," said Joad. "They were following their own paths. The trail leads not only to Android Lovethorn. The trail flows everywhere, to the left, to the right, forward, backward, and up and down. Its purpose is different for each man who has to travel it. Its direction depends on the traveler."

"So this journey is specific to me?" asked John. He stood and walked out of the shade of the bloodwood tree, looking up at the overcast sky. And the trail of clouds above El Camino de la Muerte slowed to a creeping pace, as if waiting for John to start walking the road again. "The red brick road flows in a direction toward my ends? Is that what you're saying?"

"What do you think?" asked Joad, swatting at and smashing a munkle fly that was biting his arm, drinking his thick blood. He looked at the smashed bloody mash of munkle fly mess and grimaced, then wiped his hand on a high limb of the tree.

"I think I agree."

John sat down at the tree again and pondered his journey.

And much of what Joad said made sense. It did feel as if there was a deeper purpose to walking the road than just getting back home. It felt to John as if he were getting to know himself better than he ever had before, even though he could not remember his life prior to the red brick road. And he realized that he liked himself. A feeling settled in his head, as if the meaning of his travels were starting to gel, as if he were near to grasping a purpose for it all. He closed his eyes and ruminated on the matter. On the backs of his eyelids, the ten thousand things flashed as a galaxy of twinkling stars and they swirled and rearranged into constellations of snakes and bears, donkeys and long-eared dogs. A sparkling picture show danced before him in the blackness. And just as it felt like it was all coming together...

"...Halloooooo," said Two-Dogs-Fucking. "I see you are lacking in motivation. A good nap will do you just fine."

And the Melungeon's voice snapped John out of his reverie and set him on edge. But John did not open his eyes, nor did he acknowledge Two-Dogs-Fucking. John sat with his back against the tree, eyes closed, and tried to picture the constellations on the backdrop of his eyelids. But the visions vanished and refused to return. His heart beat rapidly, fueled by his irritation. And the recharge of a midday siesta evaded him. Once he knew for sure that Two-Dogs-Fucking had risen and resumed walking, John stood and stretched. The sun was sinking, its rays diffused by the ash clouds above and casting a blood red glow over the land. Settling down for the evening made no sense when there were still several hours of daylight left. So John grabbed Alf the Sacred Burro's rope and led him away from the tree. Alf rubbed the side of his face against John's hand and looked up at him with dewy eyes. John scratched the donkey's head. Joad and Santiago once again followed John as he set out on the red brick road.

And that evening, when they settled on a campsite, Three Tooth and his men struggled into the camp. Joad stood at the edge of the piss perimeter, looking down at the sorry looking band of men who dragged themselves before him. Three Tooth, Crazy Talk, Heap-o-Buffaloes, and Throws-Like-Girl barely managed to stagger into the camp. The open, seeping sores on the scurves had crusted over but still bubbled with infection. Three Tooth dropped to his hands and knees and dragged himself to Joad's feet, gazing upward at the towering giant.

"John said you would come," said Joad. He picked up Three Tooth, dwarfing the large scurve, and carried him like a new-born to the fire. John sat beside Three Tooth and laid hands on him while Joad lugged the afflicted men to the fireside. The blazing river of flames and the emerald light of the star Wormwood cast a flickering green and orange glow over their camp as John tended to the men.

There was no sleep that night for John. His healing hands kept busy on Three Tooth and his men all night and into the next day. Nor did Joad enjoy any rest. Instead he stood sentry at the edge of the camp. The scurves' seeping sores and infected abscesses dug in and fought against the healing, but John was stronger. And he drew out the sickness and feasted on it, turning it into his strength. The sick men moaned and John vented the foulness with great bleating farts and burps. John did not stop until Three Tooth, Crazy Talk, Heap-o-Buffaloes, and Throws-Like-Girl were cured. When the morning sun peeked over the horizon and burned the sky red, Three Tooth and his men all passed out from exhaustion, but not John. He switched from man to man, laying on his hands and soaking up the infections like a sponge. When John was satisfied that his job was done, Joad lifted the men, one by one, and carried them into the shade of a bloodwood tree to shield them from the burn of the desert sun.

Neither Santiago nor Two-Dogs-Fucking concerned themselves with tending to the sick. Two-Dogs-Fucking found level ground off of the trail, well outside of the protective piss perimeter, spread out under the night sky, and slept deeply the whole night through. Santiago fell asleep, face down on the ground beneath the bloodwood tree, dead to the world, and did not awaken even as Joad hefted the recuperating men and lay them on the ground all around Santiago.

When the laying on of hands finally concluded, all present slept in the shade of the bloodwood tree until darkness once again draped itself over the land. All slept, that is, but John, who sat with his back against the tree, eyes closed. He felt no need for sleep. Energy buzzed through him and he felt it in every part of his body. When he did open his eyes, he saw different objects wavering almost imperceptibly. Alf the Sacred Burro gave off a green nimbus and his body vibrated, resonating with the buzz of a small swarm of munkle flies. The leaves on the tree threw off an almost unnaturally bright shade of green. The bloodwood fruits, red and spotted with purple blotches, gently throbbed in time with John's heart. Each and every aspect of John's surroundings registered with him. Every smell, every sight, and every sound checked in and found a place to settle in his consciousness. Before he realized it, the two moons were rising in the sky and the trail of clouds changed color to a low burning red, and random flames flickered in the clouds until the trail in the sky ignited and burned as a river of fire above. And with the onset of the evening, Three Tooth began to stir. John was aware of this, too, although he kept his eyes closed.

Like sand slugs surfacing on the desert floor with the turn of night, Three Tooth, Crazy Talk, Heap-o-Buffaloes and Throws-Like-Girl all felt the pull of the moons and awoke. The two half-moons hung low in the sky and slowly drifted toward each other as if attempting to jettison their dark halves and join together in a single glowing orb. The men slowly stirred like cave-bears waking from a long hibernation.

Two-Dogs-Fucking stumbled into camp, his face cramped with disappointment. "I'm so glad that no lunkheads found me," he said. "I accidentally fell asleep away from the camp and could have been ravished if I would have been discovered by another roving group of lunkies." But his face showed no relief, instead looking sad and lonely.

And Santiago still slept, unaware that Crazy Talk had cuddled up next to him in his sleep. Even though he was waking, Crazy Talk stayed in spooning position, his arm slung over the sleeping Santiago. Two-toned braying and cruffulous coughing from Alf the Sacred Burro woke Santiago, who threw Crazy Talk's arm from him. Santiago jumped up, spitting and hissing. "Gods damned Injun," he spat. "Can't a man go to sleep without being felt up?"

"That's what I'm saying," agreed Two-Dogs-Fucking, unconvincingly.

Heap-o-Buffaloes chuckled to himself but said nothing.

"Jump back and kiss myself," said Crazy Talk, licking at the palms of his hands and slapping them to his head, flattening his fine, blond hair. "Thatwise I am the zombie woof. And I gots me a zombie toof."

"Jumping Jehoshaphat!" said Santiago as he leapt toward Crazy Talk, murder in his eyes. The negative space between Santiago's outstretched hands formed into a perfect semicircle to fit around Crazy Talk's neck. But before Santiago throttled his throat, Crazy Talk held out a wineskin heavy with chicha. Santiago's hands closed around the skin and his face softened. His threatening demeanor immediately changed, facial expressions shifting randomly and settling on pleasantly surprised. "Is this what I think it is?" he asked.

"It is the spit of the gods," said Crazy Talk. "Thatwise I brought it just for you."

"Well, why didn't you say so, you crazy son of a niksik." Santiago put one arm around Crazy Talk's shoulders and tilted the wineskin back, draining a gut-full of chicha down his throat. Halfway down his esophagus the chicha turned against him and struggled to spew back out of his mouth. Fighting the urge to puke, Santiago coughed and gagged and forced the stinking spit-brew down, holding it there. He passed the wineskin back to Crazy Talk and dropped to his knees in the sand, battling the chicha revolt in his stomach. Alf the Sacred Burro took Santiago's fits as a reminder that he hadn't coughed up anything of substance in hours. The donkey joined in the coughing and gagging and spat up a bezoar coated in donkey slime and half-digested grickle grass. Throws-Like-Girl retrieved the bezoar and studied it, ignoring Santiago and Crazy Talk. Both Santiago and Alf concluded their coughing fits at the same time. Then, Santiago's body accepted the putrid liquid and the accompanying all-over warmth. And he craved yet another snort of chicha but had to wait until it had passed around through all of the men.

Joad accepted the skin and tilted it back, draining most of the liquid down his throat. "Mmmm," he grunted, suffering no ill effects, and nodded his head pleasantly at the others.

John opened his eyes and rose from the ground. He took the wineskin from Joad and drained the last of the drink. Everyone else had already suckled at the chicha teat and suffered the initial shock. They watched as John choked it down and refused to let it back out. Joad stood over John, ready to help him if necessary, and watched. Munkle flies alighted on Joad's face and forehead. Like Alf the Sacred Burro, he ignored the flies, even as one slowly crawled across his eyeball. Joad focused on John, concerned about his wellbeing. Only when John's stomach contractions ceased and his body accepted the drink, did Joad move and wave away the flies.

And Three Tooth was at John's side, hand on arm, leading John away from the tree, away from the road. "Come now," said

Three Tooth. "Come to our kiva and palaver with us."

"But I cannot leave the path," said John. "If I do, I'm lost. All is lost. I have to stay with the trail."

"The trail leads in many directions," said Three Tooth, and the tear dribbling down his cheek lent a sweetness to his gentle, gummy smile. He waved a hand before them and John saw that the trail did indeed lead in the way that Three Tooth was urging him. And the river of fire in the night sky tracked along with the trail.

Heap-o-Buffaloes ran well ahead of the group, giggling and mumbling to himself. And the entire crew followed along, passing skins of chicha and a pipe stuffed with burning bezoars. Intoxicated on chicha and the comfort of camaraderie, the men took their time winding along the meandering trail. Santiago and Crazy Talk walked with arms thrown over each other's shoulders and drunkenly crooned songs about the moon and the mountains and scorpions and wolves. Joad stayed toward the back of the group, scanning the land ahead for danger. Alf the Sacred Burro hung back with the giant, occasionally rubbing up against Joad's leg to prod a head scratching. Throws-Like-Girl flitted about the moving group, distributing the chicha and pipe to the needy. And Two-Dogs-Fucking strayed from the path as he felt was necessary and returned for tokes on the pipe and draws from the wineskin.

And the road collided into a roof-like structure of beams covered in juniper bark and adobe. A large rounded adobe chimney jutted through the center of the roof, belching smoke and steam into the moonlit sky. The edge of the roof rested on the ground, hinting at a subterranean pit below. A glowing flicker of orange light illuminated a round opening at the edge of the roof where it met the red brick road.

"Follow me," said Three Tooth as he stepped through the hole. The light of the fire within the structure tinted Three Tooth orange and made the hieroglyphic brands on his arms appear to dance the ghost dance. "This is our kiva. We will be safe here."

John and the others followed Three Tooth down the hole. Once inside, John saw that they were descending stone stairs that hugged the walls of a rounded, deep hole in the ground. The pit was ten cubits deep and twenty wide. The floors and walls were all formed from carved stone. Four massive tree trunks sat on carved discs of stone and supported the heavy, low roof. The chimney sat on four short stone columns, with a ventilation tube resting above a pile of burning juniper logs. Shadows of the men flickered on the stone walls in the kiva pit.

Only Joad did not descend into the kiva. He stuck his massive head through the entry hole but his shoulders proved too large to fit through the opening. Realizing that he was too large to enter, Joad sat outside of the kiva with Alf the Sacred Burro. And while the men on the inside of the kiva spoke, Joad and Alf sat on the ground watching a lively meteor shower draw bright streaks across the sky.

Inside the kiva, Crazy Talk, Heap-o-Buffaloes and Throws-Like-Girl pulled melon-sized rocks from the fireplace with large tongs. They placed the smoking stones in bins built from flat stones and dumped water over them. Steam hissed from the rocks and mingled with stray smoke that refused to exit through the chimney. Three Tooth pulled covers across the kiva's entrance and also over an opening at the opposite side of the pit, trapping the steamy smoke. Two-Dogs- Fucking sat on a stone bench and yawned, looking ready to bed down for the night. In front of the fire, Santiago sat, cross-legged, rocking back and forth and singing quietly to himself as he stared wild-eyed at the flames.

John walked the circumference of the pit, studying the walls and the stone benches and structures. On the walls someone had scratched and burned hieroglyphics similar to those on Three Tooth's arms. The flicker of the fire made the wall paintings seem to dance. Just feet in front of one of the benches was a hole in the floor four cubits in diameter. John sat on the bench and leaned over, trying to look down into the hole. But the pit was deep and a cloud of the smoky steam hung just over it, obscuring the contents of the opening. A stone dropped down the hole gave no report of hitting bottom. And Three Tooth sat on the bench beside John.

"What is the hole for?" John asked, dropping another stone and hearing no report.

Three Tooth stared forward, not looking at John, not looking at the hole. A tear dribbled down his cheek. "It's a portal from below. There are others like it that appear and disappear as they will. They are the doors of perception. The doors that some, like you, use to enter this world. They claw their way up from wherever it is that they come. Most perish and return to where they came from. Some stay. Some move on."

"Move on to where?"

"I am a simple man," said Three Tooth. "Do not look to me

for answers. I barely manage to keep my men out of trouble. I have no advice that is worthy of you."

A thick cloud of smoke and steam hovered around Three Tooth and John. Putting his hand on John's back, Three Tooth urged John up and guided him from the hole. "Come," said Three Tooth. "Sit a spell by the fire and let your mind relax."

And they all sat around the fire. One large stone seat that was big enough to fit Joad's backside sat empty. Crazy Talk stood and went to the wall, returning to the fire with a wineskin full of chicha. The men's throats were scratchy and dry from the bezoar pipe, and the smoke from the fire made them cough until their throats were raw. The chicha numbed the scorched throats, numbed the brains, numbed the pains. Conversation was not necessary. The flickering flames spoke to the men and reached them in a way that words could not. Glazed eyes zoned in and out on the blaze. The steam opened pores and purged the men of their toxins. Heat from the fire seared their faces, reddening them and tightening the skin. But the men sat transfixed and removed from the discomfort they should have felt.

Behind John, from the bottomless pit, a scream rumbled low and quiet, ratcheting up in volume and pitch until it crescendoed to an eardrum-piercing, murderous shriek. The scream made the hair on John's body stand on end and his heart race. The others sat oblivious, staring into the fire before them and passing the wineskin. And though the skin seemed on the verge of emptiness, it always contained enough for the next person to suckle at it. The scream continued and only John moved, turning to look toward the ruckus transpiring behind him. And John saw hands of fire clawing at the edge of the hole, dragging the hands' owner from the depths of the pit and leaving scorch marks on the ground. And from the pit crawled a man formed from flickering flames. A flowing beard of fire draped down over the man's chest. Long hair flamed and framed his face. His jaw moved back and forth, grinding fiery teeth as the scream subsided to a low growl. Embers fell from his mouth as he suffered a brief coughing fit. Blinding light beamed from each eye, as if they burned hotter than the rest of the flaming body. The man wore a robe of fire and his entire being burned as the fire in the fire pit.

John looked into the blinding eyes of the man and knew that he was looking at himself. He put his hand to his own face and felt his own flowing beard. He ran his fingers through his own long hair. And though he had not seen his own reflection since the time that he first arrived in the foreign desert world, John knew that he was looking at an image of himself rendered in flames. The burning man walked across the kiva, crackling with sparks and trailing streamers of fire behind him. He sat in the empty seat at the fire and faced John. And though the burning man blazed, John felt no heat emanating from him. On his left shoulder appeared a tiny flaming image of Santiago. On his right sat a miniature version of Joad. And the chicha continued to make its way around the fire and into everybody's bloodstreams. But the other men moved at half the speed of John and Burning Man. And they did not notice, nor did they pay attention to their conflagrant guest.

"You are me," said John.

Burning Man nodded. And his booming voice, the same voice

John first heard when he awoke in his cave, echoed in the kiva. "I am in your mind. You are in your mind. This all is in your mind."

"Are you trying to tell me that this is all a dream?" asked John. "Because I don't believe that. This shit has gone on too long and it's been too real. I don't know what this is, but it's not a dream."

"I didn't say that it was a dream," said Burning Man. "This is real. But, like I said, it's in your mind. It's another realm. Your physical body is in another place, in a hospital bed, comatose. You are everything that was good about you, the essence of your goodness. There was not much when you first arrived here. Mostly you were rotten inside. You hurt others, destroyed lives. Your purpose was entirely self-centered and destructive to all that came in contact with you. And the kernel of goodness that you possessed has been planted in this realm and it has flourished. All of the bad is festering in the body in that hospital bed, like a black cancer consuming you. You are here to grow strong so that when you go back – when you reach Android Lovethorn and go back – the good in you will prevail over the evil. This is your chance to make everything right again."

"I'm not so good," said John. "There's nothing so great about me."

"You've stayed the course," said Burning Man. "You've followed the path. You help others when they are afflicted with open, oozing sores. You saved your friends from sure death back at the Chelloveck village. You do no wrong and help others as you follow the path. The you that is atrophying in the hospital bed would have done nothing of the sort. With the powers that you are gaining in this world, the other you would have wreaked havoc on the entire land. Android Lovethorn would pale in comparison. But you, this you, is humble and good and right. And this is the way that you are supposed to be."

"So what does this all mean?" asked John. "What are you and what do you want with me?"

"I told you, I am you. I am the link between you in this world and the other you in another place."

"So what do you want?"

Burning Man said, "I want you, the good you, to prevail. You need to force Lovethorn to send you back. If you do not succeed, if you stay here, you die in both worlds. You need to continue to follow the path, no matter what. And when you reach Lovethorn, you need to force him to send you back. Do not harm him. Just make him return you to yourself."

"I don't get it," said John. "This isn't right. I know this is not all going on in my head. Too much has happened and it's all too real. And I'm kind of starting to feel good, happy, you know. If things are so shitty wherever I came from, I don't know that I want to return. Maybe I make Lovethorn stop with the plagues. Maybe I confront him and force him to stop. Then I stay here. I like it here."

"You cannot stay here," said Burning Man. "You are the guy. You're the one. Go back and save yourself. If you stay here, you die in both worlds."

"What if I take down Lovethorn?" John asked. "What if I make him stop? I can stay here and everything will be okay.

And what's it matter if some rotten part of me dies in some other place. That sounds like a good thing."

"You cannot do that. You will die. You cannot take down Lovethorn. He is too powerful. Even if you are able kill him, it will mean sure death for you. If you stay here, you die. If you die here, you die there. If you die, this entire world perishes."

John said, "So you're saying that if I stay here, it means sure death for me, as well as Lovethorn? That doesn't make sense. He is trying to keep me from reaching him. He wants me to stay here. Why would he want me to stay if it meant death for him, too?"

"He doesn't understand," said Burning Man. "Lovethorn came into being with your appearance here. Your presence gives him his power. He doesn't want to give that up. He thinks that as long as you do not return to where you came from, his strength will grow. The only way to stop Lovethorn and save your own life is if you make him send you back. You cannot stay here and you cannot kill Lovethorn."

And the miniature flaming Santiago on Burning Man's shoulder threw a fit, pulling at his beard and tearing off his fiery little loincloth, growling and shouting. "Fuck that shit," he yelled. "Fuck that. Take him down, Johnny. Take down the king in the corruptible crown. We gotta shake up some shit here, brother. Don't listen to this flaming piece of shit. He can't be trusted."

And Burning Man swatted at the tiny Santiago on his shoulder, knocking the small flaming image backwards and smashing him on the ground in a burst of flames and sparks. "Silence," boomed Burning Man. And the voice echoed and bounced about the kiva. Three Tooth and the others sat, unawares, passing the chicha and bezoar pipe and staring blankly into the fire. "Enough from you."

The miniature flaming Joad sat on Burning Man's shoulder, a pensive look on his face. "You know," he said in a voice with far too much bass tone for such a small form. "This fellow here may have a point. Approach Android Lovethorn from the way of the path, and Lovethorn will have no power. Not that he is not powerful, but his power will not be harmful to you and those you watch over. As for how to deal with Lovethorn when you reach him, look within yourself for the answer. No one but you can make that call. If he must die, you will know. But do not go in with a rigid mind that is set on destroying him. Let the path lead you to where you need to be and allow yourself to wash along with its flow. You will do what is right."

Burning Man reached up and smacked at his shoulder, knocking Fire-Joad to the ground where he exploded in a bright flash of white light and sparks. "Fools!" boomed Burning Man. "Do not listen to them. You have the power to set things right. Take my word and do not betray me. Convince Lovethorn to send you back and do not harm him. I command you!"

Before John could respond, Burning Man leapt into the fireplace and exploded. The concussion of pure force, blinding light, and searing heat from the explosion knocked John and the others from their seats, slamming them against the walls of the kiva. A pillar of flames shot from the chimney, a fireball blasting into the sky and crashing into the river of fire flowing above. And briefly the river exploded, raining down fire on the desert below, before it collected itself and resumed its flow in line with the red brick road.

The blast in the kiva flung Throws-Like-Girl through the air, lifting him on a wave of white light, and landing him half on the floor and half in the bottomless hole. Unconscious from the blast, Throws-Like-Girl fell down the shaft and was no more. Just before passing out, John looked to the blackness on the ceiling. And from the blackness he saw the ten thousand things swirling, tossing off strands of cool blue and flecks of gold. And then, blackness again.

At the sound of the blast, Joad stopped stacking dead bodies and ran for the kiva. Fire rained down on him from above, but he let that worry him not. Alf took shelter under the cover of a fully dressed bloodwood tree and the fiery rain droplets bounced off the cloak of leaves, dripping to the ground and burning in a circle around the drip line of the tree. Not a single fiery droplet penetrated the foliage to burn the donkey. Although it wouldn't have mattered much to Alf – he had been through worse.

Putting his head down, Joad ran for the kiva and ripped off a massive chunk of roof. A rush of scalding steam and smoke washed over Joad and knocked him back a step. But the steamy smoke did not turn him away. Joad dropped himself into the Kiva and pawed around until he felt a body. He grabbed onto an arm and dragged Three Tooth from the kiva, effortlessly

lifting the large scurve out and setting him on the ground outside of the pit. The air in the kiva cleared more as the large hole
in the roof vented a plume of smoke toward the sky. And Joad
dismantled more of the roof, tearing off beams and flinging
them far to the side of the road. With the hole in the ceiling
opened more, and the smoke settling to little more than a thin,
moist smog, Joad pulled John, Santiago, Two-Dogs-Fucking,
and Crazy Talk from the kiva, setting them beneath the bloodwood tree with Alf. He returned one final time to retrieve
Heap-o-Buffaloes. Joad lifted the lifeless body – the head
cocked at an unsettling angle, dangling on a broken, floppy
neck – and carried it to the bloodwood tree.

   As quickly as the firestorm started, it cleared away. Dim
early daylight shone down on the fuming desert ground. Joad
stood on the road, his afro singed and smoldering, and stared
at his new friends, hoping they would be all right. A sickly
dirt-rat scampered just in front of Joad's feet and crossed to
the other side of the path. Joad lowered himself and squatted
on the trail, watching and waiting for movement from John.
The big man felt that he should be doing something, anything, to help his friends. But his mind locked up as he tried
to contemplate the best course of action. So he squatted and
watched.

   And before long, John stirred and sat up. He put his hands to
his temples and groaned. Next Santiago did the same, then
Three Tooth. And they all regained consciousness and commenced grumbling. Joad retrieved skins of water from the de-
molished kiva and brought them for the men. They drank the
water and grumbled more. Eventually, all but Heap-o-Buffaloes

rose and found themselves to be substantially intact, with only a smattering of contusions and scratches. No bones were broken, no organs punctured. Other than ringing ears and some minor injuries, the living men were healthy.

Three Tooth first looked to Heap-o-Buffaloes' lifeless form and then noticed that Throws-Like-Girl was missing. So did the rest of his pack. But they did not ask about their friends. A sadness enveloped them and they huddled together, arms around each other's shoulders, shifting back and forth together and chanting low and slow. Three Tooth and Crazy Talk and Two-Dogs-Fucking did not invite John or Joad or Santiago into their embrace; and it was understood that the exclusion from the huddle was not personal and was necessary to Three Tooth and his men. So they were left to grieve the loss of their friends in their own way.

And then John looked to Joad. In Joad's forehead was a grape-sized rock – a rusty red hunk of chert – embedded there as if it were a precious gemstone perfectly set in a crown. Joad picked at the stone with thick, ham-handed ineffectiveness, and tried to wave away John's effort to help. Joad's large fingers pushed the stone deeper, failing miserably in the attempt to remove it. Realizing the futility of his efforts, Joad once again allowed John to help him. With surgical delicacy, John pinched the stone between his forefinger and thumb and wiggled it loose from a deep crease in Joad's protruding forehead. And what looked like a pebble when it was set in Joad's boulder of a head turned out to be a fist-sized chunk of chert when John removed it. A trickle of thick brown blood, similar in color to the chert, dribbled between Joad's eyes and split into two rusty runs that stained dark trails along the sides of his nose. John handed the stone to Joad.

"Thank you, I..." Joad started to say. But John slapped the palm of his hand against Joad's head and the smack sent a jolt of energy that nearly melted the marrow in the giant's bones. When John pulled his hand back, a scabbed-over spot took the place of the open and seeping hole where the stone had been. For just a moment, a golden glow radiated from the scab. The physical transaction energized both men. John held out the chert stone in his open hand. Joad grabbed the rock and heaved it high and far. They watched the stone until it disappeared from their view far off in the distance.

Off to the side of the road a fracas erupted amongst a flock of turkey buzzards. The hisses and grunts and sounds of harsh regurgitation drew John's attention. He looked and saw a pile of dead men stacked like firewood, five cubits high. And the buzzards woke early and came down from their high perches to undress the corpses. Dead grey flesh tore off easily in the beaks of the hunch-shouldered birds. Entrails streamed from gashed abdominal cavities and the vultures tore at the viscera, tossing their heads back to engorge the meat. Before long, a fighting and scratching blanket of carrion scavengers writhed atop the stack of bodies. And the birds gorged themselves and shat out white chalky feces at the same time. As if on cue, the buzzards all began hopping and awkwardly flapping their wings, eventually achieving graceless flight and leaving behind a pile of clean bones for the sun to bleach. The kettle of buzzards in flight momentarily blocked out the sun and then dispersed into hundreds of dark brown blots on the sky, heading in different directions and settling on any manner of available roosts.

John and Joad and Santiago stood as witnesses to the entire the spectacle, all fascinated by the work of the turkey vultures. When the feeding frenzy ended, John looked to Joad and asked, "What of this? Who were those men and what happened to them?"

A thoughtful look fell over Joad's face and he picked at the scab in the middle of his brow. He peeled away a small piece of the scab at the edge and a flicker of light briefly glittered out from the fresh wound until it scabbed over again. After moments of thinking it over, Joad said, "They were sent by the Man in Black. While you were in the kiva, the men approached and attacked me. I threw a number of them high in the air and they did not land so well. The donkey kicked one in the head and he did not fare much better. They came at us with weapons and their hands. I told them that if one of the men could take me out on his own, I would allow all to pass and do as they would. One man, smaller than the rest and closer to being a boy than a man, came forward and challenged me. He flung four stones at me with a sling. Mostly the stones flew askew and buzzed right by me. But the fifth one struck me above my eyes and stuck there. It fazed me just briefly and I may have stumbled backwards a bit. And then the men were on me and it is mostly a blur. I know that Alf kicked out at some of them and I snapped many in half. When the dust settled, I was still standing and the Man in Black's soldiers were scattered and broken in a circle around me. I stacked them and waited for you."

"Why didn't you call out for us?" asked John. "There were many of them and one of you. We could have helped. You didn't need to do that alone. Weren't you scared of death?"

"I was not scared," said Joad. "I know how to live. I walk abroad without fear of the rhinoceros or tiger and I will not be wounded in battle. For in me, the rhinoceros can find no place to thrust his horn, the tiger no place for his claws, and weapons no place to pierce. This is so for I have no place for death to enter. So I did not fear those men. And I did not need to endanger you. It was all taken care of and all is well. You are safe for moment and the buzzards are well-fed."

"Well, if that ain't almost as big a load of donkey nuggets as the shit that I spout, I don't know what is," said Santiago over John's shoulder. "But I can tell you both one thing: we better get moving and fast because there's a nasty storm rolling up on us from the rear and I don't think we're going to want to get stuck in the middle of it."

Up in his tower, Android Lovethorn yowled at the sky, livid at the loss of his men to the blockheaded giant. A fury driven by fear of John gripped Lovethorn. He could not let John reach him. And the failure of his men brought the problem closer to home. Lovethorn tore at the black robe he wore and ripped out clumps of his greasy black hair. He threw his arms to the sky and howled a bitter, searing scream. He spat over the edge of the tower and called on the four winds to stop John. "Pluck him from his path," shouted Lovethorn to the winds, "and fling him to the far corners of this land. Make him leave his path and lose his way and he will be forever lost, and helpless, and harmless. Do not kill him. And do not fling him over the bottomless sides of this land. Or we will all be doomed." Lovethorn called to the guard in the tower's doorway, beckoning him. Obediently, the guard came and put up little fight as Lovethorn hoisted him overhead and threw the man over the side of the tower as a sacrifice to the four winds. The winds converged in a swirling vortex and plucked the man from the air, carrying him off, far away and out of Lovethorn's sight.

Far behind them a swirling, roiling, black cloud devoured the nigrescent sky, creeping in their direction, casting a dark blanket of dread over the ground. John, Joad and Santiago approached Three Tooth and his huddled friends. "I do not want to interrupt your grieving," said John, putting a hand on Three Tooth's shoulder, "but I think that we have a big problem headed our way."

Three Tooth broke from the huddle of grief and looked at the tempest brewing in the direction from which they came. A tear dribbled down his cheek and he turned back to John. Lightning shot from the clouds and slammed the ground. Tornadoes swirled and tore about the desert, ripping up the red brick road and uprooting bloodwood trees. "We must go now," said Three Tooth, and a steady stream of tears flowed from the corner of his leaky eye. "You need to move on, too. Keep the donkey and Two-Dogs-Fucking with you. They may become necessary."

Three Tooth turned back to Crazy Talk and pointed toward a ridge far off of the red brick road. And the men did not hesitate. Three Tooth hefted Heap-o-Buffaloes' corpse over his shoulder and sprinted away from the trail. And though he was burdened with the deadweight of his friend, Three Tooth outran Crazy Talk as they dashed for cover. Two-Dogs-Fucking remained, shuffling about in circles, looking dejected and sad.

"We need to move, too," said John, grabbing at Alf the Sacred Burro's rope and tugging him into action. Alf rose from his sitting position and nudged his scarred, patchy muzzle against John's leg, giving him a donkey hug. "Those long black clouds coming down over us are the work of Lovethorn. And I suspect things are going to get rough."

Two-Dogs-Fucking plopped down in the middle of the road. "I don't feel like going on," he said. "I've lost my motivation again and I don't expect it to return. Perhaps I'll just sit here and let the rains wash me away."

The palm of Santiago's hand smacked hard at a sensitive place on the back of Two-Dogs-Fucking's neck. And the force of the smack stung Santiago's palm. He pulled it back and rubbed his hands together nervously. "Did you not hear the man?" shouted Santiago. "He said it's time to go. If we sit around here waiting for you to get your shit together, we'll be here a thousand years more."

Two-Dogs-Fucking held a hand to the back of his neck and looked up at Santiago stomping around on the ground in front of him.

"Perhaps," said Two-Dogs-Fucking, "if you just give me a minute to gather myself, I will find the desire to move along with you. Maybe it would help if you just give me a moment."

"Maybe I find spirit of caveman and thump your ass with a club if you don't start moving," yelped Santiago, and he leapt at Two-Dogs-Fucking with a clear intent to inflict damage. Before Santiago landed on the sluggish Melungeon, the large, thick hand of Joad redirected his flight, setting him on the ground several feet to the side of Two-Dogs-Fucking.

Santiago spat at the ground, tugged at his beard, and said, "You big dumb oaf. Let me at him. I'll give him the sting of the scorpion and the bite of the wolf. He'll get moving before I'm done with him."

But Santiago stayed feet away from Two-Dogs-Fucking, only because Joad's mammoth hand held him back. And with his other hand, Joad grabbed the front of Two-Dogs- Fucking's bath towel and lifted the plump Melungeon off of the ground, dangling him at the giant's side. "John asked us to move," said Joad, his voice low and clear and determined, "and he meant all of us. Understood?"

Two-Dogs-Fucking nodded his plump head, his bearded jowls jiggling in concurrence. Joad set him on his feet and pulled his other hand away from Santiago, who no longer looked ready to attack. "Now I think we all should move," said Joad. And the men listened. They followed John and Alf the Sacred Burro at a rapid pace, fleeing on the red brick road in a direction away from the oncoming storm. And the crack of thunder and rumble of the churning sky dogged them in the distance, approaching nearer by the minute.

And though they moved rapidly, the storm proved to be faster. When it caught up, plum-sized hail pelted them, knocking them to the ground. Lighting struck the land on both sides of the path. Wind threatened to lift the men from their feet and carry them off to their deaths. They tried to shield their heads and faces from the icy pain of the hail storm. They narrowed their eyes to slits to avoid the sting of the whipping wind.

When it became apparent that the storm would not relent, and that they would eventually be pummeled to death by the enormous hailstones, John stopped. He raised his arms and eyes to the sky and shouted, "Stop! What is this that the sky opens and dumps on us like this? Be done with us, storm. Let us pass in peace." He spread his arms and the hail stopped pounding his face and head. The storm continued but was divided by a clearing that rose from the red brick road and up to the river of clouds mirroring it. On both sides of the road the storm raged, and the hail and lightning pounded the ground, beating down barrel cacti, bloodwoods, and pinyon pines. A small tornado headed straight for John and the men. But, as it neared, the twister turned and tore up the ground all along the side of the red brick road. All that they felt from the tornado was a light breeze that dried them and speckled their skin with gooseflesh. John and the others were spared the storm's assault. The light of the sun, diffused by the river of clouds, shone through and tinted the road and everything on it with a rose hue.

And though the storm raged, they were safe from it as long as they kept to the road. So they walked along with the sky venting its spleen to both their left and right. And they did not talk, for the storm roared loudly enough that they could hear nothing else. As the rosy tint of the sun through the river of clouds dimmed, and the river above the road turned to fire, the storm continued to churn and tear up the desert as if it were waiting for them to set foot off of the road. There was no need to set up a protective perimeter; any lunkheads would have been ground into a fine paste by the relentless hailstone assault. So they slept on the road, all but Joad who stood guard the first half of the night, and then John, who took the second shift.

And the next two days and nights were the same – walking all day without talking, and sleeping on the road at night. And the storm continued, even increasing in intensity. But it did not touch John, nor did it deter him, as Lovethorn had hoped. Instead, it strengthened John's resolve to follow the trail and seek out the Man in Black.

On the fourth morning of the atmospheric onslaught, the storm intensified in one last-ditch fit. Ball lightning dropped from the sky and tore up trees and ground. Fist-sized hailstones pounded every accessible spot. Flash floods rumbled through the desert and wiped out entire communities and species. And still, the storm left the road and all on it unmolested. As they awoke to the red tint of the sun blazing through the river of clouds, John, Joad, Santiago, and Two-Dogs-Fucking watched as the storm relented, and the hail lessened in both size and intensity, until a drizzle of rain spat in disgust at the desert. And then, finally, nothing. The clouds cleared, except for those drifting above El Camino de la

Muerte. And the sun shone down on the desert, quickly dry-
ing the battered ground. A haze wafted off of the desert floor
as the puddles rapidly evaporated. The morning air – cool
and clear and perfect for walking – energized the men. After
a quick breakfast of jerky, pinyon nuts, and water, they set
out on the road again.

As the sun squatted directly over them at midday, the flora
of the desert began to look healthier and less battered. And
more animals began to appear. Dirt-rats poked their heads out
of holes in the ground and chattered at one another. Turkey
buzzards roosted in bloodwood trees and the cracks and crags
of high cliff walls. Munkle flies flitted about Alf's face but he
ignored them and tore fresh green grickle grass from a spot
where he stopped beside the road. Atop a ridge, John saw a sil-
houette of Three Tooth sitting atop Morticia, hand shading his
eyes and staring in John's direction. Though John could not see
his face, he suspected that a tear may be dribbling from Three
Tooth's weepy eye.

Santiago stopped them at one point. "There's a muffugin'
colony of dirt-rats grooving over there. They wasn't washed
out by the big bath," said Santiago. He skipped off the side of
the path and ran for the holey ground of the dirt-rat colony.
Before long, the entire rat colony gathered around Santiago.
And he sat still, a beatific look on his face, occasionally scruff-
ing a rat and using the ground to knock the life out of it.

"He's right," said Two-Dogs-Fucking. "This area was not hit
as bad. Over yon is a bloodwood tree whose roots remain in
the ground. And the shade that it's casting makes my eyelids
heavy." Without further consultation, Two-Dogs-Fucking

waddled to the tree and plunked himself down in the shade for what he considered to be a much needed siesta. The tree's branches and leaves drooped as if exhausted from the storm, but the ripe fruit was not ripped from the limbs and the branches were unmarred by lightning.

And John felt like moving. He felt like plodding on down the trail, working his way to Lovethorn. But even Joad and Alf seemed disinclined to movement for the time. Joad flopped back into a deep, cool puddle on the side of the road and basked in the sunlight that he had not seen for days. "Puddles are nice," he said. "I like puddles." He slapped his hands in the water like a toddler enjoying a bath and grinned a dopey, big-toothed grin. He lay back in the water and sat up, shaking the beads of moisture from his thick Afro and returning it to a dry look before dipping his head back into the water. The phrase *happy as a pig in shit* occurred to John as he watched Joad.

Alf plopped his backside in the water beside the giant and bent down to lap up hydration. And the donkey drank with such gusto that he inhaled puddle water and choked, gagging himself and coughing up a bloody bezoar. Joad fished the donkey vomit from the water and flung it to the side. Alf, thankful for the lack of judgment from Joad, rubbed his patchy muzzle against the giant. Without thinking about it, Joad scritched Alf's head. And the two relaxed in the water with no apparent intent to get back up.

And the realization hit John that his crew needed rest. As bad as he wanted to move on, John realized that he needed Joad and Santiago and maybe even Two-Dogs-Fucking. So he found a level spot of ground beneath the bloodwood tree and lay back, head on his hands, and allowed his mind to drift. And without expecting it, a nap came to John. As he drifted off, the voice of the burning man whispered to him, "The path begot one. One begot two. Two begot three. And the three begot the ten thousand things."

Two-Dogs-Fucking woke first from the siesta. A weight pressed down on his thick belly. Hands slapped at his plump man-boobs. At first he thought that a gang of libidinous lunk-heads were once again dragging him from sleep. Still half asleep, he immediately sprouted an erection under his dirty bath towel and thrust his hips upward toward the warm weight on his belly. His puffy hands reached out to latch on to whomever was atop him.

And then Santiago's ranting woke the others as he jumped off of Two-Dogs-Fucking. "Don't thrust that dirty rod at me, brother," Santiago shouted at the sluggish Melungeon. He stomped around, kicking dirt, and threw a dead dirt-rat at Two-Dogs-Fucking. "I was merely trying to wake you, not arouse your passions, dig? Up now, sluggard, and waste not life. In your grave there will be sleeping enough."

"You frightened me," said Two-Dogs-Fucking. He rose to his feet and adjusted the slight protrusion at the front of his bath towel. "I thought I was going to be ravished by lunkheads again." But instead of fear, disappointment smudged his face.

John and Joad and Alf the Sacred Burro all rose to the sound of Santiago raving. And they saw Two-Dogs-Fucking standing before them and sporting a pathetic erection under his towel. Beside him stood Santiago. Around Santiago's neck hung a string of dirt-rat skins that he had stripped from rats while the others slept. The meat from the rats, skewered on pointed sticks, cooked over a small fire that Santiago built. So they ate the dirt-rats. With their bellies full and heads rested, the men were ready to walk.

And then they were on the road again. The trail twisted and rose and dipped. Pinyon pines spread their twisted limbs to the sky. Bloodfruit trees stood, strong and healthy, unmarred by any storm. They left the storm-ravaged land behind them and all looked right. Twisting and squirming above, in concert with the red brick road, the river of clouds traced a white zig-zag across the otherwise blue sky.

The men, well rested from the siesta, marched with determination. Santiago sang songs about dirt-rats and bigheaded giants, clapping his hands but never keeping good time. And though his voice never quite hit the right notes and his rhythm was off, his songs rang out with the passion of old time spirituals, and put a bounce in the other men's steps.

Joad and Alf the Sacred Burro pulled up the rear. Joad tried to step in time with Santiago's songs but the fluctuating beat threw off his already awkward stride. He hummed along with Santiago when he could glean the melody, his deep voice providing a complex bass tone for Santiago to work with and against.

Even Two-Dogs-Fucking kept pace with the others, never once complaining about a lack of motivation or need of a nap. He kept to the road and stayed with the group.

John led the pack, feeling as if he were being drawn forward by some unseen source. He kept his head high and his eyes scanning the land before him. To the sides of the road, natural arches opened in cliff walls and hinted at strange lands to both sides of the road. While he felt curiosity about what lay through those arches and beyond, John stayed true to the path and continued slapping his feet down on the red brick road. Besides curiosity, a rumble in John's stomach demanded his attention. A hunger for food came on him, but he also felt a hunger lower than his stomach, a need in his loins that had not visited him since he loosed a hoard of jizz-critters outside of the Chelloveck mesa. And John walked faster, trying to ignore the growing desire.

Far off in the distance, steam rose from the ground around the road, distorting the air. John wondered if it was a mirage and he did not mention it to the men. But as they neared the steaming ground, they could see pools of water dotting the distant landscape and steam rising from the pools. Alf the Sacred Burro pulled up alongside and nudged at John's leg.

"Hey there, Alf," said John, scratching the donkey's scabby head. "How you doing, old man?"

But Alf did not answer immediately, because donkeys do not talk. He thought it over and brayed at John instead because that was the best response he could come up with. The burro stopped walking so that he could clear his throat of a fuzzy bezoar that had been bothering him for hours. He coughed and convulsed and brought up the stinking donkey-ball. Before the warmth could drift away from the bezoar, Santiago fell on it, plucking it off of the ground and stashing it in a bag sown from rat skins that hung from the string around his neck. Alf cleared his throat with a loud bray and then ran to catch up with John.

"Well, there you are again, old man," said John to Alf. "What do you think of all of this?" he asked, not expecting an answer. Alf merely nudged his head against John's leg to prompt scratching.

From the back of the pack, Joad answered for Alf, saying, "The donkey thinks one thing, and he that burdens him another." And the giant picked up his pace and appeared at John's other side. To John, Joad asked, "What do you think of all of this?"

"I think we need to keep moving. I think something good is just ahead. Look up there." John pointed toward the steaming ground in the distance. "I don't know what that is, but I have a good feeling."

Santiago moved to John's side. He looked to where John was pointing and his body set to trembling and convulsing. "Holy moly and great googly moogly!" said Santiago, his neurons misfiring with the excitement, making him twitch and shiver involuntarily. "We hit the big one, boys. That's Aguacaliente." And then he tried to run. But his twitching muscles rebelled at the physical effort and Santiago fell to the ground, still trembling, his face shifting through his range of expressions and settling on a glazed look of desire. "Gods damned Aguacaliente!"

John and Joad bent over Santiago and held his head and arms while he twitched and raved about Aguacaliente. John jammed one of his sandals in Santiago's open mouth to keep him from chewing off his own tongue. Santiago involuntarily bit down upon the shoe and his jaw continued to grind. John said, "What is he talking about? What is Aguacaliente?" Joad wrapped his arms around Santiago and held him tight, waiting for the seizures to stop. "It is said," began Joad, "that Aguacaliente is a body of water fed by hot springs. But the springs are shifting, disappearing and reappearing in different places at random times. Those who find the springs are said to be blessed with longevity."

"What is so special about the springs?" asked John.

Joad, still holding Santiago in a bear hug, said, "I've always thought that it was just a myth, but I have heard that the springs are the birthplace of blumpkins."

"Blumpkins and niksiks," interjected Two-Dogs-Fucking, the pitch of his voice rising noticeably on *niksiks.* "I think that this may be worth checking out, this Aguacaliente."

A calm settled over Santiago and his twitching spasms faded, leaving him with his usual deranged look. Joad released his hold and Santiago sprang to his feet.

"Why'd you hold me back, Bigg'un?" said Santiago to Joad, and he twitched several times before regaining control of his body. "You trying to keep me away from Aguacaliente? You don't want me to get to the blumpkins? You afraid I'm gonna break all the toys? Listen up you sons of motherless goats. I'm going and diving in head first, and you all can't stop me." And Santiago sprinted toward the hot springs, kicking up a cloud of dust at his heels as he ran. He shouted back over his shoulder, "Last one there has to fuck a niksik."

And they did not know for sure if it was Aguacaliente before them, or what such a place would hold in store. But, the lure of the steaming water in the distance, along with Santiago's enthusiasm, pulled strongly on John, Joad, and Two-Dogs-Fucking. Even Alf seemed to have springs in his old donkey legs. So John threw himself fully into the current of the path and was rapidly washed along behind the sprinting Santiago. As he walked, John allowed himself to consider the possibility of encountering women. He had not even been in the presence of a female since his appearance in the cave. Memories of his interactions with women in his other life eluded him and mostly all he felt was shame and guilt when he searched his brain for information about his prior dealings with the other sex. Despite the sinking feeling in his stomach when he tried to dredge up the elusive memories, John also felt nervous anticipation about what lay in store ahead at Aguacaliente. He allowed his mind to formulate lustful scenarios to the point where he realized he was noticeably aroused. He pictured curvy babes in scant clothing, lounging by the edges of the hot springs. He imagined long flowing hair, plump lips breathing hot air on his neck, teardrop shaped breasts capped with large pink nipples, round, firm asses and long, fit legs. As the mental images formed and bent to John's will, his pace quickened. Initially concerned about his semen and the resulting jizz-critters, John forgot his worries. Like a magnet, Aguacaliente's attractive force latched on to John's uncomely parts and dragged him across the desert like a testosterone-bloated pull toy.

Before long, the red brick road led the men to a steaming pool of deep blue water. The men found themselves standing side to side at the edge of a pond ringed with enormous royal

palm trees. John scanned the area and felt great disappointment when he saw nothing but steaming water, palms, El
Camino de la Muerte, and more desert. And then, from somewhere below the water, continuous streams of air bubbles surfaced. The perfumed smell of flowers and citrus permeated the
air. Muffled harmonies, the same as those John heard in the
Chelloveck Tent of Meeting, floated off of the surface of the water and rose with the steam.

"They're down below," shouted Santiago as his body resumed its manic twitching. He peeled off his stained loincloth
and the string of dirt-rat pelts around his neck. He tore off his
lunkworm bag and tossed it with the rest of his belongings.
The rail thin, twitching and naked man stood at the edge of the
springs, convulsing and struggling to regain control of his muscles. And when the twitching subsided, and his face had shifted
through his range of emotions and settled on lustful, Santiago
tugged at his hair and beard and shouted. He gripped his rigid
erection and yelled down at the water, "Lookie out below, cuz
I's coming to get you." And the little man leapt high and dove
with perfect form. At the apex of his arc, he kicked his legs
above him and stretched out his arms to meet the water. His
hands parted the water and plunged beneath it, followed by
arms, head, neck, torso, plumped up member, legs and feet.

Santiago disappeared below the surface of the springs, and the
waters settled again. Even more bubbles surfaced, bringing with
them fuller harmonies. John, Joad, Alf the Sacred Burro, and Two-
Dogs-Fucking stood still, watching the water, waiting for Santiago to come back up for air. Minutes passed, but still no Santiago.
John gazed down at the water and saw his own face – covered

with a long, thick beard and framed by his wild, long hair – staring back at him. The lines on his face gave testament to his burdens. But he looked healthy, and happy. John and his reflection smiled at each other. Intrigued with his new appearance, John studied his reflection and forgot about Santiago. He saw that his fine linens remained crisp and white, despite his travels. He noted a healthy glow about his own face and a resolve in his eyes. He gazed deeply, engaging himself in a staring contest, falling into an introspective trance.

And that spot of water that held John's reflection wavered. His concentration broke and he became aware of movement just below the surface. At that spot, Santiago burst through the water. In his arms he held ball of peach colored flesh the size of Joad's head. Santiago threw the ball at John's feet and dragged himself onto land. John stared in shocked wonder at the object at his feet. Two-Dogs-Fucking gasped in horror and tripped as he stepped backwards.

The creature was moist and glistening with beads of water. And it was beautiful, gently rolling back and forth before the men, pulsing. Full breasts and randomly placed labia covered the ball. Thick puffs of black, kinky hair encircled the muliebrous slits. And the flowery citrus aroma wafted up from the fleshy folds, intoxicating the men with desire. Several toothless mouths with full lips and smooth, glistening gums, were situated about the ball. And the mouths opened their moistened lips and hummed in harmony with each other.

"What the hell is that?" John asked, contemplating his mixture of wonder, arousal, and confusion.

"It's a blumpkin," said Santiago, "and it's ready for a little sumpin' sumpin'. So I'm gonna carry her over there and do some humpin' and pumpin'." And the madman shivered with anticipation. He shook his head to throw the crazed look from his eyes and rid himself of the involuntary twitches of desire.

Doing his best to ignore Santiago's throbbing hard-on pointing at him, John said, "I thought blumpkins were women, you know, females."

"Call 'em whatever you want: women, females, blumpkins or fuck-balls. Call this one Pamela if you like. I don't care. This is the opportunity of a lifetime and I'm done talking." Santiago lifted the humming blumpkin in his arms and carried her to a mossy spot under a royal palm, whispering softly to her all the while. Laying the blumpkin gently on the ground, Santiago turned his back to the others and took a step back, tensing his muscles like a ram getting ready to jam a lamb. He shook off a spasm and lowered himself to the ground, wrapping his arms and legs tightly around Pamela the blumpkin. They rolled about on the moss, Pamela crooning and pulsating and throbbing, blasting the perfume of passion from her unoccupied orifi. And Santiago, shouting "Yeah, baby! Yeah," thrusting himself into the blumpkin and groping at the multiple breasts as if trying to scoop them up and smash them into one big, fleshy mound.

Two-Dogs-Fucking shook his head and said only, "Disgusting! Just disgusting." He adjusted his filthy bath towel around his girth and waddled away along the edge of the steaming pool. Off to the side of the pool sat a smaller puddle of burbling muck. Two-Dogs-Fucking stopped and sat by the stagnant pond, his back to Santiago, watching large bubbles pop on the surface and inhaling deeply the rancid stench of the rotten puddle.

John looked up at Joad. "So those are blumpkins?"

"Blumpkins, they are," answered Joad.

"And," ventured John, "they're for fucking, then, right?"

"If that's what you call it."

"And you like them?"

"Blumpkins are nice," said Joad. "I like blumpkins."

John and Joad stood and watched, unashamed and unembarrassed, as Santiago pleasured himself with the blumpkin. And then it ended with Santiago rolling off of Pamela and onto the ground, chest heaving to drag in fresh air, spent from his passions and staring at the palm fronds above him. Pamela rolled up over Santiago's body and to the edge of Aguacaliente, exhaling sweet smelling breaths of perfumed air in short puffs that went *pahhhhhhh* as she rolled.

Pamela sat at the edge of Aguacaliente, singing and throbbing and sweating, turning red. Every few minutes her pitch climbed and dropped wildly, and then returned to the normal soothing song. And the frequency of the wild singing increased, getting closer and closer in time. All of the throbbing localized on one orifice that swelled and dilated. Pamela's entire being contracted and relaxed, contracted, spasmed, and relaxed. Santiago remained on his back beneath the royal palm, ignoring Pamela's distressed condition and puffing on a bezoar in the peace pipe.

"Shouldn't we do something?" said John, alarmed and starting toward the blumpkin. "Something is wrong with it. We need to help."

"Do you really think we can help it?" asked Joad. And he put his giant hand on John's shoulder. "Just let it be. This is natural. This is the way these things work. She is not in pain."

The confidence in Joad's voice calmed John. He felt assured that Pamela was not suffering but instead doing whatever it was that blumpkins were supposed to do. So John and Joad sat and watched Pamela sweat through the increasingly frequent and strong contractions, doing nothing to help her.

And then the throbbing mound on Pamela blasted a crimson spray of chunky goo into the water. Following the initial eruption, Pamela spat bone-white pods the size of bloodfruits into Aguacaliente. After lobbing twenty pale, slime- covered pods into the water, Pamela slowly rolled herself back into the steaming waters of Aguacaliente and floated toward the center of the pool. The pulsing larvae-pods and viscous pond-spunk floated toward the blumpkin as if drawn by some unseen force. She lowered the volume of her song and blew off a rapid succession of sweet smelling *pahhhhhhh, pahhhhhhh, pahhhhhhhhhs*. With each puff of her scent growing more fragrant, Pamela sunk into the water until she dropped below the surface and out of sight. The pods and their shimmering slick of spew sank, too, as if following the blumpkin.

John and Joad stared at the spot in the pool where the blumpkin dropped from sight. And the waters calmed again, only disturbed by the constant flow of bubbles percolating up from below. And they fixed their eyes on the spot and sat, unmoving. John mulled over the situation and felt a stirring in his loins. Joad sat still, waiting to see what John would do. Two-Dogs-Fucking remained at the stagnant puddle, his back to the others, staring at the muddy muck.

John and Joad sat, gazing at the bubbles until they stopped rising. And the surface of Aguacaliente smoothed over, glassy and steaming, still emitting the blumpkin harmonies and aromas.

"Well, what are you faggots waiting for?" screamed Santiago from behind John and Joad. Before they realized it, Santiago was already flying high in the air and dropping toward the center of Aguacaliente. He pulled his knees to his chest and tucked his chin down just before his rump smashed the surface of the water and threw a heavy spray all around, soaking John and Joad. And then he disappeared again for minutes into the depths of the spring, reappearing in front of John and Joad with another blumpkin, this one larger but looking much the same as Pamela. He set the creature at John's feet and wiggled his thick unibrow lasciviously. He said, "This one's for you, brother. She'll treat you so many ways, you're bound to like some of them." And then Santiago jumped backwards and disappeared again into Aguacaliente.

Without hesitation, John bent down and lifted the blumpkin off of the ground. Her soft smooth skin warmed John's arms and torso. The perfume wafting off of her made John woozy with desire. "Wow," was all he could say as he studied the creature's surface. Like Pamela, a multitude of female openings covered the blumpkin. And heavy, soft breasts capped with swollen brown nipples, hung all about her.

"What are you going to name her?" asked Joad, the question snapping John out of his daze.

"I don't know," said John. "I think she looks like a Barbara. What do you think of that, girl?" he said to the blumpkin. "Can I call you Barbara?"

And she quivered joyously in John's arms. Her mouths puckered and sang soothing blumpkin tunes.

"Then Barbara it is," said John. Barbara pulsed. Her swollen nipples contracted and sprayed warm, sweet blumpkin milk in all directions, soaking John and even getting some on Joad. "Alright, girl," John laughed. "Alright. Calm down." He stroked Barbara with one hand in an effort to calm her. But it seemed to excite her even more. In the process, John realized that he was wildly aroused.

"Don't you think you should take her over in the shade of one of those palm trees?" asked Joad.

John took Barbara in the shade of a royal palm and laid her on the soft covering of moss. He filled wineskins with warm water and gently cleansed her. He rubbed at her and caressed her and relished the feel of her warm flesh pressing on his. Everything else happening outside of the shade of the palm tree faded into nothingness.

John was unaware of Joad diving into Aguacaliente and retrieving an enormous, bloated blumpkin for himself. John did not notice that Santiago had set a hardy looking blumpkin down beside Alf the Sacred Burro and that Alf was sniffing the creature with great curiosity. John did not see that Santiago had stacked a small pyramid of blumpkins for himself under another palm and commenced fucking them like a horny bonobo with attention deficit disorder. John did not see that Two-Dogs-Fucking was retrieving something for himself from the stagnant puddle beside Aguacaliente. John did not see these things and would not have cared even if he had.

The stroking and cleansing of Barbara drove John into a frenzy. And when everything felt right, John mounted the receptive blumpkin and filled her with his seed. He suckled at her lactating teats and gulped the sweet milk that flowed from them. Time became meaningless as John and Barbara rolled about in the shade of the palm. When they finished, John – covered in a glaze of sweat and blumpkin milk – rolled off of Barbara and onto his back. He did not know if their encounter lasted two minutes or two hours. But, he was physically drained and feeling a deep serenity. He did not feel love for Barbara, but he did feel a strong bond, a need to protect her and care for her. He closed his eyes and contemplated how he could bring Barbara along on the road with him. Did she need to stay in water? Would she be able to survive in the glare of the desert sun? Could she be strapped to Alf's back or would Joad be willing to carry her? John found that he did not like the thought of someone else touching Barbara and decided that either he or Alf would have to be responsible for her transport.

Ignorant to John's musings about their future, Barbara rolled toward Aguacaliente, leaving John to his dreams and schemes.

John lay on his back, eyes closed and unaware of Barbara's departure, concocting a plan to bring the blumpkin along with him on his journey. Barbara throbbed and pulsed at the edge of the hot springs, signing her blumpkin song, her periodic labor contractions growing nearer to each other, and each becoming more intense than then last. And as John drifted off into a deep nap, Barbara tensed up one last time before blasting a slick of blumpkin spew and pods into Aguacaliente. With a trumpet of sweetly sad *pahhhhhhs*, Barbara rolled into the steaming water and floated toward the center. Blumpkin spew and pods gathered around her and followed as she sank back down to the depths of Aguacaliente, leaving her quickly fading blumpkin scent as the only evidence of her existence.

A melancholy haze settled on John when he awoke to find Barbara gone. And even though the sadness pained him, John was glad that he had at some point developed the emotional capacity to feel it. His plans for Barbara were sincere. Although John still had no memory of his other life, he somehow knew that he never experienced such emotions for any of the women he had known. That was a part of his spirit that was missing from him in the other place. Something about the sadness, though, increased John's feeling of strength and confidence.

So John stood and looked around. A row of gravid blumpkins lined the shore of Aguacaliente, throbbing and spitting pods into the waters. Blumpkins floated into the steaming pool and slowly sunk beneath the surface, dragging the pale, pulsing pods down with them. Under one palm tree, Santiago lay recumbent on the mossy ground, his legs and arms splayed out and mouth agape. Several blumpkins waited for him to regain consciousness and give them a turn. Joad sat beneath another tree, embracing the enormous blumpkin that he pulled from the waters while John was entangled with Barbara. John could hear Joad whispering sweet nothings to the blumpkin but could not make out the words. Alf the Sacred Burro lay on the ground by Joad, twitching and moving to some donkey dream.

Two-Dogs-Fucking walked around the edges of Aguacaliente, carrying in his arms what John assumed to be a blumpkin that had been out of the water too long. And when the towel-wrapped Melungeon approached, John saw that what he first thought to be a blumpkin was something entirely different. Instead of perfectly formed breasts and inviting labia gracing the form of the fleshy ball, John saw puckered assholes ringed with course hair and oozing gelatinous goo. A crusty scab covered the one orifice that slightly resembled female genitalia. Open sores bespotted the mouths on the fleshy ball, and thick black mustaches highlighted the lips. Instead of healthy, smooth gums, broken brown teeth sprouted inside of the mouths and dangled by their roots. Sweet blumpkin harmonies did not emanate from the mouths, but instead a constant, high-pitched squeal dragged long fingernails across the chalkboard of John's soul. The puckered assholes blew raspberries of foul fumes that were not the sweet perfumes of the blumpkins, and instead stunk like a week-old shallow grave.

"What is it?" asked John, almost knocked breathless with revulsion at the appearance of the creature.

"Yeah," said Two-Dogs-Fucking, mistaking John's shock for envious wonder. "She's beautiful, isn't she?" Several of the mouths on the ill-favored creature creached the high-pitched screech. Two-Dogs-Fucking looked down at the screaming mouths and gently shook the thing in his arms. He smiled down at it and said, "Oh, come on now, sweetheart."

"What the hell is that thing?" asked John again.

"Why, it's a niksik," answered Two-Dogs-Fucking. "It's basically the same thing as the blumpkins that you fellows have been enjoying. They just look a little different. It's really just a matter of personal preference. I find the blumpkins to be rough on my eyes, but I could stare at my little niksik all day. Some people don't like the smell of the niksik, and I can understand that. It is a foul bit of feculence. But rubbing a sourmint leaf on your upper lip masks the odor. And I don't care about the smell, anyway. This niksik's special. She's my little Missy. Yes, I think that's what I will call her, Missy."

"That's fine and all," said John, turning his head to keep Missy the niksik out of his line of view and the odor from his nose. The sight of the writhing ball of assholes made him sweat a stinking, nervous perspiration, and tickled at his skin like the itch of grickle grass exposure. "But just take her back over by her pond. Her screeching is setting me on edge and the stench makes me want to puke."

Santiago woke and shouted in support of John, "Yeah, get that filthy ball of assholes far away from us. I was just kidding before when I said the last one here had to fuck a niksik, you dang numbskull!"

"Please," said John. "Take it away now."

"As you wish, m'lord," said Two-Dogs-Fucking, bending his knees, bowing his head, and dipping low in an exaggerated curtsey. He promptly and enthusiastically carried Missy the niksik to a spot by the stagnant pond from whence she came, leaving behind the heavy stench of Missy's acrid flatulence that burned John's nose and throat. Under the shade of a tattered, sickly palm tree, Two-Dogs-Fucking wooed the niksik and consummated their relationship with a coupling that consisted mainly of him fondling, fingering, fisting and fucking the multiple anuses located about Missy's body. Unlike the blumpkins, when the deed was done, Missy remained by Two-Dogs-Fucking's side as he lay back on the ground, succumbing to a lack of motivation and napping.

The day gave way to the light from the river of fire and the star Wormwood. In the glow of the green and orange light, blumpkins surfaced. And John, Joad, and Santiago, drunk on the wine of fornication, took turns with the various visitors on the soft mossy ground beneath the palms. Alf the Sacred Burro relaxed in the shallow waters at the edge of Aguacaliente, occasionally partaking in the blumpkin orgy, too. But mostly the donkey relaxed and enjoyed the warm comfort of the steaming waters. Two-Dogs-Fucking intermittently woke from naps and rolled about on the ground, fucking and fisting his niksik.

And as dawn greeted the land, the last blumpkin floated toward the middle of Aguacaliente and sunk to the bottom, taking with it a slick of blumpkin spew and pale pods. With the submersion of that last blumpkin, the harmonies drifting from the steaming water faded to silence, and the constant flow of bubbles from below ceased. The sweet aroma of blumpkin kisses dissipated and gave way to the smells of the desert. John and Joad and Santiago waited at the edge of Aguacaliente for more blumpkins to appear, but none did. Santiago dove in the water and remained under for what seemed longer than possible. When he returned from the depths of Aguacaliente, he dragged himself onto land and gasped for air. "They're gone," Santiago said between deep breaths. "Vanished. No more."

The absence of the Blumpkins was reason enough for John to move on. So, that morning, John, Joad, and Santiago decided to set their feet to the red brick road again. But, Two-Dogs- Fucking stayed behind with Missy. "Go without me," he told them, expecting someone to protest and looking disappointed when nobody argued the point. "I am staying with my Missy. She cannot survive away from her waters and I cannot bear to be without her. You move on, gentlemen. I wish you the wind at your back and good luck in your endeavors."

The sun assaulted the desert and scorched every living thing exposed to it. As John walked away from Aguacaliente, the steam from the springs hissed into the air, but no more blumpkins surfaced. The only action in any of the waters occurred between Two-Dogs-Fucking and Missy the niksik as they frolicked in the stagnant pond. Two-Dogs-Fucking and Missy emerged from the puddle and sat beneath their palm, watching John, Joad, Santiago, and Alf the Sacred Burro disappear out of sight on El Camino de la Muerte. And though he felt a slight twinge of sadness at the departure of the men, Two-Dogs-Fucking had never been happier than he was at that moment, holding Missy in his arms and gently jamming a thumb into one of her windy assholes. Missy, likewise, found that there was no place that she would rather be. And she creached in her two-toned screech and pooted fetid, joyous vapors.

El Camino de la Muerte led John on a twisted path through the desert. Red stone and sand gradually gave way to more verdant lands. The Badlands faded into the past. Natural arches disappeared and lush foothills, covered in ancient trees and vegetation, replaced them. Beyond the foothills, hiding behind fog and clouds, steep mountains jutted from the ground and poked at the sky's belly. And the path meandered in the direction of the vague mountain forms. The trail of clouds above grew fuller, heavier, and ready to burst. A watery murmur drew attention to the stream that paralleled the red brick road. Symmetric rows of date palms lined the stream.

"Dates are nice," said Joad. "I like dates." He stepped off of the red brick road. Alf followed. Joad stood on the tips of his toes and plucked ripe dates from a tree, occasionally pricking his hand on the tree's thorns but not caring about the pain or the blood that trickled down his wrist. In the shade of the tree, the giant and the donkey sat and gorged themselves on a load of the sweet fruit.

John and Santiago kept walking the trail as Joad and Alf the Sacred Burro feasted on the fruit of the palms. Far off of the trail they saw small huts with sod roofs grouped together. But the inhabitants of the small villages either did not see the men passing or intentionally avoided them. Dirt-rat colonies no longer proliferated at the edges of the red brick road. New animals, stripe-dogs and beggar-monkeys, sat placidly off of the road, their eyes following John and looking as if they were judging him as he passed. Giant fluff-hens scampered across El Camino de la Muerte and pecked at the ground. The green and red birds with their oversized, pointy beaks, settled in open nests and did not flee from the men.

And Santiago screamed, "Yahhhhhhhhhhhhh!" He darted from the path and charged a fluff-hen's nest, waving his arms and flapping his tongue, leaping spastically, as if possessed by idiot demons. The fowl fluffed to twice its size and charged Santiago, pecking and clawing at him, trying to keep him from her nest. Feathers and curses and blood flew from a raging dust cloud as Santiago clutched at the bristled bird. The razor-talons of the fluff-hen sliced through the air and found the skin easy to gash. Santiago's hands found a firm grip on her neck and squeezed until the fluff-hen's claws ceased trying to rip his flesh. And the bird grew limp in his hands. Santiago tossed the fluffed up ball of feathers to the side and looked down at the oozing gashes on his arms and abdomen. He drew his fingers across a flow of his blood and then brought the stained fingers to his cheeks, painting red swipes, like war paint, across his face.

"What the hell was that about?" called John from the road. "Was that really necessary?"

Hands on knees and drawing in deep breaths, Santiago laughed his manic laugh. "I thought she'd skedaddle and leave her eggs for us for dinner. Didn't think she'd want to feel the sting of the scorpion or the bite of the wolf. I didn't know those things would put up a fight. Can you dig it?"

Joad and Alf the Sacred Burro, done with their date feast, appeared at John's side. "Those are fluff-hens," said Joad in his low-key, muffled tone. "They will fight to the death to keep predators away from their eggs. Mostly they are left alone because of their ferocity. But their eggs are nice. I like their eggs."

Three green eggs, speckled with red dots, sat motherless in their nest. Santiago plucked the large eggs from the nest and carried them to the road. "Dinner," he said to his friends, placing the eggs in Alf the Sacred Burro's saddlebags.

Sitting on the other side of the road, a stink-pig watched on with interest. Neither John nor Joad nor Santiago noticed the tusked boar with the coarse, bristling Mohawk stripe of hair running the length of his spine. But the boar noticed them. From a distance he followed the men as they walked on down the road. The stink-pig did not set foot on the red brick road, nor did he want to. But as he dogged John, other stink-pigs joined in – boars, sows, gilts, shoats and piglets – and trailed the group of men. Still, John, Joad, and Santiago failed to notice the sounder of stink-pigs following down wind from them. The number of the beasts gave the group a collective bravery and the stink-pigs approached closer, their grunts finally attracting the attention of the men.

When the swine sensed that the men were not interested in them, they approached the humans and walked ahead of, alongside, and behind them, just off of the red brick road. In the midst of the stink-pigs, their presence was undeniable. The animals fumed with a rancid, musky mixture of piss, ammonia, and sulfur. Despite their fearsome appearance – the muscular upper bodies, stubble-covered lips sneering over dagger-like tusks, the always-bristling strip of hair down their backs – the stink-pigs made no aggressive behaviors toward the men. Instead, the hogs moved along at the same rate as John, their long, tufted tails flicking in the same manner as a happy dog's.

"Do you think we need to worry about these pigs?" said John to both Joad and Santiago.

"I think we need to huff and puff and blow their house in," said Santiago. "We need to nibble the meat off their big bones. We need to dine on green eggs and swine." He gazed at a large stink-boar as if he had not eaten in twenty days and twenty nights. The boar edged to the outside of the drove of stink-pigs, putting other potential victims between himself and Santiago.

"I think there is not so much difference between these stink-pigs and us," said Joad. "There is no difference between a pig and a man. They are both intelligent living beings. We are following the path. The stink-pigs follow the path. For us to make a distinction between ourselves and those pigs is merely a human conception for our own advantage."

Santiago twisted his face through the range of expressions and ended up with an arched unibrow and an incredulous smirk. "Now who you jiving with that cosmic debris? You saying we ain't no better than those stinking beasts? You saying we ain't in danger of the pigs? You saying we shouldn't eat them? You saying you don't like stink-pig ribs?"

"No," said Joad, flashing a smile like a mouth full of river stones. "I like ribs. Ribs are good."

"Then what are you saying?" asked John. "Because I'm not so sure I get it either."

"I'm not really saying anything," said Joad. "Just talking to hear myself, I guess. Sometimes the rumble of my voice calms my head. Do I think that we are in danger from these animals? No. Alf doesn't seem spooked by them. And look, they wag their tails like they're happy. I sense no danger."

"Well, they reek like festering meat shits," griped Santiago. "We need to ditch them or get upwind of their stank." He ran toward the side of the road, waving his arms, jumping from foot to foot and howling like a coyote. But the stink-pigs paid him no mind. They neither shrank from his madness nor returned the strange display of aggression. They merely moved along with the flow of the path, keeping in stride with John.

"Can't we do anything to scare these things off?" asked Santiago, recognizing the futility of his tactic. He looked to John. "Can't you bring down fire and thunder to scatter them to the corners of this land?"

"I don't think I can," said John. "It doesn't really work like that."

"Well, how does it work, brother?" said Santiago. "Because this stench is getting the best of me and I don't think I can endure it much longer."

And it was true. The stink-pig fumes burned the men's eyes, raped their noses, and scorched their throats. A hot, itchy burn dragged itself across their skin. No matter whether they tried to cover their faces or fan the fumes away, the stink-pig atmosphere assaulted them.

"I don't know how it works. I only know when it will and won't work," said John. "And, I just know that there isn't anything I can do to get rid of them. For some reason, it seems like they should be here."

"I think I know what to do," said Joad. He stepped to the side of the road and knelt down. The soft whistle from his lips beckoned a young stink-bitch to his outstretched hand. The pig approached without hesitation and took a ripe date out of his palm. "Hey there, girl," Joad said, patting at the stink-pig, ruffling the strip of coarse hair on its head. Alf the Sacred Burro stepped several feet back and dropped a pile of donkey mud to try to cover the stink-pig stench.

The stink-bitch looked into the eyes of the stooping giant. Its sneering lips turned to a sweet smile and its thin tail wagged enthusiastically from side to side. The stink-bitch rested back on her haunches and let Joad scratch between her ears. Soft grunts of pleasure escaped the pig's snout in response to Joad's gentle touch. His other enormous hand reached out and scratched the stink-pig behind the ear. And the pig looked into his eyes and realized only too late that Joad was not in love with her. And Joad locked his massive hands around the pig's neck, cutting off the flow of blood and oxygen to her brain. She managed a sharp squeal before losing consciousness, alerting the rest of the stink-pigs to the peril of coming too close to the men. And the sounder of swine backed away, their wary eyes locked on the giant.

And Joad felt remorse. He did not want to hurt the stink-pig. He lifted the pig and estimated its weight at somewhere around three talents. He noted that the stink-bitch was clearly an adult and probably a recent mother judging by her swollen nipples. But he knew it was the only way to scare the other stinking pigs far enough away that their stench would not sicken the men. It would have been a shame to pass up perfectly good pork, so Joad hefted the weighty stink-pig, wrapped it around his neck and over his shoulders, and carried it to a kapok tree beside the road.

With the sun fading out for the day, Joad hung the stink-pig by its back feet from the kapok tree. He tied her front legs together to prevent her from struggling. The pig swayed in the breeze and Joad whispered to it, "I'm sorry I have to do this to you, pig. But it is necessary. And I won't let you go to waste."

The sounder of stink-pigs all watched from a distance. Snorts and squeals traveled on the wind and stung Joad with their accusations. The cries of some of the stink-piglets sounded disturbingly like the weeping of freshly orphaned children.

Joad circled his victim, justifying his actions to the stink-pig. Meanwhile, Santiago jumped around just outside of Joad's reach and chanted, "Kill the pig. Cut her throat. Kill the pig. Bash her in." And he stuck his fists against his sides and flapped his arms like wings, prancing about with his legs bent and bowed, chanting all the while, "Kill the pig. Cut her throat. Kill the pig. Bash her in."

Joad shouted at Santiago, "Stop it. Show some respect for life and death. After all, we are not savages." And his arm shot out, the fleshy palm of his hand finding the side of Santiago's head, knocking the madman to the ground.

"Oh sure, get mad at me," spat Santiago, laughing his nervous titter. Ass on the ground and hands propped behind him, he laughed at the giant and said, "Yeah, I'm the problem. Like I'm doing something to hurt piggy. We mustn't let anything happen to piggy, must we? Look here, brother, I ain't the one that choked out that stink-bitch and set her to swinging in a tree. That was you. Now let's get her ready for dinner." And he started chanting and dancing, now out of Joad's long reach. "Kill the pig. Cut her throat. Spill her blood. Kill the pig. Cut her throat.

Spill her blood." But he stopped and backed quickly away as Joad moved toward him with surprising agility and speed. And though mad, Santiago knew well enough to stop and let Joad take care of the stink-pig in his own way.

John and Santiago sat on the road and watched Joad tend to the suspended stink-bitch. Santiago said, "That boy ain't right. Look at 'im, babbling his gobblety glibbety gangly goop to that stink-bitch like she can understand him. Ahhhhh!" he shouted. "Go ahead and kill the pig. Cut her throat. Spill her blood." And he shut up just a quickly as Joad turned and stared him down.

Ignoring his audience of men and pigs, Joad sat on the ground, looking up, and spoke to the pig. He stood and circled her, patting her on the back and rubbing her head. With one hand locked onto the strip of hair running along the stink-pig's neck, Joad drew a dagger from a sheath that hung on his leather and bronze kilt. The knife slashed a clean part of the stink-bitch's throat skin. With a mere wee wiggle and one tiny squeeee, the stink-bitch gave up and spilled death onto the soil beneath the tree. Once drained of her blood, Joad commenced butchering the stink-pig.

And that night they did dine on green eggs and swine. A lone dire wolf howled a low, sad howl, as if mourning the loss of the stink-bitch. Though the meal was delicious, and though they enjoyed it greatly, John and Santiago said nothing as they ate. Joad's solemn demeanor demanded respect and the men gave Joad his due. When the fire died down to embers and the two moons rose in the sky, the men pissed a protective circle around their camp and lay themselves out on the ground. The wistful song of the dire wolf yowling at the two moons played like a lullaby that sang the men and Alf the Sacred Burro and the congregation of stink-pigs to sleep.

And as John and Joad and Santiago slept, Android Lovethorn's guards dragged a group of four sickly desert scurves before him on his throne. Ragged buckskin pants and shirts, bones that had broken and reset wrongly, greasy, torn heads of hair, crumbling teeth and festering sores. These were the physical attributes of the desert rats. Other than their copper complexions and crudely crafted clothing, the men bore little resemblance to Three Tooth. Where Three Tooth stood straight and strong, the men standing before Lovethorn hunched over before their captors and flinched at any sudden movements.

Lovethorn waved his guards out of the hall and said, "Leave now." He rose from his seat and descended the three steps that led to the platform on which his altar and throne of bones sat. The guards turned and quickly exited the cavernous room, slamming the doors behind them.

Paralyzed with fear, the trembling group of men cowered and covered their heads and faces as Lovethorn approached them. The frailest among the captives, One-Eye, lost consciousness and went limp at the approach of Lovethorn. Lovethorn bent and lifted the monocular man from the ground and carried him up the steps, gently laying him on the altar. Looking down on the scrawny little man, Lovethorn saw that the empty eye socket had been sewn shut long ago but the scars from the stitches were still red and raised. Lovethorn pushed on the empty socket and felt resistance from the skin, but nothing beneath it. The Man in Black smoothed One-Eye's oily hair back and petted the sickly man's head until he regained consciousness. One-Eye's one eye blinked frantically upon waking and seeing Lovethorn's grim countenance looming over him. "Jeepers creeper," said Lovethorn with a dry laugh, "where'd you get that peeper?" And, the frightening sight of Lovethorn, as seen by the one good eye, blacked out as Lovethorn unexpectedly jammed his thumb into the socket and plucked the eyeball from One-Eye's head.

With just a slushy pop, the eye vacated the socket and left in its place the burn of raw nerves. One-Eye screamed unintelligibly and once again lost consciousness from shock. Lovethorn said, "and thine right eye has offended me, thus I plucked it out and cast it from ye." And he threw the smashed orb to the floor in front of the other captives, but they continued to cower and kept their eyes to the floor for fear of being the next to draw Lovethorn's damning attention.

The blackness of the freshly exposed socket called to Lovethorn. He lifted One-Eye from the altar and bent over his face, kissing the open eyehole. Moist sucking sounds filled the air. Lovethorn's dry lips smacked at the edges of the eye socket and his tongue flicked at the fresh wound, lapping up the blood until the flow slowed and stopped.

One-Eye's blood still flowed through his veins. And his mouth struggled to drag air into his lungs. But he did not see and he did not feel. He did not think. His heart was black, and his lips were cold. Lovethorn's demons infected One-Eye's being and corroded his already weakened spirit. And the forces that pumped the scurve's blood and drew air into his lungs were malevolent and rotten. One-Eye's skin and bones remained but his essence trickled into Lovethorn's mouth and almost completely expired with the exhalation of his tormentor's stale breath. The scrawny scurve dissipated, leaving almost nothing but a glove of flesh to hold the stinking rotten sampling of Android Lovethorn's sickness.

"Take your friend from here," Lovethorn said to the other scurves. "Take him along El Camino de la Muerte. Take him as far away as you can manage, but stay on the road." And he dropped One-Eye to the ground and turned to walk back up the steps to his throne.

One-Eye's friends did not move to help him. They did not look up at Android Lovethorn. They waited, sitting still, eyes downcast, afraid to do anything.

"Do it now," boomed Lovethorn, his voice a hollow, ricocheting echo in the large room. He stood from his throne and advanced on the men, who wilted at the hostility of his approach. "Do it now and you will live. Wait any longer and I will strike you down and grind you to dust. I will wipe your names from the annals of this land now. And those who knew you will not remember your names and faces. All that you will know is the eternal sting of my wrath, and unbearable pain. So take your friend and be gone from my sight. Be gone and be fast about it."

Lovethorn turned and stomped out of the room. The sound of his voice, shouting at guards just outside, prompted the men to action. And they grabbed One-Eye and dragged him out of the room, out of the fort, and onto El Camino de la Muerte.

And a fluff-cock crowed thrice before John awoke that morn-ing. The stink-pig pork from the night prior churned in John's gut and fought hard to resist digestion, provoking painful cramps and rank gas. Meat farts, burps stinking of undigested pork, and the stench of the slaughtered stink-pig hung heavily in the air about the camp. Joad stirred in response to the roost-er's raspy cock-a-doodle-doo, and, still asleep, rolled onto his stomach. His giant ass arched high in the air and released a mephitic blast that that shamed the stink-pigs' stench into submission. The rumble startled a group of turkey buzzards that had descended in the early morning and torn apart the remains of the slaughtered stink-pig. And Joad's noises set the buzzards off into a drunken flight pattern above the camp. When it became clear that the men were no danger to them, the vultures again descended and finished their breakfast of putrid stink-pig carcass.

Santiago sat up and rubbed at his bloated gut, admiring the taut belly filled with an abundance of gas. Bile bubbled halfway up his throat, trying to escape on the wave of a rotten burp. "I should'a known better than to dine on that cloven hoofed swine," he said to himself. Palms pressed to the sides of his head to calm the throbbing, Santiago rocked gently back and forth and moaned, "Awwww, damn. Should'a known better."

Like an angel of mercy, Alf the Sacred Burro appeared at Santiago's side. Alf's body convulsed rhythmically and the thud of his throat opening and closing announced the imminent birth of a bezoar. And the burro coughed and heaved until he laid a fist-sized, hairy, donkey-nugget at Santiago's feet.

"Thank you, you stinking donkey," said Santiago as he grabbed his pipe and stuffed the bezoar in the bowl. He looked up at the ragged old beast, and the sun positioned itself perfectly behind Alf's head so as to make it appear that the sacred burro had a fiery red halo glowing around the edge of his head. Alf whinnied and held his head still while Santiago scratched his chin.

The stink-pig meat sat, rotten and festering, like a load of hot sand in John's stomach. He plopped down on the ground beside Alf the Sacred Burro and scratched at the donkey's head. Santiago passed the bezoar pipe to John without saying anything. And they sat silently, scritching Alf and passing the bezoar until the healing donkey-ball soothed their stomachs and calmed their throbbing heads.

And though they felt better from the bezoar, neither John nor Santiago ate any breakfast that morning. Joad, though, woke up with a great hunger. He stood, stretched his arms wide, arched his back, and blurted out another bum-rumble that once again set the turkey vultures to flight. While it was clear to John and Joad that the stink-pig meat had also turned on Joad, Joad did not realize it. He sat by the embers of their fire from the night before and gnawed on the charred remains of a rack of stink-pig ribs. John and Santiago looked on in disbelief as Joad polished off the remainder of the ribs.

"What?" asked Joad. "I'm hungry. And ribs are good. I like ribs."

And then they set out and walked on down the road, John,

Joad, Santiago, and Alf the Sacred Burro. Walking helped them to shake off the last vestiges of stink-pig sickness, all except for Joad's curdled meat farts. But Joad walked behind and downwind from John and Santiago and exhausted his foulness into his past and toward the sounder of stink-pigs. And the swine squealed and oinked and walked along the sides of El Camino de la Muerte, keeping a safe distance from the men. The stink-pigs always seemed on the edge of fleeing, especially if Joad slowed his walk and turned to look at them. But the pigs were no longer in danger of becoming dinner. Their fallen family member sat like shame in the men's bellies and made it so that stink-pig was the last thing they wanted to eat. Gradually, the stink-pigs sensed that they were safe, and they followed closer, but still out of reach of the giant. Not out of fear, but out of a recognized pecking order, the pigs waddled along at the back, and as a part of, the caravan.

With each step the men took, the mountains in the distance seemed closer. The hazy skies diffused the sunlight and cast a red glow over the land. The cold air blew down at them, carrying with it the smell smoke and decay. Beneath a grand trufulla tree, along the side of El Camino de la Muerte, John saw movement. A small group of men lounged under the tree and did not rise at the approach of John and his entourage.

As they neared the strangers on the side of the road, John saw that it was a group of sickly desert scurves. He stepped toward the men with a determined stride. But Joad stepped in front of him and blocked his path. Joad said, "Let me approach them. I will find out what they are doing and what their intentions are."

John said, "Look at them. They are frail and sick. They are small and we are large. They are ill and we are healthy. What do we have to fear from those little men?"

"There are no small enemies," said Joad. "Something's wrong. Those are desert scurves but this is not the desert. They do not belong here. Something's wrong." He looked down at John but neither the sincerity of Joad's glare nor the imposition of his size deterred John. And Joad knew that he could not take control of the situation if John did not agree. So he stepped aside and let John take the lead.

And when they approached, they saw the Indians scattered on the side of the late-morning's highway. Three of the scurves lay dead and bleeding. Their ghosts swam off on the chill breeze that blew along the path. One scurve writhed on the ground, holding his hands over his eyes and kicking his feet in the air. He screamed over and over in a language that John did not understand: "Deah ym fo tuo teg. Deah ym fo tuo teg."

"He's rotten with demons," said Santiago, squatting in front of the man and sniffing at the air like a dog catching a scent. "He doesn't even know we're here, dig?"

John looked down on the scene and saw that the dead scurves had been attacked and hacked at. And there was blood on the ground from the dead desert scurves. Blood on the street in the land with no name. Bloody red sun beating down on the death scene.

Santiago walked around the scurves, surveying the situation. And he bent down and grasped the head of one of the corpses, looking into the dead eyes, Santiago said "Injun, Injun. What did you die for?"

But the scurve said nothing at all to Santiago's inquiry. The dead eyes, they saw nothing. The dead ears did not hear the question. The dead mouth, it spoke not. The only sound coming from the group of scurves was the buzz of the munkle flies and the ranting of the man with his hands held tightly to his eyes. And he covered his eyes because his sight had been ripped from him. John knelt in front of the scurve whose name – One-Eye – no longer suited him.

"Do not touch him," warned Joad, but he made no move to stop John. "There is something wrong here. He may be small and sick, but there is something wrong with this whole situation. I smell a trap."

Before Joad could say any more, John laid his hands on One-Eye and received a jolt that momentarily stopped his heart. One-Eye's body jumped and his mouth screamed in the foreign tongue, "Deah ym fo tuo teg. Deah ym fo tuo teg." But John held tight to the emaciated scurve's head and drew the sickness from the little man. John realized that Santiago was right, that the man was rotten with demons. And Joad was right, too – it was a trap. John could not have removed his hands from One-Eye even if he wanted to. He kept his hands on the scurve and consumed his sickness. But it was unlike the illness John had taken on before when he laid hands on the sick. This did not give him energy or power. It felt like he was sucking up rot, like something foul had been festering deep in the scurve. And when it was only too late, John realized that the man was rotten with demons and that he had removed the demons from the scurve and taken them on himself. His hands locked onto One-Eye's head and the spirits flowed like the rapids of a river from One-Eye and into John.

When it was all done, both men fell to the ground, unconscious. John's body trembled, it rolled and it tumbled. He did not speak. His eyes squeezed shut. His lips tucked in and his teeth chewed at them. Shivers overwhelmed his body, and heat poured off of him like the steam from Aguacaliente.

Then John and One-Eye splayed out on the ground beneath the truffula tree and, but for the occasional tic, appeared as if they were no more living than the three dead scurves. Out of nowhere, John randomly smacked at his head and chewed at his own tongue. And One-Eye's strange words now flowed from John's mouth: "Deah ym fo tuo teg. Deah ym fo tuo teg." One-Eye, he now said nothing, but still drew in shallow breaths, the slight rise and fall of his chest giving the only indication of the spark of life.

Munkle flies laid their eggs in the eyes and noses of the dead scurves. And the size of their swarm grew at the same rate as the stench of the corpses. Joad lifted the lifeless bodies and hauled them far downwind from the camp, where the smell blew away from them and the flies would bother them no more. The pile of dead scurves drew not only the attention of munkle flies, but also turkey buzzards and stink-pigs. The creatures growled and shrieked and spat and tore at each other in claims of ownership of the dead meat. And the carrion feast ensued, the beasts and birds quickly undressing the desert scurves down to the bones.

While Joad cleared the area under the fluffy truffula tree, Santiago and Alf the Sacred Burro sat vigil over John's twitching body. Alf coughed up bezoars and Santiago placed the healing vomit balls in John's shaking hands. When John's arms flailed, Santiago sat on his chest and pinned the arms to the ground. When John's teeth ground at his lips and tongue, Santiago stuck a truffula branch in his mouth to keep him from chewing anything off.

For the next three days and nights, John suffered the demons under the truffula tree. He shook and sweated and cried out at nothing. His arms flailed and his legs kicked out at the air. Wild bloodshot eyes bugged out and stared a fearful stare at nothing. Santiago stayed on the ground by his side, sleeping during John's calm periods and pinning him to the ground when he cried out and thrashed about. And when the demon seizures stopped, Santiago dribbled water into John's mouth and wiped the sweat from his brow.

While Santiago tended to his friend, Joad brought water from the river that paralleled the red brick road. Joad retrieved fluff-hen eggs and figs and bloodfruits, but Santiago refused the food, only taking water after giving it to John. And John, twisted and deranged by Lovethorn's demons, accepted no sustenance other than the water. Joad tended the camp and pissed a protective circle around them each night. He kept watch, always alert and never sleeping, ready to dispatch Android Lovethorn's men or lunkheads should they attack.

And the stink-pigs gathered and stood in a circle around the trufulla tree. More and more pigs arrived and joined in the vigil, scratching their feet and snouts at the ground, squealing and stinking up the air. By the third night of John's ordeal, nearly a thousand stink-pigs amassed around the site of his possession.

The pigs did not move from the site and they neither ate nor slept. The rank stink of their feces and urine polluted the air and sickened Santiago and Joad, but the men did not move from the site and they failed at their attempts to chase the stink-pigs off. Joad reluctantly snapped a stink-bitch's neck to scare the pigs off, but they did not shy away this time. Instead, the remaining pigs merely made a small clearing around the dead pig, marking the spot of Joad's offense against them.

On the third night under the trufulla tree, John's heart beat an off-tempo rhythm and his breathing slowed. One-Eye lay on the ground beside John, marinating in his own piss and shit, his breath, too, growing shallower. And John screamed at the sky: "Deah ym fo tuo teg. Deah ym fo tuo teg." He inhaled one last time and then deflated with a soft hiss.

And while Joad and Alf the Sacred Burro retrieved more water from the river, Santiago slapped at John's face and chest, trying to make him wake up. He stood and kicked at John's legs and arms. "You sad, sorry ass, piece of donkey shit," he screamed, accentuating his words with light kicks to John's defenseless body. "Suck some air into your talk-hole. Get up and get moving again, brother." But the random onslaught of kicks did nothing to revive John. And Santiago, thinking his friend dead, fell to the ground and beat at it with his hands and cried a great sobbing boo-hoo of a wail.

The river of fire above roiled and tossed off a fury of flames. And from above, a ball of fire hurtled downward and crashed at the foot of the trufulla tree. The explosion temporarily scattered the gathering of stink-pigs and slammed Santiago to the ground, knocking him unconscious. Stepping from the fire,

John's flaming doppelganger strode toward him and bent down at his head. Fire-John knelt and straddled John's chest. Bending down with his face inches from John's, Fire-John whispered, "*Exorcizo te, omnis spiritus immunde.*" He spat fire on his flaming hands and clapped them to John's face, touching John's ears and ramming his fiery thumbs into his nostrils. John seized, his back arched, and he tried to buck his doppelganger off. But Fire-John rode out the effort and stayed on John's chest. He bent again, his thumbs still jammed in the nostrils, his hands still touching the ears, and whispered into John's ear, "*Ephpheta, quod est, Adaperire.*" And John's eyes flew open. They burned with madness. Fire-John continued, "*In odorem suavitatis. Tu autem effugare, diabole.*"

John's body bucked like a brainsick bull and unsuccessfully tried to throw Fire-John aside. Fire-John gripped at the thick beard on John's face and once again rode out the seizures and spasms. John spit and bit and fought and fit, but Fire-John held on. And he leaned in again and whispered in John's ear, "*Exorcizo te, omnis spiritus immunde.*" And John screeched a two-tone discordant creach that made the surrounding stink-pigs panic. And the pigs crashed into and trampled each other. This time when John's body flailed and lurched, Fire-John did more than ride out the spasms. Fire-John balled up his flaming fists and slammed them against the sides of John's head. He beat the fists on John's chest and neck and face and chanted, "*Exorcizo te, omnis spiritus immunde.*"

And at that place on the ground, under the fluffy trufulla tree, the flaming being on top of John exploded in a white-hot burst. And fire and smoke and screaming demons poured from every hole in John's struggling, shaking body. The unclean spirits tore at John as they exited him and left bloody streams flowing from every orifice. In their haste to find hosts, those demons (those sick and broken bits of Lovethorn's essence) dove into all other living beings surrounding John. They penetrated and possessed Santiago, and his body leapt from the ground and danced a herky-jerky jig like a marionette under the control of a mid-fit epileptic. And the spirits, they possessed each and every one of the stink-pigs that milled about around the trufulla tree.

And outside the circle of demon-infested pigs, Joad and Alf returned with water. They stood, shocked and confused as the entire stink-pig gathering ran around and past them, like a wild river flowing around a solid rock. And the pigs tore at each other as they ran, some gashing at others with great bloody tusks. And in the maddened torrent, Santiago's possessed body ran past Joad and Alf the Sacred Burro. Santiago screeched the same words as John, "Deah ym fo tuo teg. Deah ym fo tuo teg," and tore thick clumps of hair from his head and face as he ran stumbling along with the stink-pigs.

The entire community of demon-infested swine ran away from El Camino de la Muerte and down a steep embankment, crashing and splashing into the river. Santiago ran with them and collapsed, facedown, into the river. His face remained in the water and his body struggled and thrashed. And then he calmed and gave up the ghost. The bedeviled pigs swam no better than Santiago. They tumbled down the embankment and into the river, kicked about, and drew water into their lungs until they were no more. The current of the river carried the stink-pigs away. And just before Santiago's limp body caught the strong current, Joad rushed into the water and tossed dead and dying stink-pigs out of his way. He fished Santiago from the water and carried him back to the trufulla tree. He lay the madman's corpse on the ground beside John and One-Eye.

Still unconscious, but no longer bewitched, John remained on the ground. The trauma floored him. He lay exhausted from the ordeal and did not regain consciousness. One-Eye also rested easier but still looked little better than a lunkhead. Joad saw that all were safe and then he collapsed under the trufulla tree. The combination of a deep sadness and three days and nights of sleep deprivation won over and Joad leaned his back against the trufulla tree. And though he only intended to rest his teary eyes momentarily, sleep crept up on him and temporarily rescued him from his grief.

By the time Joad awoke, John had already risen and dragged Santiago's body off to the side of the red brick road. All alone on the side of the road, John dug a shallow grave and piled rocks on top of the corpse until Santiago's final resting place was covered with a waist-high mound of small boulders and stones. John piled the rocks until he could find no more of them. He said, "This will save you from the buzzards, my friend, and leave you to become one with the land." And that pile of rocks remains there to this day.

The heavy hand of Joad fell on John's shoulder. He moved beside John at the grave and got down on his knees out of respect for Santiago. His head now at John's level, Joad said in his deep rumble, "His return to the soil is peaceful. It is the flow of nature, an eternal decay and renewal. Accepting this brings enlightenment. Ignoring this brings misery."

John said nothing. He stayed and knelt at the pile of stones with a bowed head. Alf the Sacred Burro approached, sat on his haunches, and heaved up a large bezoar at the head of the grave. Tears stained a streak on each side of his ratty donkey snout. And he brayed a sound of pure misery at the sky.

"Do not let it bring you down," said Joad to John and Alf the Sacred Burro. "Since life and death are each other's companions, why worry about them? All beings are one. He is not gone. He is in the rain and the dirt and the dire wolf that howls at night. He is in the fluff-cock that crows in the morning. He swims in the flow of the river of clouds and walks the path with us."

"Yes," agreed John. "He is one with us and one with all. I don't grieve his loss because he is not lost. He is here," he patted his chest. "And here," he pointed to his forehead. "And here," he grabbed at his crotch. "He is not lost to me because he is me. He is in me."

Alf the Sacred Burro brayed in agreement and coughed up another fuzzy donkey-ball. They all hung their heads in a moment of silence.

And while they marked the passing of Santiago, One-Eye awoke from his catatonic state and ran an all-out wild sprint, fleeing in blind fear from the trufulla tree. And he ran for miles in a straight line, miraculously not bumping into anything, until being intercepted by another desert scurve. One-Eye tried to keep running, but Three Tooth held tight onto the back of his buckskin jacket. The sight of the sickly scurve with one sewn-up eye and one empty socket drew a heavy tear from Three Tooth's weepy eye. So Three Tooth invited the wreck of a man into his misfit tribe and One-Eye gladly accepted.

When John and Joad and Alf the Sacred Burro turned away from Santiago's grave, they saw that One-Eye had left them. John scanned the land on both sides of the red brick road and did not see One-Eye anywhere. He said, "I hope that he's alright. He has left the path and we can't go searching for him."

Joad said, "Every man has his own path that he must follow. It is not up to us to make that decision for him. The best we can do is hope that his path takes him to his destination."

Alf blew a rancid donkey burp in agreement. And they decided it was time to move on. So they set their feet to a steady rhythm and walked the red brick road as it wound its way to the distant mountains. They allowed the flow of the path to wash them along. Alf stuck close to John's side and Joad walked behind them, scanning the land for Lovethorn's men and other perils. They did not talk because they didn't feel like it. Mostly John either thought of Santiago or just shut his brain down and let his legs carry him forth. And though he missed Santiago, John did not feel a void where his friend should be. Instead, he felt that Santiago was with him. He felt an urge to eat and to fight and to fuck and he knew that that was a part of Santiago that he took on himself. The urges were something that he accepted and welcomed like an old friend.

And they walked for days, not encountering people or peril or problems. The sun warmed them and the cool water from the river refreshed them. Their supplies did not dwindle and their sleep did not suffer. As the flow of the path pushed them along, the snow-capped mountains seemed to creep their way.

"La Montaña Sagrada," said Joad, sweeping his thick hand before him. "That is the name of the mountain directly before us. It is part of the LaSals range. It is beautiful, isn't it?"

"It is," said John. He looked to the sky and saw that the river of clouds crashed into the side of the mountain and broke up into a spray of disorganized fog that rose and swirled in a giant vortex just above the snowy peak. "And I'm guessing that is where I'm supposed to end up."

"It would seem that you are right," said Joad. "It appears that is where your path leads."

And they continued walking. La Montaña Sagrada loomed over them as they neared. As the red brick road sloped upward and the ascent became steeper, the land grew greener and fuller. Along the side of El Camino de la Muerte, enormous red poppies with plump black stigmas at the centers bloomed on woody stalks, their blossoms growing as large as John's head. Among the poppies thrived other flowers of red and white and black. As they neared the base of La Montaña Sagrada, the poppies grew fuller and crowded out the other flowers. And the crimson carpet of flowers grew so thick that it completely covered the ground on both sides of the path. The sweet fragrance of the poppies filled the air and lightened the men's steps. And as they pushed on, the meadow of red flowers crept over the path, obscuring the red bricks and slowing the men. John and Joad swept their feet across the ground, uprooting flowers to make sure they were still on the red brick road.

And then Alf the Sacred Burro stopped. He sniffed at an enormous poppy blossom and shivered with delight. He brayed a happy donkey sound that caught both John and Joad's attention. And they turned to see Alf chewing a mouthful of red, velvety petals. In front of Alf stood a headless poppy stalk – the victim of his hunger. They watched as Alf chomped down on another blossom and swallowed all of it, except for the scraps the fell from the sides of his mouth.

"He really does like those flowers, doesn't he?" said John.

"He does," said Joad. "Perhaps the donkey is onto something." Joad tore the bloom from a poppy and sniffed at it. His eyes glazed over and he pushed out a satisfied, low rumble of a grunt. He nibbled at the petals. The sweet and silky flavor of the flower filled his mouth and fed a hunger he did not even realize had existed.

John saw the delight that the flowers brought to both Joad and Alf the Sacred Burro. And a flood of childlike sayings flashed through his head. "Monkey see, monkey do," said John, pulling a poppy bloom from its stem. He plucked off the top of the flower and laughed, saying, "Momma had a baby and its head popped off." He crammed the poppy into his maw, and the taste of the flower was delicious and satisfying beyond all that he expected.

And a gluttonous frenzy of a poppy feast ensued. A cacoethes for the petals possessed them. Leaves and stalks and the occasional non-poppy flowers flew about in the air as they tore at the blossoms and crammed them in their mouths. And before they realized it, their stomachs were bloated and taut. The red from the petals stained their lips and faces, making John and Joad look as if they had baked in the sun too long. And the rouge from the flowers reddened Alf's full donkey lips. John and Joad laughed loudly and too much at the foggy vision of the jackass with the sensuous lips. Sensing that he was becoming a spectacle, Alf lay himself on the poppy-covered red brick road and closed his eyes.

"I think the donkey has the right idea," said Joad, plopping down to a sitting position on the road. "I am suddenly exhausted." Before he could say more, the giant's body slumped and he thumped over on his side, fast asleep and beyond reach.

John laughed a thick, drunken laugh at Joad and Alf. "What has become of you fellows?" he said. And he sat on the red brick road in front of his friends and laughed that they should be so tired. John held the stalk of a flower before him and gazed into its round, black center. And the flower's center looked like a dead, blank eye staring at him. He bit at the flower petals and ruminated on them like a cow chewing its cud. Without realizing what had happened, John's muscles turned to jelly and he found himself with one cheek pressed to El Camino de la Muerte. Alf's tired old face confronted John. The donkey's lips, covered with dirt and bits of chewed flowers, funneled off stinking donkey drool from his rotten old mouth. One glazed eye remained open and Alf breathed heavily. All muscle-control left John and he lay on his side, staring into the donkey's blank eye and allowing himself to drift off. And the plump black button at the center of John's poppy blinked at him just before he slept.

Android Lovethorn's eyelids blinked over his dead black pupils. From his tower he looked down to the valley at the red swath of the poppy field. And though he was too far above to see it, he knew that John had fallen under the spell of the poppies. He knew that John would sleep long and deep and that when he awoke, he would be driven to eat more of the sleep-inducing flowers. And the cycle would continue and keep John close below in the valley, unconscious and harmless, where Lovethorn could draw on John's power. Despite his attempts to keep John far away, Lovethorn now found that he liked having such power over him. He could feel the energy buzzing up from the valley, tickling at his feet and coursing all up through his body. And he laughed and stared down at the poppy field for hours before turning away. Once satisfied that John was locked in sleep down below, Lovethorn threw a handful of blood red poppy petals into the wind, and they blew down the mountain toward John and Joad and Alf the Sacred Burro.

And it was all a blur. John slept and he dreamed and he awoke. The hunger and the crushing headache gripped him with each waking and he crammed the flowers into his mouth to stop the pain. Joad and Alf the Sacred Burro did the same. With faces full of poppies, and blurried vision, they stood and stumbled and dropped again to the ground like dopey baby birds failing miserably at flight. And each time they nodded, the vines grew all around them and the flowers flourished, completely obscuring the red brick road. They lay that way for twenty days and nights. As they lay comatose, the vines crawled around their arms and legs and bound them to the road to the extent that they no longer rose when they awoke. The vines did not allow it. They only allowed John and Joad and Alf the Sacred Burro to raise their heads and feed on sweet, full flowers. Above El Camino de la Muerte, the trail of clouds stalled during the day and the river of fire refused to move at night.

On the twentieth night of the stupor, John dreamt of Android Lovethorn. In his dream, John was chained to a post on the red brick road. And on the cross-bar of the post, coarse ropes bound his wrists so that he could only move at the expense of his own pain. His tongue was thick and his head heavy. He thought to himself that nothing seemed to change and the bad times all stayed the same. Android Lovethorn – dressed in his priestly collar and black leather pants, his eyes hidden behind the mirrored sunglasses – walked in circles around the post and laughed at John. Lovethorn ripped a poppy from the ground and with great violence crammed the flower into John's mouth, bloodying his lips and loosening teeth. John's numb tongue refused to cry out in rebellion and the sweet petals in his mouth blocked any protest. He chewed at the petals and swallowed the black juice that the flowers produced. And Lovethorn pulled off the sunglasses and revealed the rotting sockets where his eyes should have been. John's revulsion at the sight humored Lovethorn. He put the glasses back on and puked out a sick laugh.

"What do you want from me?" asked John, red petals fluttering from his lips on a wave of sour breath. "Why do you torment me?"

"I have not even begun to torment you," said Lovethorn. "But I will. And I will thrive and drool on. I have cut off the toes and thumbs of kings and had them grovel under my table for scraps, and I shall do the same to you."

Lovethorn approached with a dagger and slashed a slit in John's favorite wrist. John cringed and closed his eyes against the pain. Lovethorn held a crystal goblet beneath the cut to catch the flow of blood. And when John opened his eyes again, he found himself still bound to the post, but now the ornate walls of a dimly lit cathedral surrounded him. Gargoyles, not unlike the jizz-critters in appearance, twisted their mouths up in snarls on the walls.

And at his pulpit, Lovethorn cried, "Most precious blood." He held the goblet high above himself and tilted his head upward at the ceiling. Behind him, a choir of castrati sang in eerily high-pitched voices that were more appropriate to young boys. Their voices climbed the scale, rose in volume, and wavered on an unnaturally high note. Lovethorn swooned and sang over and over to the cup he held high, crooning, "*In saec-*

ula saeculorum, in saecula saeculorum, in saecula saeculorum..."

The congregation before Lovethorn cringed and cried and chanted along with their leader, "*In saecula saeculorum, in saecula saeculorum, in saecula saeculorum.*" They shook their balled-up fists at the roof and averted their eyes when Lovethorn looked out into the crowd.

The Man in Black stomped about before his followers and kicked at the post that held John. And the post groaned and canted toward the floor of the sanctuary. But the cross remained embedded in the floor and did not completely tip. Greasy black hair tumbled over Android Lovethorn's forehead and clung to his mirrored sunglasses. He flipped his hair back and ripped the shades from his face, revealing the gaping sockets that glared out at the congregation. He smiled at the congregation, and the black rot festering at his gum line stood in stark contrast to the blindingly white teeth. And though he had not so much as a limp, Lovethorn grabbed an ornately carved cane and used it to help him pace before his followers. The tip of the cane tapped out sharp clacks on the wood floor.

"You," boomed Lovethorn, and he pointed the cane at a man in the front row of the nave. "Come forward and taste the blood most precious."

And the gaunt man struggled to push himself up from the pew. He shook from hunger and fear and exhaustion. When he reached his position in front of Lovethorn on the stage, the man fell to his knees and averted his eyes to the ground. But Lovethorn did not offer the goblet to the sickly man. Instead he asked, "Who are you and why did I call you forward?"

The man said, "I am but a memory of the man on the post. I am a story in his head, a picture in his mind. I am nothing more than a wisp of smoke."

Lovethorn did not give the man a drink of John's blood. He asked the man no further questions. Instead, he lashed out with his cane, knocking it solidly into the side of the man's head. And Lovethorn said, "A whip for the horse. A bridle for the donkey. And a rod for the backs of fools." He struck out with the cane and thrashed the man until he moved no more. Lovethorn panted and stood over the limp body, winding up to smack it again. As he brought the cane down one last time, the man disappeared in a puff of black smoke that fumed up into the Man in Black's face.

Lovethorn called more followers before him, one after the other, and beat them until they dissipated in whiffs of smoke. And each time, he breathed in the smoke and exhaled with a look of ecstasy. In between each thrashing, he sipped John's blood from the goblet and muttered to himself, "Blood most precious."

And John could do nothing to stop Lovethorn. Even if he could escape his bindings, John felt his strength waning with each thrashing Lovethorn dealt out to his congregation. With each time Lovethorn drank his blood, John found himself drifting closer to oblivion. He watched the Man in Black call one more of his congregants forward. The first lash of the cane knocked Lovethorn's victim to the ground. John watched, helpless, as the cane thwacked at the defenseless man. Android Lovethorn stopped beating the man and turned toward John with a look of surprise and anger on his face. At the same time, the rope around John's wrists loosened and he fell from the post, smacking his head on the floor. John's vision tunneled as Android Lovethorn ran toward him. But before the Man in Black reached John's place on the floor, Lovethorn dissipated in a puff of screaming smoke and left a black stain on the floor. The smudge on the floor filled John's view, and his vision contracted to a black pinpoint.

And John regained his vision. The red glare of the sun assaulted his eyes and blurred his vision. Many hands tore at the vines that covered him. The many hands freed John from the poppy tangle and helped him to sit up. And he blinked his vision back into clarity and saw that he was surrounded by many versions of himself. The men all sported the same beards and flowing hair. Their faces were identical to John's. He reached out and touched one's face and stared into the eyes and knew that he was looking at himself. And the other John stared back and smiled.

"I'm still dreaming," said John, his mind reeling from twenty days of ingesting the poppies. "I'm still stuck to the ground and I'm still dreaming. This is just another dream, but much nicer than the last."

Another John lookalike handed John a skin filled with cool water. The water soothed his scratchy throat and helped to bring more clarity to his poppy-addled brain. "Thank you dream-clone," said John. He struggled to stand and the other

Johns helped him to his feet. "Thank you all. Who are you and why are you here?" But the other Johns said nothing and only nodded at him.

And the red poppies flourished and filled the air with their sweet perfume. But, their spell, having been broken, no longer held sway over John. The scent was pleasant, but it no longer compelled John to eat the flowers. Instead, he only felt thirst. And he quenched the thirst with the entire contents of the water skin that was given to him.

The water washed away the haze in his head. As he looked around, John saw men tearing vines from Joad's and Alf the Sacred Burro's unconscious bodies on the ground. Closer inspection showed that the men clearing the vines were more of John's doppelgangers. Also helping Joad and Alf were carbon copies of Santiago and Joad. They helped Joad and Alf sit up and gave them full skins of cool water to drink. John watched in amazement as the men helped Joad shake off the ill effects of a poppy hangover. Alf sat up, lapped at the water spilling from a skin that a Santiago held for him, and choked on something stuck in his throat. He brayed and blew a spray of water from his lips, and puked up a bloody bezoar that looked more like an enormous, glistening ruby than a donkey vomit-ball.

John looked around and as far as he could see, there were clones of him, Joad and Santiago. And there were donkeys that looked like Alf the Sacred Burro. And the clones all milled about in the red pasture, trampling the flowers and nodding and smiling at each other, but saying nothing. And then from behind him, John heard it...

"Hallllooooooooo!" said the voice, starting low and climbing to a falsetto *ewwwwwww*. And then Two-Dogs-Fucking burst out in his overly joyous laughter, "Bwaaa-ha-ha-ha."

And the multitude of Johns and Joads and Santiagos finally made noise, mocking Two-Dogs-Fucking with their own attempt at his laugh. Throughout the valley, the sounds of "Bwaaa-ha-ha-ha" rang out. And the sound went into Alf the Sacred Burro's ear and pierced his brain like a spike. The donkey rose to his wobbly legs and brayed his loudest in protest. The Alf clones brayed in response. And the braying spurred the men to further mimic the ridiculous laughter.

Two-Dogs-Fucking laughed more, along with the crowd, and then smiled at John. And the teeth missing from his broken smile told a tale of serious injury. In addition to his mouth, Two-Dogs-Fucking sported a multitude of bodily injuries. Scabs covered his arms and legs and torso. Abrasions and contusions and lacerations throbbed and leaked and glared an angry red. Scratches streaked across his face and told of fingernails scraping away flesh and beard. Stretch marks radiated from his chapped lips. The ragged bath towel, cruddy with grime and blood and crust, barely clung and hung at his rotund waist, threatening to drop and reveal perhaps even more startling injuries.

Two-Dogs-Fucking held a poppy in his hand and nibbled at its petals.

"Don't eat those," John warned, trying to snatch the flower. "They will kill your mind. They will drain you of your will."

But Two-Dogs-Fucking dodged John's attempt to take the flower and bit off more petals. "Nonsense," said the Melungeon with the bloodshot eyes, smiling at John. "I have been eating these all morning and have never felt better. It is amazing the energy that I feel right now."

And then all around them, the clones of John and Joad and Santiago began dropping to the ground with flowers in their hands and petals falling from their lips. Donkeys fell over on their sides, thumping on the ground. And while the flowers had the opposite of the normal effect on Two-Dogs-Fucking, they managed to lure in the extra Johns, Joads, Santiagos, and Alfs, and knock them unconscious.

"See," said John, waving his hand at all of the unconscious men on the ground. "See what the flowers will do to you?"

"Funny," said Two-Dogs-Fucking. And he took another bite of petals from his poppy. "I'm not tired at all."

"Who are these men?" asked John. "Why do they look like me and Joad and Santiago? Where did all of the donkeys come from? What is going on here?"

"These are your sons," said Two-Dogs-Fucking. "These are the children you made with the blumpkins. Don't tell me that you didn't realize that you were reproducing?"

"Blumpkins," said John, shaking his head. "The blumpkins made these?"

"Well," said Two-Dogs-Fucking, "you had a little to do with it, too. Didn't you, now?" He winked a lascivious wink and let loose with his laugh, "Bwah-ha-ha-ha."

"So, I screwed some blumpkins and they created adult-sized clones of me?"

"That's about how it happens," said Two-Dogs-Fucking. "Except they are just babies at first and then they grow quite rapidly. Your sons are all only one moon's phase old. They are as physically mature as adults but still are like children intellectually. But all aspects of their development occurs rapidly. Any day now they should be talking and working on complex thoughts. They have all of your knowledge and memories that you imparted when you coupled with the blumpkins. Before you know it, they will be both physical and intellectually on par with you."

"So that's how Chelloveck had so many sons," said John. "And why he was not despondent at the loss of some of them. He really could make more just like them."

"That sounds right," said Two-Dogs-Fucking.

"And that's why Chelloveck was so upset with Santiago," realized John. "Because he was going to have a small army of Santiagos in his camp. The blumpkins were most important to him and Santiago fouled them with his seed. And to add insult to injury, Chelloveck is going to have to see Santiago's twitchy, bearded face everywhere he looks."

"Wouldn't that upset you?" said Two-Dogs-Fucking.

"I suppose I can see his point," said John. "But I do find it kind of comforting seeing his face again." He looked at all of the sleeping Santiagos strewn about in the poppy field and smiled.

"What of the donkeys?"

"What of them?" said Two-Dogs-Fucking. "The donkey also had knowledge of the blumpkins, didn't he?"

"Okay, maybe that's more than I want to think about," said John. He looked at the clones on the ground and shook his head. "So, I'm a father now. Why did you bring them here?"

"I stayed at Aguacaliente at first so that I could be with my Missy Niksik. Oh, she was a beautiful ball of sphincters," Two-Dogs-Fucking sighed as his countenance took on a dreamy look.

"But after several days, our lovemaking was interrupted when your sons began crawling from the springs. And I had to take care of them, feeding them and teaching them to walk and whatnot. I'll tell you, I was not motivated to get up from my Missy, but I also felt an obligation to your sons. So I nursed them and cleaned them and helped them along."

"Well, thank you," said John. And he looked around at the unconscious versions of himself scattered about on the bed of flowers. Powerful feelings welled up in his chest. His eyes leaked warm tears. The sight of his clones moved him. A strong emotion, one he assumed to be fatherly love, burned in him. "Thank you for bringing them here. I assume it must not have been easy."

"It was not easy," said Two-Dogs-Fucking. "I neglected my Missy Niksik and one day, she pooted her rotten air, spit one of her teeth at me, and rolled back into her bubbling cesspool. I thought that she was just moistening herself for me. But, before I even realized what had happened, she sank into her puddle and did not return."

"I'm sorry," said John. He patted Two-Dogs-Fucking on the shoulder as a showing of sympathy. But the act was not sufficient to comfort the Melungeon. And before John had time to step back, Two-Dogs-Fucking quickly embraced him and cried and snotted into John's shirt. Uncomfortable and disturbed by the physical interaction with Two-Dogs-Fucking, John patted him awkwardly on the back and said, "there, there."

And when Two-Dogs-Fucking pulled away from John, his scabs and scars and weeping wounds were gone. The healing touch from John made him healthy again.

And John drew rejuvenating power from the healing. His body buzzed. His senses sharpened. And the grogginess from the poppies evaporated and blew away on the wind.

"I feel much better," said Two-Dogs-Fucking, talking both about his physical and mental wounds. "It really was a hard time, you know? A gang of lunkheads attacked at Aguacaliente at one point. I did what I had to keep them away. I led them on a chase away from the springs and from the babies. But I tired quickly and had to rest. They caught me while I napped and were awfully rough with me. They had their way with my face and nethers over and over. And I could only pleasure them for so long. I was unable to walk for several days thereafter. It was horrible." But the tone of his voice sounded as if he were relaying the details of a pleasant meal instead of a brutal rape. He smiled and gazed toward the horizon as he spoke, as if watching for someone. "Just horrible."

"Well, I thank you," said John. "These are all my children. And Joad's and Santiago's, of course. And Alf's, too, I guess. You did a fine thing in protecting them. I will not forget that."

Two-Dogs-Fucking nibbled at his poppy and smiled at John. "I would do it all again...for them, of course."

John and Joad walked about the poppy pasture, studying their clones in amazement. John knelt down before one of his copies and swept the man's hair from his closed eyes. He stared at the face and knew that he was looking down at himself. Slapping gently at the face did not rouse the man. Neither did shaking his body. The poppies' power took hold over the field of unconscious men, and it would be some time before any of them awakened.

A great sadness stirred in John's chest. For perhaps the first time, John recognized and understood the emotions that bubbled up in him. His heart hurt because he did not have time to stay and tend to his children. But, the river of clouds above resumed its flow and the current of the path pulled at John. Though conflicted, an urgency compelled him toward Android Lovethorn. And he decided that he could not wait.

"I need you to stay with the children," said John to Two-Dogs-Fucking and Joad. "They will need you. And I have a feeling that I'm going to need them. So stay and tend to them. Be here for them when they wake and do not let them eat any more flowers."

"You cannot go up the mountain alone," said Joad, and his deep voice cracked with heartfelt concern. "I will go with you. I will fight for you. I will fight with you if you try to stop me."

John said, "No, I have to go by myself. I'm not worried about Lovethorn's soldiers. You don't need to protect me from them. They won't harm me. I'll cut through them like the birds through the sky. Android Lovethorn cannot keep me away. I just know this. And I know that I have to go alone."

Joad wrinkled up his bony brow and cleared his throat while he gathered his thoughts. His voice, deep and muffled and forceful, flowed slowly from his chapped lips like lava down a slight incline, "Nothing ever exists entirely alone; everything is in relation to everything else. I will stay here with our children. But, I will be with you, too. My spirit carries on the flow of the path with you. My will is born over to your plan. I am here and I am with you. You will not go entirely alone; an empty sack cannot stand upright; a wheel is useless without its spokes. I am your spokes and I am the content of your sack. I will be with you, no matter where I am."

"I, too, will be with you in spirit," said Two-Dogs-Fucking. "I will do anything that I have to. I don't even care if more lunk-heads come along. I will divert and distract them, even if it means them ravishing me again."

"That will not be necessary," said Joad, smashing a fist into his open hand. "I can take care of any problems that come along."

Disappointment washed over Two-Dogs-Fucking. In a flat tone, he said, "That is quite a relief. I don't know that I would survive another attack from those beasts." He crammed the rest of his flower into his mouth and ground it between his molars. His already slumping shoulders sloped even more.

"You won't be left behind," said John to his friends. Alf the Sacred Burro nudged up against him and rubbed his ratty head against John's hand. "I take you all with me here," and he placed his hand over his heart. "But I have to go alone. And I need you to stay with the children and be ready. If I need help, I'll scorch the sky with fire and rain down lightning. You will know that your time has come when I send my signal. And when that time comes, bring our children and bring your fury on all that block your path. And we will be together again when it is all done."

And John was on the road again, followed only by Alf the Sacred Burro. John reluctantly turned his back to his children and friends and set to walking the path again. Poppies grew thick on El Camino de la Muerte and obscured the road. John kept his eyes on the winding river of clouds above to make sure he followed the trail. The road emerged from the poppy pasture and snaked up the mountain. The bricks, now free of the poppy vines, glowed a bright red in the glaring sunlight. Far above him, John could see a dark fortress near the top of the mountain. Behind him, John knew nothing of the arrival of Three Tooth's tribe at the poppy field.

The red brick road led John up the mountain in a slight but steady incline. And the road cut into the mountain, zigzagging up the slope in a series of sharp switchbacks. Stately ponderosa pines lined one side of the road and a precipitous drop down the mountain comprised the other side. And had he turned and looked down the mountain at the poppy field, John would have seen that an army of Chellovecks were gathering below. He would have seen that his children and the children of Joad and Santiago were stirring and being helped back to consciousness by Joad and Three Tooth's men. But John's eyes were locked on the fortress above and he was drawn forward on the road to the castle.

John's steady and determined march up La Montaña Sagrada never faltered. But, occasionally Alf stumbled over roots that grew up through the red brick road. Sometimes the donkey sat and wheezed away a brief attack of asthma or worked to bring up a hairy bezoar. When that happened, John plopped down on the bricks beside Alf and waited for the ailment to resolve itself (as it always did with Alf). Although John was compelled to move toward the top of the mountain, he did not rush the donkey, nor did he leave Alf behind. When the burro recovered, John walked again and Alf followed.

And the road cut into the mountain and across ridges, switching back again and again. Dark caves appeared along the side of El Camino de la Muerte as the road rose higher and higher on the great hill. A complete absence of sound thrummed from the caves, sapping those parts of the road of noise and echoes. John did not talk to Alf the Sacred Burro as they passed the caves. He felt that if he did, the words would drop, stillborn, from his mouth. And a weight pushed on his chest at those parts of the road, making it a chore to draw in breath. But the caves not only affected the sound and John's respiration, they also muted his emotions, leaving only a deep depression and anger. Once they passed the caves, John breathed easier and the pressure on his chest abated. His ability to feel returned and the anger and depression evaporated, leaving him with a healthy balance of emotions. He talked to Alf, once clear of the caves, saying, "Those caves don't seem right to me," and felt relief at the sound of his voice. In response, Alf just rubbed his head up against John's hand for a scritching. And John always obliged.

The forest of ponderosa pines gradually thinned as they ascended the mountain, until the tall, proud trees grew no more and were replaced by stunted, densely matted bushes. And the air became dry and thinner, making the ascent difficult. But John and Alf the Sacred Burro did not stop walking until they found themselves standing at the tall iron front door of Android Lovethorn's mountain fortress, Abaddon. Alf plopped his posterior on the ground and looked at John, as if to say, "What now?"

And John realized that he was meant to enter the fortress alone. "Go back down the mountain," he said to Alf. "Go back to our friends in the flowers."

But Alf the Sacred Burro did not move. He plopped his rear end down on the red bricks and whinnied at John, asking to stay with him. Alf did not want to leave his friend. And he did not want to walk past the silent caves again. Milky, cataract-afflicted eyes begged John to take Alf with him.

"Go now," said John, regretfully ordering his donkey friend back down the mountain. He pulled the saddlebags from Alf and flung them over his own shoulder. "We'll see each other again. And when we do, I'll feed you all of the bloodfruits a donkey could want and scratch your head for you."

Alf did not want to go. But he did reluctantly turn and slowly walk away from John. Once several cubits away, the sacred burro turned one last time and gave a pleading look.

John did not acknowledge the sad gaze and merely said, "Be gone now, donkey. Be gone and be glad. For the next time we see each other, it will be as old friends celebrating a victory." And then Alf the Sacred Burro disappeared from John's thoughts and sight. John turned toward the imposing iron door of the fortress and studied it, considering his next move.

Mounds of mountain dirt clung to girthy Asherah poles like prolapsed rectums on unlubricated phalli. The carved poles stood sentinel to the front door of Android Lovethorn's mountain fortress and stretched upward, outreaching the top of the stony walls by cubits. Twin turkey vultures, plump and sluggish, lurked at the top of the poles, hunched over and looking down for the food that always fell to the ground right in front of the fort. Instead of the dead meat that the birds preferred, they saw a long-haired, bearded man dressed in clean, white, freshly twisted linens, standing before the fortress with his hand poised to knock on the door.

John stood in that spot, contemplating his situation. Iron rods barred an opening at eye level and gave him a limited view into the murky interior behind the door. And then he did the only thing that he could think to do. He rapped his knuckles on the iron door and the sound clanged off of the mountain and echoed down the road. Immediately, in response to the knocking, a face appeared behind the bars. An old man with a tiny head and a long, crooked nose gazed out at John. Beneath the man's nose, a full white mustache, like that of an elderly walrus, sprouted and obscured his upper lip. And the mustache wiggled and wriggled like the whiskers of a prawn prodding the seafloor for food. Below the mustache, the puckered mouth spat out words.

"The master says to go away," said the man behind the door,

his mustache twitching and flicking erratically. And his right eye set to fluttering. "Go away says the master."

"I cannot," said John. "I am John the Revelator and I am here to see Android Lovethorn. He is expecting me. I need to see him."

"Well, you can't see him," snipped the man, his whiskers twitching wildly. "Not nobody gets in to see Reverend Lovethorn. Not nobody. Not no how."

"I demand to see Lovethorn," commanded John. He balled up his hand and beat his fist against the door several times until the little man recoiled at the banging.

The doorkeeper turned and limped on a gimp leg into the darkness of the fortress, saying, "Not nobody gets in to see Reverend Lovethorn. Not nobody. Not no how." And the clop-drag sound of his twisted gait carried the little man into the fortress and away from John.

"I will wait right here," shouted John. "I will wait until you grant me admittance and I see Lovethorn." So he dropped to the ground, crossed his legs, and leaned his back against the door. And because he had not a clue about what to do next, he sat there until the day turned to dusk, and dusk to night.

The river of fire flowed above in the sky and crashed into the top of La Montaña Sagrada, erupting in an explosion above the peak. The two full moons in the sky reflected the fierce red intensity of the sun. And the haze in the sky wreathed the moons with twisting, smoky halos that diffused the glow. Every so often John stood and beat his hands on the iron door, calling out for somebody inside to grant him entry. When nobody opened the door for him, John closed his eyes and spoke to the sky. And though he knew it was useless, he tried to summon lightning or wind or a pillar of fire to rip the door from its frame. But nothing that he did would cause the door to open. And he would not walk around the walls of the fortress to locate an entrance; the red brick road met the iron door and, John assumed, led right into the fortress. Should he leave the path, he would lose the path and be lost to the path.

So John sat again with his back to the iron door and pulled a wineskin from the saddlebag that Alf the Sacred Burro left him. The chicha choked him at first but then went down smoother than before. John found it far too easy to drink the drink, and before he knew it, it was hard to think. He drank the brew down to the dregs and tossed the empty wineskin down the side of the mountain. And he pulled two more wineskins from the saddlebags, pushing one through the iron bars on the front door as an offering to anyone willing to grant him entry, and tying it to the bars with the skin's rawhide strap. The other skin he opened and drained down his throat, ignoring the burn and the stench and welcoming the numbness that would soon follow.

With his vision fogged from chicha, and his thoughts muddled and befuddled, John shut his eyes to put an end to the double vision. And troubled sleep pounced on him, making him toss and turn on the red brick road. John dreamt that he was walking down a long hall with red brick walls that curved up to meet in a point. At the end a the hall an iron door, much like the front door of Lovethorn's fortress, waited. No matter how far he walked, the door always loomed the same distance away. John tried to run toward the door but his body felt as if it were running in water. So he slowed his step and focused his eyes on the ever-distant door.

"You're never going to get there like this," said John's voice. But the voice came from John's fiery doppelganger, whom appeared at his side. "Take your gaze off of the door and turn it inward. That is where your strength lies. That is where you will find your power, not behind some door. Focus on yourself and the doors will come to you."

"And why should I care about reaching the door?" said John. "Lovethorn wants to kill me."

"No," said Fire-John. "Lovethorn wants to hold you captive and suckle at your energy. He does not want you to die and he definitely does not want you to leave. He wants you alive and weak because that makes him stronger. You must meet him face to face and make him send you back. You must make him return you to yourself so that you can be complete. Otherwise, you die there, and you die here, and all is lost."

"That just doesn't seem right to me," John argued. "I've grown strong here. I have power. And I don't see how it is that I could die if I stay here. I don't care about the other part of me dying. I don't know that part. I don't remember that part of me. And, from the little that I can tell, I was an awful person."

"You were a wretch," agreed the doppelganger. "And the only way to set things right is the reunion of your two halves. The good and the bad. And your light is now strong and will not be swayed by the dark. That is why you are here. That is why you split, so that you could plant the seed of goodness here and let it grow inside you. And that is what you have done. You are ready. When Lovethorn comes to you, meet with him and force him to send you back. Because you have the power and Lovethorn is the only one that can return you to yourself."

"I don't know..." said John.

But before John could finish his argument, the fiery doppelganger boomed, "I do know. And you must do as I say or all will be lost." And, as if avoid any further argument, the fiery apparition ran toward the end of the hall and crashed into the door, knocking it from its frame with the concussion of his impact.

The blowback from the explosion knocked John to the ground and thumped his dream-head on the dream-bricks. And the flames from the explosion blazed through the door like the light of the red sun and burned John's eyes closed.

And when John awoke and opened his eyes, he found himself laid out on the red brick road. Above him, two shriveled, shrunken heads looked down at his face, one grinning and one scowling. As his vision focused, he saw that the two tiny heads both sat on the same set of hunched-over shoulders. The shoulders shared the same thick, hunchbacked torso and the torso shared the same two legs. The grinning head on the left looked to the one on the right and, in a high-pitched voice, said, "I don't know, Magog, I do believe he is the one. He's the guy."

"Come now, Gog. He can't be the guy," said the scowling head, his voice slurring but also shrill. "Just look at him with his tangled hair and face. Look at his crusted, dull eyes. He is not the one." The right hand of the shared body lifted the wineskin that John left hanging from the door, and slopped a snootful of chicha into Magog's mouth.

"Is," said Gog, his voice clear and his enunciation sharp.

"Is not," said Magog. The left hand tried to grab the wineskin from the right. But the right hand held it out of reach and the left flailed ineffectually at the air. Magog laughed in Gog's face, and the hand under Magog's control kept the wineskin out of Gog's reach.

"Give me that skin," said Gog.

"Won't," slurred Magog. "It's mine."

"Give now," snapped Gog.

"Can't," said Magog, laughing again.

And Gog's left hand shot out for the wineskin. But the right hand, under control of Magog, pulled away. "Give," shouted Gog. "Won't," replied Magog. Gog's hand chased Magog's and their shared body spun, an ungainly flailing top in that spot, until the conjoined twins grew dizzy and fell to the ground. And while Magog tried to clear his head of the titling, swirling vertigo, Gog snatched the wineskin (now mostly drained) and flung it down the side of La Montaña Sagrada.

John rubbed the drunken, crusted sleep from his eyes and watched Gog and Magog argue. The scene intrigued him to the extent that he did not even realize that the door to the fortress hung wide open behind him. He could not tear his eyes away from the altercation happening right in front of him.

"You're a fool," screamed Magog. "That was the spit of the gods and I was obtaining enlightenment."

"Were not," said Gog. "You were obtaining a state if idiocy."

"Was not," said Magog. "'Twas enlightenment." And his fist swung up and back, crunching Gog's mouth.

"You swine," said Gog through a fattened lip. "You pus-infected cum bubble. You bloodstained undergarment. You pusillanimous pinhead. I'll rip your head off and fuck it with our dick." And Gog looped a left hook around and smashed Magog's nose to the side of his face.

"Will not," screeched Magog in a warbling falsetto. Blood bubbled from the squished pulpy glob that was his nose. "I will rip your head off and shove it up our ass, you dog-humping, finger-sniffing, microcephalic moron."

Gog and Magog thrashed about and struck at the small targets of each others' heads. And they kicked up dust from the road and cast aspersions like stones until John could not tell which head was flinging which insults. The barbs and threats shot out in a random, jumbled mess while fists flew and feet kicked. "You anal-dwelling felch bucket...fanny-diddling queef huffer...I'll rape your throat and make you eat feces...rotten corpse-loving semen demon...I'll rip open your face and fill it with diarrhea so that it stinks for ages...I'll fistfuck your dirty whore mouth...choke on cock, bitch-hole..."

Gog's fist pulled up short and close and walloped Magog directly on the chin. At the exact same moment, Magog looped around with a full-force swing and smashed Gog in the ear. And for just a second, the shared body dropped to the ground and both heads flopped back. The grey static of disconnect from consciousness buzzed in their apple-sized noggins. Then, Gog and Magog shook their heads, and their body raised up on its elbows. And as if the blows had reset their brains, Gog and Magog looked at each other and smiled.

"It looks like we've done it again Brother, doesn't it?" said Gog, rubbing his hand on his ear.

"Does," agreed Magog, the unhinged joints of his jaw clicking with his words. His hand gripped his chin and pushed it back into position. "Sorry."

"It's okay."

And when they looked back to the spot where they first discovered John, he was gone. And the door to the fortress was closed behind him.

"How now, Brother?" said Gog, pointing at the closed door. "It looks as if he is on the path. He is the one. He is the guy."

"How now, yourself, you fool," said Magog. "He's gone on by himself and we were supposed to put him to the scales. Lovethorn will put us to the wheel if we don't catch him."

"Well, we better intercept him then," said Gog.

Gog-Magog lunged at the door and found that John did not lock it behind himself. They ran into the dark halls, flung open doors, and scampered through a labyrinth of low-ceilinged, low-lighted, low-level tunnels until they reached the room.

With his pupils constricted to pinpoints from the chicha hangover and unable to adjust to the almost nonexistent light in the tunnels, John fumbled blindly through the dark halls of Abaddon, fleeing the strange two-headed man, and hoping that he was on the path to Android Lovethorn. The walls jumped out at him, scuffing his elbows and sides, and doors unexpectedly blocked his way. John opened the doors and walked on down the hall. He stumbled along, trusting his gut that he was still following the proper path.

And then he came to a door that did not want to open. He kicked at the door and heard the latch that held it on the other side loosely jangling as if it were not securely fastened. He backed up and charged the door, leading with his shoulder. Along with the flare of pain that flooded his shoulder and arm, the door burst open and John crashed into the room, falling to the floor.

Before he could stand, the men were on him, pinning his body to the ground. Gog and Magog hovered over John and looked down at his face.

"That's him," said Gog.

"It is," agreed Magog.

Gog said to the men on top of John, "Strap him to the scale and then be gone."

The short, muscular guards wore bronze helmets and breastplates and back plates. They lifted John to his feet. They kept a tight hold on each arm and wrist and led John to a seat positioned at the middle of a large beam. And the beam rested on a center-situated triangular fulcrum and held a gold plate at each end. The men quickly bound John's arms and legs, strapped him snug to the seat on the scale, and fled the room.

"Such is the way of the wanderer," said Gog, hocking a gluti-
nous loogie into an earthen bowl filled with grit and gunk. Dipping his left hand into the bowl, he rubbed burnt ashes
between his fingertips and smiled at John. Smudging the soot
and slobber and smoot between his fingers, he said, "This is the
way. The way is the truth. And truth is not knowledge.
Knowledge is not wisdom. Wisdom is not beauty. Beauty is not
love. Love is not music. Music is the best." Gog smeared the ash
on John's face and neck. And from somewhere beyond, the
clear, powerful voices of a castrati choir pierced the walls of
the room.

Gog-Magog strode around the room, placing candles in
sconces on the wall and lighting them. The strains of the castrati swelled and ebbed in time like the respiration of some
great beast, and the candles flickered and fluttered as if being
blown about by the eunuchs' song.

Gog-Magog picked up the saddlebags that John dropped
when he burst into the room. "Let's see what we have here,"
said Gog, opening the bags and thrusting his hand into them.

"Let's," agreed Magog.

And Gog-Magog retrieved the oversized deck of cards that
John had collected from bloodwood corpses. The conjoined
twins' hands worked in concert, flipping through the deck and
examining the cards with anxious wonder. John said nothing
and kept his protests to himself, somehow sensing that whatever happened was something that was meant to be, and
something that simply had to be endured. And he felt no fear,
merely impatience at the current inconvenience.

"The cards will tell us if he is the guy," said Gog.

"Or if he isn't," countered Magog.

"Let's do the deal, then," Gog and Magog said together. And they dropped the deck to the red brick floor and knelt in front of the jumble of cards. In the flickering light of the candles their hands whipped the cards around, like a child sloppily shuffling a deck, mixing the cards in a random order. Still they worked as one, gathering the cards together again and straightening them into a newly shuffled deck. "Let's do the deal, indeed," Gog and Magog said together.

Magog pulled the top card and looked at it. "Ah, the two of hearts," he said. And the image on the card was the face of a woman with her eyes and mouth stitched shut, bloody tears streaming down her cheeks. "And it looks like you were not very nice to somebody somewhere," Magog said to John, his high voice assuming a sharp prosecutorial tone. "That doesn't sound to me like somebody who is the guy." With a flip of his wrist, Magog flicked the card in John's direction and it landed on the gold plate on the left side of the beam. John felt the level of the beam tilt down to the left very slightly. "Not the guy," said Magog.

"Let's see what I find," said Gog, and he plucked the ace of spades from the top of the deck. Gog's confident smile faded and he said, "Oh my," as he took in the card's image of a faceless man dangling from a noose. "Well I'm sure there's an explanation. We cannot judge him on a single act, can we? We have to evaluate the whole man." And Gog flipped the ace of spades in the direction of the scale, landing the card in the gold plate on the left side of the beam. When the card landed, and the beam slanted to the left a little bit more, Gog cringed.

Gog and Magog pulled more cards from the deck. Magog smiled and commented on the blackness of John's soul and John's contemptible treatment of his fellow man. Gog's face demonstrated his disappointment and concern more than his words did. And the indictment of the cards weighed heavily on the left side until the downward left slope of the beam forced John to shift his position on the seat to avoid the feeling of sliding off.

John cared not to witness the proceedings against him. Clearly Magog opposed him and was prevailing. And Gog tried to come to John's defense, but with little success. To have come so far and see his quest shut down at the hands of shrunken-headed Siamese twins was more than he could accept. John closed his eyes and directed his thoughts upward, trying to call down a pillar of fire. But he was too weak, or the walls of the building prevented it. *Or maybe*, John thought, *maybe this is all a big joke and I don't have any powers. Maybe this is a dream and I should just wake up.*

So John closed his eyes and ears to the proceedings, not wanting to hear as Gog and Magog went into more detail about the meaning of each card they pulled, about the meaning of John's past. John hummed to himself to block out their words and give himself something to concentrate on. On his eyelids, the flickering flames of the candles played out a picture show of dancing, indistinct black images on a red backdrop.

"Don't you think you should be paying attention?" said a voice. And John kept his eyes closed, but on his own eyelid picture show, John saw that his fiery doppelganger stood before him, frowning and shaking his head, disgusted. "They are taking account of all of your life up to this moment. They are measuring the ledger of your actions, weighing your spirit, quantifying your value. This is your story. Don't you want to know these things?"

"I do not," said John. And he realized that he could keep his eyes closed and be confronted by his doppelganger, or open his eyes and watch Gog–Magog level harsh accusations against him for things he could not even remember. John clenched his eyes even tighter, opting to argue with himself. "That doesn't matter. I don't know about anything I did before I came to this place. And I don't care about all of that. Whatever that was, it's not me now. I'm not bad. I'm not evil. I don't do anything to intentionally harm others. I've actually helped people, laid hands on them and cured them. I know there is good in me. I've seen it in the eyes of my friends and felt it when I looked down at the faces of my children in the valley."

"Of course there is good in you," said the doppelganger, sitting on a flaming stump and leaning his back against John's clenched eyelid. "What do you think this is about? I've been telling you, you split. The skuzzy loser that was you is lain up in a sickroom, rotten with festering bedsores and weak with atrophy. That is the blackness that consumed you and it is growing weak, losing its energy. And that's because you are here and you are good and growing stronger. You are doing that because you are meant to go back and unite your split halves."

"I call bullshit," said John. "I'm here and I'm happy and strong. I'm good and this is what I was meant to be. I think that's why I'm here. It's me moving on from what I was. I cannot and will not go back. If that other me dies, then it's all for the better."

And Doppelganger leapt up from his stump. His white hot hands buzzed with electricity as they throttled John's neck. "If your other half dies, you die, I die, everything here dies. Say that you will go back. Say that you will make Lovethorn send you back or I will end it all for us right here. I will choke the life out of you and give you what you are going to cause if you do not return. Your path is one back to yourself. And if you are going to stray from that path, then there is no point in struggling on any further. If that is your goal, then we are all going to die anyway and I will end it here and now for us."

But the burn of Doppelganger's hands did not hurt John's neck, nor did the pressure of the throttling. Doppelganger's touch shot John full of energy. And from somewhere within, John drew the power to break Doppelganger's grip and throw him against one of John's eyelids. Doppelganger fell to the floor but left a burning smudge on the wall of John's eyelid, and the fire blazed and formed into the image of a burning eye staring back at John.

"Do as I tell you or we are all dead," shouted Doppelganger, and he disappeared in a burst of flames, leaving only the smoldering fire-eye on John's eyelid.

"I will do as is right," said John to himself. "I will go where the flow of the path takes me. If it takes me back to myself, then so be it. But if the trail ends here, then here I shall stay."

And when John opened his eyes he saw Gog and Magog before him, their shared body flopped over the wooden chair like a wet towel set out to dry. John realized that the belts that had bound him hung from his chair. And the beam he sat upon tilted to the right. Cards littered the floor, mostly scattered around the left side of the beam. More cards filled the left-hand plate than the right, but still the beam tilted to the right under the weight of the cards on that side. Both Gog and Magog drew in heavy breaths and neither bothered to stand when they saw John looking at them.

"He is the guy," said Gog, sitting up a little and lifting his weary head.

"That he is," agreed Magog.

"Go," they both said to John, waving their hands feebly as if shooing him away. "Go through the door and follow the red brick floor. It will take you where you need to go."

Behind John, opposite the door he crashed through, waited another door. John turned and looked at the door and then back at Gog-Magog. They nodded and waved him away, giving every indication that they had no more interest in him.

So he turned his back to the twins and walked to the door. Behind John, a raspy exhalation released from Gog and Magog as they fell from their chair. There they remained, deflated and defeated on the floor. John turned in their direction to help.

"Go," said Gog. "You cannot help us."

"He's right," said Magog. "Help yourself."

And they waved John away again, refusing his help. John turned back to the door and found that it was unlocked. The door creaked on its hinges as he pushed it open and a torch-lit hallway opened to him. And the red brick trail continued down the hallway. John stepped through the door and knew that he was still on the path. The flow of energy almost pulled him along. Doorways opened to unlighted paths on both sides of John as he walked on down the hall. But the red bricks did not take John along those paths. As he passed the openings, John felt the same emptiness that he experienced when he neared the caves of silence. The lack of sound thrummed from the black holes in the walls and pushed down on John's chest. The absolute void down the unbricked hallways cast John into deep depression as he passed and made him feel as if it were not worth it to go on, as if it would be better to turn off and walk down into the void. The strong current of the red brick pathway pulled him along past those dark caves of oblivion.

Once past the doorways, John felt like himself again. And he walked on down the hall. The red brick floor took John up and down ramps and around corners, twisting him around until he lost his sense of direction. The only thing he could do was follow the path to wherever it led him. So he walked deep into the cool, moist bowels of Abaddon until he felt that he must be well below the mountain. And then the path rose and twisted and carried him back toward the top of the La Montaña Sagrada and to a stubborn door.

And the door stood firm, refusing entry, despite John's kicking and slamming his shoulder into it. John stood, sweating and shaking, his shoulder throbbing from the efforts to bust the door open. He readied himself to patiently sit at the door and wait it out, just as he had done at the front gate of Abaddon, and then heard the noise behind him.

"Stand back," said the gnarled old guard behind John. He flashed a gummy, edentulous grin. "Kicking and pounding on that door is not the way to get through."

John moved aside. He did not try to run or fight with the guard, although he had no doubt that he could easily overwhelm the smaller, feeble-looking little man. There was only one way to go – forward – and someone had to let him through. So John moved out of the way and watched. The man ran a hand along the edge of the door, stopped at a spot that looked no different from the rest of the door, and pushed. And a latch the same color as the door popped out. The man grabbed the latch and pulled the door. And the guard swung the door out, instead of pushing it in as John had been trying to do.

"It only goes one way," said the guard as he opened the door. "And so does the trail. Where are you going?"

"Where is Lovethorn," asked John. He sensed that the Man in Black was close. He sensed that he was near the top of the mountain. He sensed a mounting tension just beyond the walls around him.

"He is where he is," said the guard. "I will take you to him. Just follow me."

So John followed in the draft left by the quick-moving little guard. And they climbed spiraling stairs, scaled ladders, rounded corners, all the while staying on the red brick path. Winded and lightheaded from following the guard, John found himself in circular room much like the one where Gog-Magog strapped him to the scale.

"Sit down," said the guard. "Make yourself comfortable. Someone will be with you soon."

The red brick path intersected the room and led to a door on the other side. The guard continued on the path and exited the room. And when he shut the door behind himself, it blended in with the wall, as did the door through which John entered the room. He studied the walls and felt at them where he knew the doors to be. But his eyes only saw stone walls and his hands failed to discern handles or knobs or latches for the doors he knew to be there. John found himself once again trapped and waiting at a door until someone let him through. There was no going back through the door which he entered the room, even if he would have wanted to. But John knew that the only direction was forward on the red bricks and wouldn't have turned back even if he were able.

A skylight far above him opened to the heavens. Looking up, John saw the flow of the river of clouds directly above. And as day turned to night, the clouds morphed into the blazing river of fire. The star Wormwood shone down and tinted the circular room a warm shade of green. Though he had nowhere to go and none of his supplies on him, John did not fret about his situation. He knew he was still following El Camino de la Muerte. The river of fire above confirmed that for him. So he lay himself out on the red bricks and watched the sky above, knowing that he was following the path and would sooner or later find himself face to face with Android Lovethorn.

The red light illuminated the room and the early morning chill shivered John awake. As soon as he moved, they were on him. The old, toothless guard stood above John and said, "Get him before he starts moving."

And another guard – younger and stronger and fully blessed with a wide, straight grimace of sharp teeth – leapt on John and pinned him facedown on the red bricks. He wrapped twisted hemp ropes around John's wrists and ankles, and then stood and yanked John to his feet. Holding tight to John's biceps, he leaned in close. The whiff of breath from the guard smelled of death and contrasted sharply with the bright, white grin. And he asked, "Who are you?"

"What do you mean, 'Who are you?'" asked John. "I am me and I am here to see Lovethorn."

"But who are you?" shouted Toothy in John's face, the breath as angry as the tone of voice.

"You ask me who I am," said John. "Perhaps I should be asking the same of you. I am the man that Lovethorn will see. I am the one that must get through. Can you tell me that I am wrong? Who are you?"

"Who are you?" shouted the young guard again. He smashed a balled fist to the side of John's head. And a shock of pain shot all of the way from John's ear down to his shoulder. The older guard smirked a moist, gummy smirk, and stood back against the wall, watching.

The red light of dawn throbbed with intensity, and rosy blossoms of pain pulsed in the air before John's eyes. And he shook the pain from his head like a dog shaking off bathwater. "Who am I?" John snapped. And his face flicked through a range of emotions, just as he had seen Santiago do before. The volume of his voice rose and he shouted, "I am the one that you will see coming down on a wave of fire. I am the one that will cleanse this festering cesspool. I am the one that will crash lightning storms down on your people. You will know my vengeance and my power if you do not let me go and let me through."

And then both guards were on John, pinning him to the ground and binding his wrists behind his back. They stripped him bare and sat him in a chair. They mocked him and spat in his face and slapped him with open hands.

The toothy guard smacked John hard on the cheek and left a hand-shaped welt. He said to John, "We are giving you the opportunity to turn around. You can do so now. You can leave this place and walk away and we will harm you no further. But if you insist on seeing Lovethorn, there will be a lot more of this to come before we let you through." And he balled up a fist and slammed it into John's stomach.

John said, "Ooomph," and doubled over to recapture the breath that the guard knocked out of him. And he said nothing more than the involuntary grunt of pain. He did not accept the offer to walk away unharmed. He did not answer or acknowledge the guards' questions other than to repeatedly demand to be taken to Lovethorn. Once again, John knew that this was something to be endured. There was no chance of him turning back. The red bricks led forward and he knew that it would be impossible for him to turn around and try to fight the current of the path.

More guards came into the room and they took turns beating John. They beat him until their knuckles broke and their hands swelled. With each blow, John smiled defiance and said nothing. And his sweat fell from him as it were great drops of blood, raining on the ground and soaking into the red bricks below him. And when the men could strike John with their hands no more, they beat him with rods. And when the rods snapped on his back, they flogged him and scourged him, the scourge producing quivering ribbons of raw, bleeding flesh. Still, John twisted up his battered, pulpy face and cast a serene smile at them. When they spat at John, he gave them a bloody grin in return. And when it finally dawned on them, when the men saw that John would not give in, they stopped striking him. They untied John and opened the next door for him to pass through.

John dragged his forearm across his face and brushed the sticky, blood-soaked hair away from his eyes. He struggled into his fine twisted white linens as the guards looked on and refused to help him. The gashes and lacerations seeped out and stained John's clothes the color of rust. A brick that stuck up just a trifle more than the others tripped John, sending him sprawling flat on the red bricks as he stepped toward the open door. And the men just laughed and flexed their sore hands. Not one moved to help him up. So John strained to get back to his feet and walked on down the hall.

The hallway slanted upward and culminated in a ball of red radiance. The powerful song of the castrati choir screamed from the door, as if set on fire by the crimson glare. Horrid brutes, with their gargoyle faces twisted in painful knots of hate, stood along the walls. And John walked on down the hall. Each person that he passed spat at him and threw fists and kicks in his direction. Mostly John dodged the blows as he passed. Some caught him in the head and on the neck, making John stumble, but not stopping him.

And when John reached the doorway, a blast of heat and light and ear-crushing sound blew back his hair and beard, nearly lifting him from his feet. But he fought the force and pushed through the threshold. The light of day shone down on him from above through ghastly stained glass images of torture and famine and plague. He stood for some time, looking up at the stained-glass-suffering, marveling at the grotesque scenes above and the beautiful colored light they created. And then a voice called him back to his senses.

"John the Revelator," said a raw, deep voice that sounded as if it had been soaked in chicha and dragged across a bed of gravel. John's eyes followed the red brick path that led down the aisle before him. And at the end of the path Android Lovethorn stood on a stage paved with red bricks, holding his arms out wide. Looking just as he had in John's dreams, Lovethorn waited in black leather pants, black shirt, and clerical collar. His raven hair stayed slicked back to his head. Mirrored sunglasses concealed his eyes. Lovethorn paced on the stage, his bearing like that of a caged lion, and beckoned to John. "Welcome to my home. Welcome to my church. John the Revelator, come on down."

Without hesitation, John walked toward Lovethorn. Pews lined each side of the aisle. And from the pews, deformed men, scarred from burns and gashes and blunt force trauma, shouted at him. And these men in the great hall had gathered to worship idols made from wood and metal, and to listen to the words of Android Lovethorn. John looked to the crowd and saw that there were those that were possessed by devils and those who were lunatic. Half-men writhed on the pews and shook their truncated stumps at John. And there were those who were lame and stricken with palsies. The glow of pure hatred burned in all of their eyes. They grimaced and glared and spewed hostility from their mouths, shouting over the song of the castrati choir, calling John a pig, a defiler, a murderer, a dream raper, and a hope thief. They spat thick saliva in his face and screamed for him to turn back, to leave, to never show his face in Abaddon again. They threw sticks and dead rats and rotten food at him. But, John did not stop. He shielded his head and face as best as he could and walked on down the red brick path toward Android Lovethorn. And as he reached the end of the aisle, just before he climbed the stairs toward Lovethorn's stage, a skeevy, piffulous rat of a man shot out from the pews and lunged toward John, piercing his side with a dagger. The point of the knife met with John's red, irritated, preexisting scar and penetrated the flesh. John doubled over, feeling the same pain that he felt before when his side had begun to bleed.

And with the sting of the dagger burning in John's gut, he dropped to his knees and pushed his hands on his eyes. The pain nearly sent him into shock and rendered him unconscious. He felt himself fading and pushed harder on his eyes with the palms of his hands. John saw the ten thousand things blasting their light from the backdrop of his eyelids. Inspired by the ten thousand things, John drew on his reservoir of strength. He muttered incoherently and threw his head back. And he screamed a yowl that flew from his mouth in a torrent of flame. The fiery scream crashed through the stained glass above, showering the congregation in a hail of shimmering, multicolored, shards of glass. The force flowed from his mouth and from deep down in his chest and gut and loins. It shot into the sky as a ball of fire, trailing a tail of smoke and sparks behind it. And the ball of fire rose and crashed into the river of clouds, setting the sky on fire and stirring a violent lightning storm. John opened his eyes and gazed toward the sky. When the fire crashed into the sky, a brilliant display of the ten thousand things spread out and fell like glimmering snowflakes. Bolts of lightning gashed the heavens and struck La Montaña Sagrada and the valley below, setting fire to the trees and brush and poppy fields.

The outburst laid John out flat in the middle of the aisle. And while his spirit was not ready to give up, it seemed that his body was. Though John willed himself to action, neither his arms nor legs budged to help him stand again and approach the Man in Black.

The song of the rosy-cheeked, round-faced castrati quieted and then stopped. And from the pulpit, Lovethorn looked down at John and shook his head. Android Lovethorn said, "Now look who has come to me. Look who has come before me to be returned to himself, like the dog who has returned to his own vomit and the washed sow who returns to wallowing in the mud. Look who wants to go back. That is what you want, isn't it?"

The castrati choir started again with a soft, mournful hum. And John could not raise his head or even speak to answer Lovethorn. Instead, he lay there on the bricks at the foot of the stairs and tried to muster the energy to stand and climb the steps so that he could stand face to face with the Man in Black.

"Look at this weakling who comes before us," shouted Lovethorn in the frenetic cadence of a revival minister. And he stomped about on the stage and pounded his fists on the pulpit to accentuate his words. Lovethorn ripped his sunglasses from his face and flung them aside. Bloodshot eyes burned in the sockets and threw off mad glares. "He blows his wad on one explosion and expects me to cower before him. He comes to my fair home and treats her as he would a worn out blumpkin, using her only for release. But look at him now, cataplectic and decrepit, feeble and flimsy, worthless and weak." Lovethorn commanded his crowd of followers, "Bring him before me now."

One soldier from each side of the great room moved in on John and lifted him from the bricks. His body hung limply in the grasp of Lovethorn's men and he put up no fight as they dragged him up the stairs, his feet slapping on each step. And when they hauled John onto the stage, Lovethorn cried out, "Strap him to the stake. Tie him there tight."

A beam stood strong and erect at the center of the stage. One soldier propped John up while the other lashed his limp body to the beam, wrapping the bindings around his legs, torso and throat. And they bound his outstretched arms to a crossbeam. When they finished, the weight of John's body strained against the bindings, but he stayed in place on the beam with his arms spread and his head flopped over. John mustered just enough strength to lift his head so that the weight of it did not cause him to choke on the rope around his neck. And then he slipped, his head dangling and the weight of it pressing his throat against the ropes. And just before John was about to pass out, one of Lovethorn's soldiers grabbed him by the hair and lifted his head. John once again gasped for air. And he looked to the crowd and saw that they screamed at him.

"Look at this fool who dares to challenge me," Lovethorn preached to the crowd. "Is this the man who is supposed to impose his will on me? He comes before us and defiles our place of worship."

And the crowd erupted with a wave of shouts calling for the punishment and torture and banishment of John. Some cried out for John to be locked in a cell in the bowels of Abaddon. Others screamed for him to be removed to the edges of their world. None called for his death, but many shouted for his blood to be spilt.

When the congregation called out for blood, Lovethorn flashed a pointy-toothed grin. From the pulpit he grabbed a golden cup and a dagger and held them high for his followers to see. "Blood most precious," said Lovethorn and the crowd exploded with rabid howls and more calls for blood. Lovethorn neared John's injured side and grabbed cautiously at the linen, making sure not to actually touch him. The Man in Black lifted the blood soaked linen enough to expose the fresh knife-wound. And then he poked at the wound with the tip of his dagger, slowly working the blade in. Thick blood poured from the opening like sap from a tree. Lovethorn pressed the lip of the golden cup against John's side and filled the cup with blood.

And the pain of it all jolted John and burned in his guts. He summoned enough energy to lift his head and tried to scream toward the sky again. But instead of a torrent of fire, he coughed out a small croak of smoke. As the anemic puff dissipated, John's energy ebbed and his head fell forward again, straining his neck against the ropes.

"And he cries to the sky again," laughed Lovethorn, moving in front of John, inches away and face to face, careful still not to touch his adversary. His voice rose in volume as it addressed John, "But there is no Sky God. There is no intervention from above. There is you and there is me. I can be your Sky God if you want. I can be your brother or your father or your savior if you want. But I cannot abide your brazen appearance before me and I cannot allow you to demand my audience whenever you so choose. Your presence before me is repugnant, like a blumpkin's monthly uncleanness. You have defiled my palace with your appearance and reviled my existence. So I will pour out my wrath on you. I will lay you low and watch you crawl in your own rot in my dungeon. I will not return you to yourself. I will not help you rejoin with your other half. Instead, I will remove your heart of flesh and replace it with a heart of stone, one that pumps your blood but knows not love or joy. I will return your memory so that you can know what you were, and, thus, what you are. And you can wallow in the sick knowledge and the self-loathing that will come of it. You will feel that shame and disgrace for your conduct and realize that none of the good you do can cleanse the blot on your soul."

Lovethorn turned to the crowd, "Can we abide this behavior?"

"No, Father," shouted the congregation as one, all starry-eyed and intoxicated on the Man in Black's vain and profane ramblings.

Reverend Android Lovethorn stomped about the stage and shouted back, "Does this man hold any power in our house?"

"No, Father," responded the congregation.

"Then what should we do with this pathetic scurve who shows his face before us as if we are to bow down to him and gape in wonder at his splendor?"

And the clamor of the congregation boiled over in the pews. "Slice him," some shouted. "Beat him," screamed others. "Toss him in a cell and throw away the key," one man shouted.

And then a piercing soprano scream piped out of one of the castrati, cut through the din, and rose above the uproar. "Let us drink his blood."

And the others agreed. "Drink his blood," they all chanted.

"Drink his blood it is, then," agreed Lovethorn, and he held the golden cup above his head, slopping blood on the floor of the stage. And the red bricks drank of the blood and wore its rusty stain. "Come before me, aisle by aisle, man by man, and drink from *Copa de Oro*. Drink the blood most precious. Drink from the cup full of his abominations and filthiness."

The parade of horribles, the deformed and decrepit worshippers, flowed from the pews and appeared one by one before Lovethorn. And they genuflected before Reverend Android Lovethorn and placed their sore-crusted lips on the golden cup. And as they drank, some fell to the floor and twitched and seized and rolled off of the stage. Others shook and lurched all over the church floor. Some screamed out in strange tongues and pressed hands to their faces as if restraining some great power. Others dropped to the floor and gave up the ghost.

As each of Lovethorn's worshippers drank of the blood, John felt his spirit draining from his head and his heart. His head flopped to the side and the soldier behind him righted it and held it there so that the ropes did not completely cut of John's air. And as John drifted toward oblivion, Lovethorn's body throbbed with raw energy and the potency given over by John's apparent surrender.

Lovethorn once again approached John and stood inches away without touching him. And he saw that John had no fight left in him. The Man in Black felt the energy pulsing through his every fiber and every cell. Gripped in the mania of his followers, dizzy with his new power, and drunkenly brazen from his complete and unexpected control of John, Lovethorn lifted the bloodstained linen and ogled the wound in John's side as if it were the quivering slit of a fresh blumpkin.

Lovethorn blew his fetid breath in John's face and they locked eyes. Just as John had pushed through the wall of heat and noise to enter the hall of worship, Lovethorn pushed through the almost overpowering fear he felt of John. He touched John's side and no bolt of lightning struck him down, no jolt of electricity threw him to the ground, no pillar of fire fell on him. He smiled his pointy-toothed grin and held his hand to John's side. Working first one finger, then two and three into the cut, Lovethorn tore the flesh on John's side, jamming the fingers in knuckle-deep.

The pained grimace on John's face aroused Android Lovethorn further. And the Man in Black squished his fingers in and out of the open wound as if he were popping a ripe blumpkin. And his rod filled with blood and strained against the leather pants that held it down. So he rubbed at his loins with his free hand and probed at John's side with the other. And in his fervor, Lovethorn's eyes turned down toward John's wound. He did not see John throw his head back from the jolt of energy that shot through him. He did not see the fire reappear in John's eyes. He did not realize that John now held his head up without the assistance of the soldier. Lovethorn did not realize his fatal error in touching John until it was too late.

And when Android Lovethorn felt the burning on his hand, like the sting of one thousand scorpions, he pulled his fingers from John's side and looked down in horror. His hand began to shrivel from a creeping, black, defiling mold. And the necrosis of his flesh rapidly spread, wasting the limb all the way to the shoulder. And the arm crumbled and fell from him, turning to dust as it landed on the red bricks. The weariness that had appeared in John's eyes now fell hard on Lovethorn and he collapsed on the floor of his own altar. And he realized that John's touch sapped him of his energy, it drained him of his sickness and blackness. It bled Lovethorn of the very things that gave him his power. And the blight that consumed his arm spread to all parts of his body, graying his skin and withering his substance. The red in his eyes turned yellow and his slick hair fell over his forehead, obscuring his gaze. At the same time, John fed on the sickness and took back all of the energy that Lovethorn's followers robbed him of when they drank his blood. John took on the sickness, just as he had with others, and it charged him with staggering strength.

The ropes that bound John to the cross snapped and frayed at the mere flex of his arms and legs. He dropped the ropes to the bricks and slowly stepped down from the stake. Lovethorn cowered on the ground before John and struggled to drag himself away. He pointed his dagger at John. The Man in Black hissed and spat, but lacked the energy to do anything else. Android Lovethorn's emaciated body trembled at John's approach.

John stepped toward Lovethorn and stood over him – looking down at the beast that was, and is and yet is not – feeling no fear of the shuddering husk of a man at his feet. The congregation cringed in their pews and recoiled when John looked out at them. None of Lovethorn's followers rushed in his direction. Even the soldiers who tied John to the cross had disappeared from the altar. And a voice rang out in John's head, "Now is the time. You can make him send you back. He will do as you order him. Make him send you back home. Go back to yourself."

"I don't want to go back," John shouted at the voice in his head. "There is nothing there for me. I don't remember who I was and I don't care. I like who I am now and see that only good will come of my sloughing off the rot. I belong here. And Lovethorn deserves to die."

The voice in his head trumpeted, "Do not kill him! If you kill him, you will die here, you will die there, and all that you have done and become will be for naught." And the power of the voice stabbed at John's head like a dagger, momentarily staggering him.

John stood stunned on the stage, hovering over Lovethorn and arguing with the voice in his head. Taking advantage of John's distraction, Lovethorn drew on his remaining energy and lunged forward with the dagger, just missing John's injured side by inches. And Lovethorn's final effort brought John back to the present. And he realized that he was at the end of the red brick road, standing over the man that he sought. John leaned down and took the dagger from Lovethorn's hand without a fight. And he drew the dagger back and thrust it into Lovethorn's chest, driving it into his black heart and twisting it deeper.

And just before he expired, Lovethorn loosed a furious roar like the sounds of one thousand dying men. And the deafening roar took the physical form of a black cloud pouring from his mouth and hovering above the congregation. And the black cloud exploded above their heads. Dark, writhing ribbons of smoke shot out in all directions from the explosion, many of them falling on the congregation, and others falling on the rest of the inhabitants of Abaddon outside of the temple. The black tendrils filled the mouths and nostrils of Lovethorn's followers. They breathed in the snakes of smoke. They swallowed the black tendrils. And all whom the ribbons of blackness infested, they echoed their master's scream and took on his madness.

On the altar, John stood back and watched Lovethorn's body crumble into a small mound of ashes. And the men before John frothed at the mouths and rushed the stage, seeking to avenge the death of Lovethorn. They clawed at each other in an effort to be the first to reach John. But those possessed by Lovethorn's demons were no match for John.

Powerful words, channeled from above, flowed through John's mouth and he chastised his foes, saying, "And as the storm passes through, the wicked will be washed away and the righteous will remain. Now be gone. Be gone from your nests, you pests." And, he called to the sky, bringing down bolts of lightning and pillars of fire on the den of thieves. He overturned the tables and chairs in their temple and vented his furious wrath on those who attacked him. And those who were not laid low by John's fury fled the temple and ran to the far corners of Abaddon for safety.

John did not pursue his enemies as they cut out of the temple. He stood and threw Android Lovethorn's ashes into the air. He splashed the blood of the fallen on the red bricks of the altar under his feet. And the bricks soaked up the blood like sponges. And though John did not pursue his foes when they fled the temple, none of Lovethorn's men found refuge in Abaddon that day.

Alerted by the fire and lightning that John dropped from the sky, Joad led an army out of the valley of poppies and up La Montaña Sagrada. The army consisted of the blumpkin lovechildren of Joad and Santiago and John, as well as the entire, heavily armed, population of the Chelloveck mesa. Alf the Sacred Burro and a pack of his offspring hefted much of the army's weaponry and supplies up the narrow mountain road. Staying behind at the field of poppies, Two-Dogs-Fucking complained of ennui and listlessness and bunions. He said that when he mustered the motivation, he would join the army at the top of the mountain. Waiting halfway up La Montaña Sagrada, armed with quivers full of arrows, Three Tooth and his crew joined the army.

And at the front door of Abaddon, the doorkeeper shouted out at Joad, "Not nobody gets in. Not nobody. Not no how."

Possessed with the strength of an army all by himself, Joad gripped the unwieldy front door of Abaddon and tore it from the stone wall. He heaved the door, and it flew far down the side of the mountain before reacquainting itself with the ground. And when the front door flew back, there followed a day of tumult and trampling and terror. The multitudes of John's army stormed the grounds of Abaddon and put the city to the sword. And the army gave no quarter to any living thing in Abaddon stained by the touch of Lovethorn. Even Lovethorn's beasts and bulls, and his moo-cows and niksiks were put to the sword. All the men of Abaddon – the soldiers, the guards, the cripples and crazies, the townspeople and seers and priests – fell under the crush of the attackers. And the army smote Lovethorn's men with the side of the sword and trampled them underfoot. Some stood gape-jawed, hands hanging limp at their sides and urine wetting their knees as the attackers struck them down with swords and stones. Others bemoaned the siege bitterly, screaming anguished cries at their own destruction. And there was much weeping and gnashing of the teeth.

And La Montaña Sagrada seized and trembled. The smoke from the forest fires choked the air. Lightning fell from the sky.

And still John's men smote the city of Abaddon, seeking out every one of Lovethorn's men and putting them down like diseased livestock. The sons of Santiago attacked, barehanded, and bit and tore down their foes one at a time. Joad and his sons dispatched many enemies with each swipe of their mighty swords. And the sons of John engaged in combat, swinging slings and bags filled with stones, and crushing skulls. Swinging his ear trumpet in wild looping arcs, Old Man Chelloveck cleared a path through the melee and knocked his enemies to the ground. Alf and the donkeys kicked out at men as they tried to flee. Even One-Eye joined the fray, leaping on the men afflicted with Lovethorn's taint and gouging out their eyes.

Some of the Abaddonites fled the city. They scaled the walls and crawled away through tunnels. At the tops of the fortress walls, Three Tooth and his men rained down arrows on the absconders, stopping most of them. But some of the escaped Abaddonites scrambled for the caves in the rock faces. And some hid under moldy, mossy crags. Still, John's men hunted each and every one of the Abaddonites down and put them to the sword. And the blood of Lovethorn's men flowed, knee-deep, like a river through the grounds of Abbadon and down the mountain. Blood on the streets. Blood on the rocks. Blood in the gutters. And the bloody red sun shone down on the dead.

When the screams stopped and the swords swung no more, when no more arrows fell from the sky and the red brick road drank the river of blood dry, only then did the lightning cease. Only then did La Montaña Sagrada settle. So it came to be that John's men wiped the memory of the Reverend Android

Lovethorn from the pages of the annals of the history of Abaddon. And, though all Abaddonites fell, others also gave up the
ghost in the battle of Abaddon. John's blumpkin-sons fought
fiercely to eradicate the Abaddonites, yet all perished in the
battle. And so it was, too, with the son's of Joad. One-Eye drew
his final breath while skewered at the end of a spear, his guts
pouring out, and yet still managing to pluck the eye from his
killer. The carnage halved the ranks of Chellovecks, and Old
Man Chelloveck wept and spat on the walls of Abaddon. And
though they all sported injuries of varying degrees, the sons of
Santiago suffered no casualties in the course of the carnage.

So Joad, the Chellovecks, the sons of Santiago, and Three
Tooth's band of scurves cleared the grounds of Abaddon of
Lovethorn's men and all vestiges of the Man in Black. They cast
the corpses of their enemies out of Abaddon and down the
precipitous sides of La Montaña Sagrada. A massive cloud of
turkey buzzards fell on the bodies and undressed them. And
they piled the fallen friends of John high in the central square
of Abaddon and set them to burning, their funeral pyre blazing
high into the crepuscular night sky.

While his friends cleared the grounds of Abaddon, John remained in the temple, sitting with his eyes closed, contemplating his deeds. He hoped for his fiery doppelganger to appear
and say that what he did was right and that everything would
turn out well. But no wise apparitions appeared before John. No

visions played out on the inside of his eyelids. Even the ten thousand things refused to reveal their shimmering presence. John thought that, in a way, his killing of Android Lovethorn was a copout. Perhaps he took the easy way. But mostly John just recognized himself as a flawed soul, and he accepted that some things about him might not change. And when he pondered his situation, it all made sense to stay where he was. The thought of his other body dying in a bed far away was sad and it was fucked. And he realized that maybe what he did was wrong. He could have gone back. He could have learned who and what he was and made things right in that other place. But, mostly, when he really thought about it, it seemed right. He killed Lovethorn, yet he did not die. The land John had traveled still existed and many of the people he met and cared about still lived. And he cleansed the land of the scourge of Reverend Android Lovethorn. And something about where he found himself felt like progress instead of a step backward.

So John decided that what he did was good and right. And he accepted it as the proper course of events. He even decided that it was good that the other part of him might die. Once he sat long enough to come to grips with his situation, John rose and left the temple. Outside of the door of Lovethorn's church, a flight of stairs descended to the central square of Abaddon. John stood at the top of the stairs and waited for his friends to gather at the bottom.

Chellovecks, scurves, Santiagos, and Joad looked up the steps at John and saw him standing before them, beaten, bruised, and battered in his bloody linens. Two-Dogs-Fucking rode into the courtyard on an exhausted clone of Alf the Sacred Burro. The donkey fell to its side and spilled the Melungeon onto the ground. Two-Dogs-Fucking stood and adjusted his bath towel, ignoring the distressed burro gasping for air on the ground, and joined the rest of the crowd gathered before the steps.

John spoke to the crowd, telling them, "It's a day of independence, for us and our descendants. Android Lovethorn's shadow will no more darken the land. His curse is broken. He is dead, morally, ethically, spiritually, physically, positively, absolutely, undeniably, and reliably, dead."

"He's not only merely dead, he's really most sincerely dead," shouted Joad in his deep and muffled voice. And the crowd broke out in a raucous cheer.

John shushed the men and continued, "This land is free of the curse, and so is this fortress. These grounds shall no longer be known as Abaddon, but shall henceforth be called Beyza M'Geyza. And all will be free to stay and live here if they choose."

And the men cheered John on. They stomped and shouted curses on Lovethorn's name and spat on the ground.

"Tonight," John continued, "we will celebrate. But first, bring me our injured. Bring them to the foot of these steps."

The men carried those who were alive but could not walk and set them on the ground at John's feet. And John fell to the ground and laid his hands on the bloodied men. Others dragged themselves and limped to the steps. John laid hands on each and every wounded man and healed their injuries. Even those who felt their lives leaking from them, those whiffing the stink of death's breath, recovered and walked away from the stairs whole and healthy. John stood on the steps and gave his healing touch to every last injured man until every broken bone restitched itself and every cut stopped bleeding.

As John tended to his flock, the healthy and hardy men drained the blood from the slaughtered livestock and set the meat to cooking over fires. Others raided Lovethorn's cellars and carried out barrels of wine and spirits. Three Tooth walked among the crowd handing out wineskins filled with chicha. Crazy Talk dragged a giant brass hookah to the middle of the courtyard and packed it full with steaming bezoars and called out to the men "you gotta beep a gunk a chucha, honk konk konk, yeah right!" And the men converged on the hookah, sucked at the hoses, and chased the smoke with chicha and wine. And when John was done giving his healing touch, his body buzzed with energy. He loosed a hoard of jizz-critters on the grounds for the men to slaughter for the feast.

The sons of Santiago seized all manner of instruments from the cathedral and commenced a flurry of nonstop musical entertainment. They plinked bouzoukis and baglamas. Some scraped sticks on rhythm fish. Others slapped out solid beats on hand drums. Chellovecks picked up their jazz pipes and piped screeching funk into the air. And the sons of Santiago cycled their animated features through all ranges of expression and crooned off-tune songs about the desert and death and the bloody red bricks. They sang of joy and sorrow. They pantomimed the death of Android Lovethorn to the cheers of all around them.

And the men ate scruff goat from the mountain and moo cow and grilled jizz-critters. The spirits flowed from the barrels and filled the men with great joy. And the celebration lasted for three days and three nights. And on that third night, John stood atop one of the walls that surrounded the courtyard where his friends drank and danced and laughed with each other. John raised a glass to his friends and laughed at their gaiety. And he shouted out from the wall, "I threw light on the darkness, and the darkness understood it not. And I threw myself at the grounds of this mountain nest, and Lovethorn and his people wilted like dainty flowers in the desert sun."

The men cheered and clinked their mugs together. The put their arms around each other's shoulders and stared up at John.

John continued: "And the grounds of Abaddon drank the blood of all who followed Lovethorn. And he built high walls and towers to keep out goodness and love and warmth. But Abaddon does not belong in my land. It was as useless as a gold ring in a stink-pig's snout. Android Lovethorn did not realize that he who builds high gates and walls invites destruction. And you and I, my friends, we were that destruction. We were the heavy storm that washed the grounds of this place clean. This is our place now. This is Beyza M'Geyza. And the gates to these grounds shall never be barred shut again. Evil cannot touch us here. So drink up, men. Drink to yourselves and drink to what we have done. For it is a good thing. We have taken down the one in the corruptible crown. We have recompensed him, evil for evil. Now that he is gone, there shall be no more weeping and gnashing of teeth. We shall have nothing to be troubled at, and thus, shall be troubled at nothing. We have followed the path. And the path is the way. So celebrate your-selves tonight, because you deserve it."

And the men raised their glasses. They wept tears of happiness, and camaraderie warmed their hearts. Alf the Sacred Burro and his sons ambled about the courtyard and grazed on the grickle grass around its edges. And though John still had no inkling as to the details of his other life, he knew it in his gut that he had never felt like this before. A flood of emotions washed over him and he knew and recognized each feeling and it was good. It was right. He finally felt complete.

At the end of the third night, John retired to a bedroom in the fortress and weariness overtook him. Taking a straight razor to his head, John shaved off his long hair and shaggy beard, even cutting off his eyebrows. He liked the way his shining head and face looked in the mirror. He rubbed his hands across his scalp and enjoyed the smooth, cool touch of the bare flesh on his head. And he stripped and lay himself out naked on a large mattress stuffed with the feathers of fluff-hens. The soft bedding conformed to his body and comforted him. And a fluffy pillow of fluff-hen down supported his head. John took one last look out the window of his room and wondered at the two full moons sitting low on the horizon. And the light of the star Wormwood bathed John's room in a warm green haze. John's eyelids grew heavy and a much-needed rest overtook him. Peaceful nothingness swirled around him, tossing off strands of cool blue and flecks of gold. The ten thousand things played out a fantastic lightshow on the backs of his eyelids and then fled and left in their place a cozy void.

And when John awoke, he realized that his room was no longer a room, but instead a craggy cave. His bed was now the dusty ground; his down pillow now a rock. And beside the spot where he awoke was a hole five cubits in diameter. John peered into the pit but saw no bottom. He dropped a rock, but the sound of it hitting bottom never came to him. At the edge of the pit, John saw claw marks in the sand and a trail that dragged itself to the spot where he awoke. And then John remembered everything.

He stepped out of the cave entrance and stretched the sleep from his arms and back as he stared out from the mountainside. Warm light shone down from the morning sun and tinted the mountain and everything in sight gold. And John's heart throbbed and swelled with joy as he heard the out of tune clang and bang of a guitar coming from somewhere down the hill.

MUCHAS GRACIAS

I owe many thanks to those who have helped me shape *Sloughing Off the Rot* into the big, gloopy, gooey glob of a story that it now is. Thanks for the advice, critiques, and authorly support of David David Katzman, Patrick Wensink, Andersen Prunty, Kirk Jones, and Mykle Hansen. Go out and buy their books, they are all talented and entertaining authors. Thanks to Kelli Reich for always helping to pimp my work. I couldn't ask for a better kid. Thank you to Deneen Meischker for the editing / proofreading. That was very cool and generous of you. And in return I burden you with the indelible shame of having your name included in my book. Thanks to Kelly Williams for being patient and working with me until the cover and illustrations were just right. Thanks to Lori Hettler of The Next Best Book Club for your support of my books and other independent authors. And, finally, thanks to my readers, who give me words of encouragement and support. Without the feedback that you give me, I do not think that I would bother to publish what I write. It means so much to know that there is a market for my work and that people actually enjoy my writing.

ABOUT THE AUTHOR

The Dr. Reverend Lance Carbuncle was born sometime during the last millennium and he's been getting bigger, older and uglier ever since. Carbuncle is an ordained minister with the Church of Spiritual Humanism. Carbuncle doesn't eat deviled eggs, and he doesn't drink cheap beer. Carbuncle doesn't wear sock garters. Carbuncle does tell stories. His stories are channeled through a pathetic little man who has to work a respectable job during the days in order to feed the infestation of children in his house. Carbuncle is the author of: *Smashed, Squashed, Splattered, Chewed, Chunked and Spewed*; *Grundish and Askew*; and, *Sloughing Off the Rot*. Carbuncle likes to hear what his readers think. You can let him know how you feel about his books, or just send him strange questions and/or pictures, at:

bonesbarbuncle@lancecarbuncle.com.

Lance Carbuncle can be found online at:
LanceCarbuncle.com
www.Goodreads.com/author/show/824409.Lance_Carbuncle
www.facebook.com/pages/Lance-Carbuncle-Fan-Page/132798993420266
Twitter.com/lancecarbuncle

ALSO BY LANCE CARBUNCLE

GRUNDISH AND ASKEW – Strap on your athletic cup and grab a barf bag. The Dr. Reverend Lance Carbuncle is going to kick you square in the balls and send you on a wild ride that may or may not answer the following questions: what happens when two white trash, trailer park-dwelling, platonic life partners go on a moronic and misdirected crime spree?; can their manly love for each other endure when one of them suffers a psychological bitch-slap that renders him a homicidal maniac?; will a snaggletoothed teenage prostitute tear them apart?; what is the best way to use a dead illegal alien to your advantage in a hostage situation?; what's that smell?; and, what the hell is Alf the Sacred Burro coughing up? *Grundish and Askew* ponders these troubling questions and more. So sit down, put on some protective goggles, and get ready for Carbuncle to blast you in the face with a warm load of fictitious sickness.

SMASHED, SQUASHED, SPLATTERED, CHEWED, CHUNKED, AND SPEWED – Idjit Galoot has a problem. He escaped from his master's house for a brief romp around town, seeking out easy targets such as bitches in heat, fresh roadkill and unguarded garbage cans. When he returns to his house, the aged basset hound discovers that his master has packed up their belongings and moved to Florida without him. "Smashed, Squashed, Splattered, Chewed, Chunked and Spewed" is the story of Idjit Galoot's ne'er do well owner and his efforts to work his way back to the dog that he loves. Along the way, Idjit's owner encounters Christian terrorists, swamp-dwelling taxidermists, carnies, a b-list poopie-groupie, bluesmen on the run from a trickster deity, and the Florida Skunk Ape.

ALSO BY KELLY WILLIAMS

Hello, Do You Work Here?
The Cabinet
The Hobo Kings: Bum Sub

www.ingramcontent.com/pod-product-compliance
Lightning Source LLC
Chambersburg PA
CBHW060800120626
46557CB00001B/38